"Where you going, Mommy?"

Ashley was staring at her mother, big gray eyes wide open. Always observing. Always aware.

"Just to make a phone call," Jamie told herself as well as the child. *It was only a phone call.* She'd talk to him, find out what he wanted. How had Kyle Radcliff tracked her down...and why? He didn't know— couldn't *possibly* know—about Ashley.

"Don't you want to see the movie?" Ashley's sweet voice was filled with concern. Her thumb stole to her mouth.

"Of course I do, baby!" Jamie said. She rounded the table and knelt down by her daughter's chair. "I'll hurry."

"Okay, Mommy."

Smiling, choking back tears, Jamie leaned forward and kissed Ashley's cheek.

"Love you, Mommy," Ashley said without relinquishing her thumb.

"Love you, too, baby."

Jamie fled.

D1012484

Dear Reader,

Almost everyone is biologically equipped to reproduce. But as miraculous as birth is, the true miracle comes not in the giving of life but in the nurturing of it. No job or other endeavor will ever be more important than the raising up of innocent lives. To have a child completely dependent on you for food and clothing, for safety, for emotional health, for guidance, is an immense responsibility. I've often thought you can judge people not by how they look or dress, the position they might hold in society, not by education, financial status or geographical location, but by how effective they are as parents.

Unfortunately, good people are sometimes driven by life, by circumstances, by tragedy, to make bad decisions. Yet it seems to me that a bad decision doesn't necessarily make a bad person. Sometimes, though, a person can be imprisoned by such a decision because our society tends to look only at the surface...tends not to look beyond mistakes and their consequences.

Certainly, accountability is crucial, cost is just, but one of the great beauties of life is the opportunity for second chances. I cling to that promise.

Her Secret, His Child was with me long before I wrote my first book. I'm glad to finally have the opportunity to bring you this novel and hope you will join me in celebrating the incredible strength of the human spirit as you share Jamie's story.

Tara Taylor Quinn

P.S. I'm always delighted to hear from my readers. You can reach me at P.O. Box 15065, Scottsdale, Arizona 85267-5065 or on-line at http://www.inficad.com/~ttquinn.

HER SECRET, HIS CHILD
Tara Taylor Quinn

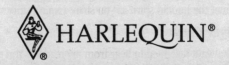

HARLEQUIN®

TORONTO • NEW YORK • LONDON
AMSTERDAM • PARIS • SYDNEY • HAMBURG
STOCKHOLM • ATHENS • TOKYO • MILAN • MADRID
PRAGUE • WARSAW • BUDAPEST • AUCKLAND

ISBN 0-373-70836-X

HER SECRET, HIS CHILD

Look us up on-line at: http://www.romance.net

Printed in U.S.A.

For Rachel. Having you made my life matter.
And for Jane Robson, whose belief in me taught me to
believe in myself.

CHAPTER ONE

"OKAY, BOYS AND GIRLS, we had Christmas in December and New Year's last week, and we said Valentine's Day comes in February, St. Patrick's Day in March and Easter will be in April. Can anyone remember what we celebrate in May?"

Four-year-old Ashley Archer put her hand up as high as possible; she couldn't wait to answer. The words almost came out of her mouth before Miss Peters called her name, even though that was against the rules. She squirmed in her seat, rising to her knees so Miss Peters would see her.

"Nathan?"

Darn it. Dumb old Nathan didn't deserve to answer this one.

"Memory Day."

Wrong. Wrong. Wrong. Ashley threw her hand up again. *I know. I know.*

"Memorial Day!" Miss Peters sounded like she just got a Christmas present. "Right!"

Right? That wasn't it.

The teacher smiled at them. Ashley settled back in her seat, although she kept her arm in the air. She liked it when Miss Peters smiled.

"Memorial Day is when we remember our soldiers who died fighting for our country."

Hmm. Ashley frowned. Maybe that was where her daddy had gone—maybe he was died from fighting for our country. Maybe that was why Memory Day was special, too.

"There's another special day," Miss Peters said. "Does anyone know what it is?"

Please ask me. Ashley waved her hand, just in case Miss Peters couldn't see it up there.

"Ashley?"

"Mommy's Day." Whoosh. There. She'd got it out.

"Right!" Miss Peters smiled again. "Mother's Day."

Ashley bobbed in her seat. She'd done it. And she couldn't wait to tell Mommy. After all, Mommy's Day was the most special day in the whole wide world. 'Cause it was all about God giving Ashley to Mommy.

God was really smart, even if He was old. 'Cause He gave Ashley the best, prettiest mommy in the whole wide world. Miss Peters baby-talked some more and Ashley sank down in her seat, looking at all the other kids to make sure no one saw what she was thinking. She didn't want them to know that God gave *her* the best mommy, 'cause that meant theirs weren't as good and that would be a not-nice thing for them to know.

She also didn't want to have bad thoughts, in case God might change His mind and give her some other mommy, instead. Like Nathan's. Yuck.

Staring at one of the bright-red flowers on Miss Peters's dress, she tried really hard to pay attention.

JUST AFTER TWELVE, Jamie Archer hummed to herself as she pulled into the drive at Ashley's preschool. This was her favorite time. Her work for the day was done; she'd finished the Worth's Flower Shop books early and was ready to start on her tax clients the next morning. The rest of the afternoon and evening belonged to Ashley.

Snuggled in her black wool jacket, she faced January's brisk cold as she raced for the door, eager to collect the girls. Karen Smith, Jamie's next-door neighbor and closest friend, had chili and crackers waiting at home for them. Karen's daughter, Kayla, was Ashley's best friend, car-pool buddy and preschool classmate. The two girls had been inseparable since the day Jamie and Ashley had moved to Larkspur Grove, Colorado, a little town outside Denver, two years before.

Jamie hated to think what would happen if the girls were put in separate classes when they started kindergarten in the fall.

"Mommy!"

Jamie's heart skipped a happy beat as it always did when she heard her daughter's voice.

She bent down just in time to catch the little whirlwind who hurled herself into Jamie's arms. Anyone might think they'd been apart for days rather than the two and a half hours it had actually been. But sometimes these preschool mornings, away from Ashley, felt so much longer to Jamie.

"Hi, punkin, how was school?" she asked.

"Good. I got to answer Mommy's Day!"

"Good girl!" Jamie gave Ashley one more hug before releasing the child. Even after four years, it was sometimes difficult to believe that this little girl was actually hers.

"Where's Kayla?" She looked around the huge room filled with miniature furniture and a confusing array of mothers collecting children.

"She had to go potty," Ashley said, trotting off to get her coat.

"Miss Jamie!"

Jamie turned as she recognized the other little voice in her life, and grabbed Kayla up for a hug. "Did you remember to wipe?" she asked. Kayla was often in too much of a hurry to finish what she started—much to Karen's chagrin.

"Uh-huh." Kayla nodded, her blue eyes wide. "Ashley knew Mommy's Day," she informed her importantly.

"I heard!" Jamie set the little girl down and helped them both zip up their parkas.

And as she escorted the two young children out into the parking lot, one tiny hand each in each of hers, she listened eagerly to their continuous chatter. There was no job more important, nothing on earth she'd rather be doing.

For the first time since she was Ashley's age, Jamie had everything she could possibly want.

KAREN RAN OUT of crackers. A near catastrophe, seeing that Ashley just *couldn't* eat chili without crackers. And besides, Kayla had already had five crackers and Ashley had had only three. Not bothering with her coat, Jamie hurried across the yard separating their homes, sure she had a box of saltines in the cupboard.

And saw the light blinking on her answering machine as she ran in the door. Hoping the light meant another client—an answer to the plea she'd sent out via Dr. Patterson, dean of Gunnison University—Jamie pushed the play-back button.

Ashley wanted to take dance lessons. Jamie needed to come up with the extra money to pay for them.

"Hi, Jamie. Kyle Radcliff calling. As of today, I'm the new English professor at Gunnison University. Could you give me a call, please?"

With a shaking hand, Jamie wrote down the number he rattled off. But as she dropped the pencil, the marks she was staring at through glazed eyes were barely legible.

She couldn't breathe. Couldn't see. Limbs suddenly weak, she clung to the counter, trying to keep down the portion of lunch she'd managed to eat.

Just like that.

He wanted her to call him.

Just like that. Her life was over.

She'd been found.

DRAWING ON the strength that came with motherhood, Jamie stood upright, forcing herself to breathe deeply, struggling to hold herself together. Ashley needed crackers. Was waiting for her mother to bring them. Jamie reached into the cupboard.

Yes. Just as she'd thought. There was an unopened box. Enough to keep both girls happy for the rest of the meal. Crackers were good. She was glad she had them.

Hugging the box, Jamie walked slowly back across the yard. The icy air didn't penetrate. She didn't notice the blue sky or the blinding glare reflecting off snow-covered yards. Ashley was waiting for crackers. Jamie had crackers. That was good.

"Mommy got crackers! Hooray!"

Jamie smiled automatically, holding up the box of crackers for the prize it was, as her daughter's greeting met her at Karen's kitchen door.

"Thank goodness." Karen rolled her eyes dramatically, grinning. She took the box even before Jamie slid into her chair.

"Thank Mommy," Ashley insisted, her brows creased with the seriousness of her correction.

Jamie's heart started to shatter.

Divvying up the goods, Karen reminded the girls that as soon as they finished their chili, they could watch *The Little Mermaid* again. Jamie heard her. Heard the girls' chorus of hoorays. She looked at her half-eaten bowl of chili. The spoon she knew she should be picking up.

"Something wrong?" Karen's voice was soft, barely audible beneath the girls' animated conversation.

"No!" Jamie glanced across at her friend. The

only true friend she'd ever had. The woman who didn't really know her at all. "Why?"

"You don't look so good."

"I, uh, just remembered I didn't return a phone call this morning and I can't afford to lose any clients."

"Then go do it. I'll watch the girls."

"You sure?"

"Of course! They'll be wrapped up in Ariel for the next hour anyway. Get out of here!"

She had to go. But she couldn't leave Ashley. Could barely wait for Ashley to finish eating so she could lift her out of her booster seat and hold the little girl's chili-smeared face against her. She'd be all right just as soon as she felt Ashley's arms around her neck.

"Okay, I'll hurry," Jamie heard herself say. And stared again into her bowl of chili. It had been good chili.

She was going to have to leave Ashley with Karen. She absolutely could not allow whatever was to come to touch Ashley's life. Couldn't bear for Ashley to know...

"Take your time," Karen said, clearing their bowls from the table.

Jamie stood.

"Where you going, Mommy?"

Ashley was staring at her mother, big gray eyes wide-open. Always observing. Always aware.

"Just to make a phone call," Jamie told herself as well as the child. "I'll be right back."

"Don't you want to see Ariel?" Ashley's sweet

voice was filled with concern. Her thumb stole to her mouth.

"Of course I do, baby!" Jamie said. She rounded the table and knelt beside her daughter. "I'll hurry."

"Okay, Mommy." Ashley's feet swung back and forth, her heels kicking the front of her booster chair.

Smiling, choking back tears, Jamie leaned forward and kissed Ashley's cheek.

"Love you, Mommy," Ashley said, pushing her cheek into the kiss without relinquishing her thumb.

"Love you, too, baby."

Jamie fled.

LEAVING ASHLEY BEHIND in Karen's kitchen was hard. But not as hard as growing up with a man who'd given her nothing—except bruises. Not as hard as being homeless at seventeen. She could do this.

She was only going next door. Yet as she walked into her house, as she picked up the piece of paper she'd left lying on her counter, the distance that separated her from her innocent little girl seemed suddenly insurmountable.

What did he want?

What could he possibly want?

He was new in town. Lonely. And somehow he knew that Jamie lived in Larkspur Grove.

He could go to hell.

She was already there.

By the time she got to the tiny bedroom she used as an office, Jamie was almost completely transformed. Encased in a hard shell of numbness her daughter wouldn't recognize, she wondered how far the word had spread. How many more of them knew where she lived?

The phone seemed to jump out at her, threatening to pull her away, back to the life she'd left behind five years ago.

Even now, even here, Ashley was all that mattered. Her daughter was everything Jamie was not. Sweet. Unsoiled. Innocent. She was the part of Jamie that had never been given a chance to live. Not since the devil himself had moved in with Jamie and her mother, just after Jamie's fourth birthday.

Jamie would do what she had to do, *anything* she had to do, to protect Ashley's right to a childhood. Her right to grow up decently.

And if that meant facing down the demons from her past—one or all of them—she'd do it. There was simply no alternative.

PHONE IN HAND, she punched in the number. *His* number. Only the shaking of her finger testified to the trauma playing itself out inside her. At seventeen, she'd survived her stepfather's debilitating advances. She'd survive this, too.

She pushed the last button. Lifted the mobile phone to her ear. Heard it ring…

The phone dropped to the floor, the ringing muffled by the plush gray carpet as Jamie flew to the bathroom and vomited. She hung over the toilet for another few minutes, just in case.

She could do this. She *could* do this.

It was just going to take a minute.

Wringing a washcloth under cold water from the basin faucet, Jamie fought the monsters she'd been fighting for as long as she could remember. Why had she ever thought she could outrun her past? She should have realized it would eventually catch up with her—destroy the present she'd so painstakingly created.

She buried her face in the cloth, welcoming its coolness against her hot skin. How had she ever been stupid enough to believe she could get away with these deceptions? That they wouldn't always be part of her?

And then she met her eyes in the mirror. Big gray eyes, just like Ashley's. Except that Jamie's had seen too much. Way too much. More than any woman ever should. The eyes that stared back at her weren't innocent like her daughter's. They were knowing. They knew just the right look to promise a man anything.

They made her sick. So did the woman they belonged to. She'd made her choices. And had to be accountable for them.

Turning away from the mirror before she threw up again, Jamie wadded the cloth in her fist. The thought of Ashley being tarnished by her sins was killing her as surely as her stepfather would have done if he'd managed to catch up with her all those years ago.

He was dead now. But the effects of his having lived would never die.

The anniversary clock in the living room chimed

the hour. She'd been gone from Karen's for more than twenty minutes. Ashley was going to start wondering where she was.

Concentrating on the child, Jamie found the strength to enter her office a second time. To pick up the phone. To dial again. She'd been facing her problems head-on her entire life, even when it meant putting her own body between her stepfather's fist and her mother's weaker frame. Her strength was the only reason she'd survived this far.

She had one focus, one goal: doing what was best for Ashley. Life on the run, hiding, wasn't it. Reaching for a recent photo of her daughter laughing at her from Santa's lap, Jamie kept her eyes glued to the image as Kyle Radcliff answered his phone.

"Yes, Ms. Archer, thanks for getting back to me so promptly...."

His voice was just as she remembered it. When she remembered it. It was so warm, almost as if he were in the room with her. She could see him sitting there on the end of the hotel bed, hunched over, his head in his hands as he told her about his mother's death. "...so I'd like to hire your services."

He wanted to hire her services. She hadn't gotten to that part of the memory yet. The part where he'd turned out to be just like all the rest. Her voice stuck in her throat.

He wanted to hire her services.

She wanted to die. Right then. Right there. What was the point of fighting anymore? She was who she was. Who she'd always been. Who she'd always be. The floor started to spin and she almost gave in, almost let that feeling of vertigo swallow her up. Almost.

And then her vision cleared again. And she could see the image she held of her laughing little girl. The trusting eyes. She couldn't let Ashley be a part of this. Panicking, she tried to think of something to say. Did he know she'd had a child?

She concentrated on the red velvet dress she and Ashley had picked out together for the much-anticipated visit with Santa.

"Ms. Archer? Are you there?" He'd called her "Jamie" before.

"Yes. I'm here." She didn't know what else to say. How to keep him away from Ashley. How to keep the woman she'd been away from her child.

"So do you think you'll be able to squeeze me in?"

Would he go away if she did?

"What exactly did you have in mind?" She hated the words, hated herself for saying them. But she was afraid that if she turned him down, he'd figure she was playing with him, would take it as a challenge, a come-on. That he wouldn't go away. After all, men like him weren't used to hearing "no" from women like her. Probably because women like her never *said* that particular word to men like him.

"You're the professional, you tell me." His voice was pleasant, calm, detached.

"You're the one paying the bill." The words practically choked her. But she had to gain some time, figure out what to do, how to get rid of him without making him suspicious—or even curious.

Her daughter's entire future depended on making this man nonexistent immediately. Forever.

She not only didn't want him to call her again, she didn't want him to *think* of her again.

"But I've never hired an accountant before—"

What?

"An accountant?"

"I'm sorry, I assumed you were an accountant," he said.

His voice carried a hint of the self-deprecatory humor that had ensnared her almost five years before. That long-ago night, his humility had caused her to let down her guard, to do one of the stupidest things she'd ever done.

"Dean Patterson gave me your name," he continued. "Said you do taxes. I just assumed you were an accountant."

"I am."

"Oh. Good. So, do you have time to take on one more client? Like I said, my records are in fairly good shape, but with the move from Las Vegas to Colorado and selling my house, I'll need all the help I can get."

Records? She'd clearly missed something.

"Dr. Patterson gave you my number?" The room had begun to spin again. Relief was making her light-headed.

"I'm sorry to impose like this on a total stranger, but the dean said you were the best."

A total stranger. "No!" Jamie's mind raced. "No, it's no imposition." The dean and his wife were good to her. They sent her seventy-five percent of her business. They had no idea who she'd been before she moved to Larkspur Grove, pregnant, single and two semesters short of her degree. She'd met them at a student-welcoming session, and for some reason Jamie had never understood, they'd shown an interest in her right from that first introduction, befriended her, helped her get established. They'd guessed, based on her silences, that she was a widow. She'd never corrected the assumption.

"You'll take me on?"

Kyle Radcliff sounded hopeful, but she heard nothing more personal than that in his voice.

She was trapped. There was no way she could decline without arousing suspicion, maybe not his but certainly the dean's. She'd just told Dr. Patterson about Ashley's request for dance lessons, the tuition, recital fees, the costumes involved. Just thanked him profusely for saying he'd send another client or two her way.

Jamie took a deep breath. "It might be a couple of weeks before I can get to you."

She'd met him once. It had been dark. She looked completely different now. She'd run into one of her college professors from the University of Nevada a couple of years ago and even he hadn't recognized her. Surely someone who'd seen her only once, at night, wouldn't know who she was.

"No problem. This all happened so fast I need a little time to unpack and find things, anyway. I just registered with the Las Vegas Educational Job Service in December and didn't expect a permanent position to come through until the fall."

The Las Vegas Educational Job Service. Which consisted of one very energetic woman, the service's owner, Wanda Kendall. Wanda had an office at the university in Las Vegas and was the person who'd helped Jamie find Larkspur Grove, the one who'd arranged for her work-study position so she could finish her degree at Gunnison. The woman who'd introduced her to Dean Patterson.

"Were you teaching in Las Vegas?" At the university? When she'd been a student?

"Yeah," he said easily. "I was head of the English department at a private college just outside the city."

A private college. With no connection to Jamie at all.

Okay. So maybe here was her chance to prove there was no part of that other woman, the woman he'd known and forgotten, still left inside her. Here was her chance to put the past behind her, once and for all. To prove to herself that she *could*. And maybe, finally, to forgive herself....

"Mr. Radcliff, you've just hired an accountant."

CHAPTER TWO

THE HOUSE WAS QUIET. Ashley slept soundly, tucked beneath her *Little Mermaid* comforter, as Ariel and Flounder smiled down at her from the walls above. Jamie had no idea how long she stood in her daughter's doorway, absorbing the comfort of her presence. Yet no matter how long she stood there, it wasn't long enough.

She'd made it through the day. Managed to convince herself that she was fine. That the phone call changed nothing. That it wasn't any big deal.

Until darkness fell. And the woman Jamie had been, the woman who'd worked nights, returned to haunt her. Nighttime was often bad for Jamie; she was used to coping. But that night, none of her coping techniques were working.

She couldn't find peace. Couldn't shut the doors in her mind. Memories flooded her relentlessly until she was drowning, suffocating beneath their weight....

Jamie had only been four, Ashley's age, when her widowed mother married John Archer. Though she'd loved her mother, Jamie had known, even then, that Sadie Archer wasn't a strong person. It was why Jamie had wanted a daddy so desperately.

She'd hoped and prayed for someone big and strong to take care of them, to keep them safe. She hadn't known, then, to be careful what she wished for.

John was big and strong, all right, but the day he'd moved into her life was the last day Jamie ever felt safe. He'd been a hard man to please, an unforgiving man. And no matter how hard she tried, Jamie never could please him. She spilled her milk; she made too much noise; she left water on the floor in the bathroom.

At first, her mother had taken the beatings for all the things Jamie had done. But it wasn't long, a few months maybe, before Jamie started getting them herself. By her fifth birthday, lying was a way of life. Stories came as automatically as the bruises she had to explain.

And several years after that, when it had become obvious that Jamie's young body was stronger than that of her frail mother, she began to take the hits for both of them. She'd been twelve the first time she stepped in front of a fist aimed at her mother's chest.

And seventeen the last time she'd felt his hands on her body...

COVERING HER MOUTH to stifle the sobs, Jamie backed away from Ashley's door. The memories weren't letting up. And Jamie couldn't bear to live through them in her daughter's presence.

She stumbled into the kitchen, as far from Ashley's room as she could get, and slid down to the hard cold tile, leaning against a cupboard. All her possessions were new since she'd moved to Larkspur Grove—even her underwear. Especially her underwear. She'd brought nothing with her. Not so much as a photograph. But that didn't obliterate the past's existence. It lived and breathed inside her. In her heart, in her mind...

The cemetery in Trona, California, was lush, green, full of flowers. And crowded. Jamie had had no idea so many people had cared about her mother. But it made no difference. Surrounded by all these people, she still felt completely alone. Apart. Frozen. It had all been for nothing.

All the struggles. The prayers. The hopes for a better day. The promises of freedom from hell. They'd all been for nothing. Her mother had lived a life of torment. And then died. She'd never escaped. The future had ended before she'd ever reached it.

"'Peace I leave with you, my peace I give unto you: not as the world giveth, give I unto you. Let not your heart be troubled, neither let it be afraid...'" The minister's words faded beneath the screaming in her mind. Peace! Not where she stood. And fear? What else was there?

"You okay, baby?" John's arm stole around her shoulders. She would have lost her lunch if she'd had any. All afternoon he'd played the role of loving stepfather. Just as he always did when anyone was around to see him. Anyone who mattered.

Jamie and her mother had never mattered.

Though she couldn't make herself respond to him, she held herself steady by sheer force of will, bearing the weight of his arm about her. She hadn't missed the tightening of his fingers on her upper arm. He'd issued his warning—she wasn't to make a scene. The warning would be a bruise by nightfall.

And no one would ever believe that John had given it to her. Everyone loved John. He was a charming, personable man with a reputation for generosity. Jamie cringed every time she heard him described as a "wonderful family man." But she knew better than to try telling anyone what had really been happening at home all these years. She knew John would deny everything in that charming salesman's voice of his. He'd talk about how difficult she was, what a burden she'd been to him, what a liar she'd become. They'd believe him. They always did.

They'd believed him that time she'd told her kindergarten teacher he'd beaten her so badly she ached all over; he'd claimed merely to have spanked her once for lying to him. He'd actually had tears in his eyes when he'd related how hard it had been to raise a hand to her, saying he'd tried everything else to stop her compulsive lying.

It also hadn't hurt that he'd been valedictorian of his class, in the same school district. Or that his parents—now dead but long revered—had both put in many years on the board of education.

And, of course, the die had been cast from then on. Jamie's word was no longer valid. She was labeled. A compulsive liar.

Her stomach cramped with fear, she hoped the bruise on her arm was the only one she'd be sporting that night. John had been the perfect stepfather since her mother's death three days before. But there had been people around. Her mother's elderly sister, who'd flown in from Florida. Neighbors. Members of the church they attended.

They'd all be gone by evening.

"'In my father's house are many mansions: if it were not so I would have told you. I go to prepare a place for you…that where I am, there ye may be also…'"

Recognizing the familiar Bible verse, Jamie felt the first prick of tears that day. If only it *were* so. If only she could be sure her mother finally had her mansion.

Her expression stoic, Jamie refused to allow the tears to fall.

And as her mother's casket was lowered into the ground, she looked not at her mother's grave, but at the people around her. Their tears flowed freely. They mourned a wonderful, giving, fragile woman.

And not one of them knew.

"Let's go," John said, hugging her close.

Longing to flee, to throw his arm away from her, to spit in his face, Jamie walked slowly beside him. There'd been times during the last thirteen years when John's softer mood would linger for a week, even a month or two. Dared she hope this was one of those times? That the mood might remain? With head bowed, she stared at the ground every time someone stopped them to offer condolences, nodding when the pressure of John's fingers forced her to acknowledge a comment here and there.

Sure they were all sorry. Sorry her mother had

died. But what about being sorry she'd lived? Was Jamie the only one who felt that? She'd rather her mother had been spared the whole sorry business.

"At least you have each other. You'll need that now." Pastor Hammond was talking to them outside the limousine provided by the funeral home.

Jamie studied the way her black dress shoes matched the darker patches in the pavement. Pastor Hammond didn't have a clue. He was supposedly a man of God. A man with divine knowledge. And he didn't have a clue. Not that she could tell him. If, by some miracle, Pastor Hammond did believe her, which she doubted, John would kill her. She could take that for granted. There was no law powerful enough to keep John from killing her.

The reception at the church passed in a total blur. Some of Jamie's friends from high school were there. She knew she spoke with them, though she had no idea what their conversation was about. Jamie was used to putting on a facade. Hell, she'd taken gym class with broken ribs the year before. No one had guessed there was anything wrong.

"I can't believe we're finally seniors," Loretta gushed, her hungry eyes checking out all the men in the room.

Following her gaze, Jamie wondered how many of those men had another, uglier, side. One the world never saw. Their superior physical strength gave them all an edge that women couldn't possibly fight.

"Yeah." Jamie finally answered Pastor Hammond's daughter. "Just eight more months." Loretta's enthusiasm to leave high school was one of the few things Jamie had in common with the other girl.

A high-school diploma meant freedom to Jamie. Without her mother there, needing her protection, she couldn't get away from John fast enough. And once she was eighteen, graduated from high school, he wouldn't be able to make her stay.

Somehow the rest of the afternoon passed, night fell, and Jamie was at home with John. Alone. Her aunt had left for the airport a few minutes before, and Jamie, having changed from her black dress to a pair of jeans, sweatshirt and tennis shoes, was hiding out in her room. Hoping she wouldn't be noticed by the man she heard slamming things downstairs. Was it possible he actually felt some compassion for her? That he'd realize how much she was hurting and leave her be?

Studying her second-story window, she thought about climbing out. The bushes below were full enough to break her fall. She had nowhere to go, but that wasn't what stopped her. It was knowing how bad things would be when John eventually got her back. He'd broken her arm the last time she'd used that window.

And then refused to allow her to see a doctor to have the arm set. It had healed eventually. But it still ached whenever she used it too much.

She'd rather just take her chances on being slapped around until John had finished venting his rage. Bruises didn't hurt much after a day or so. And they didn't last.

"Jamie!"

Her heart skidded to a stop. The bellow was ugly. *Oh, God, here it comes.*

"Yes?" She ran quickly to the top of the stairs, eager to appease his anger, not intensify it.

He was such a bastard for doing this to her.

"Get down here now!"

Fear was a familiar companion, yet it still grabbed her by the throat as she hurried downstairs. Maybe this was one of the times he'd be content just to holler at her for a while.

Her long permed hair, tied back in its familiar ponytail, bounced on her back with the force of her descent. And then she was at the door of his study. *God, if you're around, please go in there with me.*

"What?" she asked, forcing herself to sound amenable. She leaned against the door frame.

"Don't 'what' me." John's handsome face was twisted in a sneer. "You know we have some things to discuss."

Not sure what to say, what to expect, Jamie just stood there. She knew from his tone that she wasn't in his good graces. She just didn't know why. Or how bad it would be. She didn't move, barely breathing, not wanting to do anything that might further raise his ire.

"Your mother being gone changes things." He sat behind his desk, going through papers. He was still wearing his dark suit from the funeral, but he'd removed the jacket, loosened the tie. The sleeves of his shirt were rolled up past his forearms.

Trembling, Jamie couldn't take her eyes off the

muscles that flexed in those forearms with each object he moved.

"Now that your mother's gone, I owe you nothing," he said. "Not a stitch of clothing, not a meal or a bed."

Was he going to kick her out? Adrenaline pumped through her as she straightened in the doorway, waiting for him to continue. If he kicked her out, she'd know there was a God after all.

"I've been supporting you all these years out of the goodness of my heart, out of love and devotion to your mother."

If she hadn't been so excited, suddenly, sensing freedom within her grasp, Jamie would have burned with rage at his lies.

Please let him kick me out. She was barely aware that he'd stood up, that he'd walked to the front of his massive oak desk and rested his lean body against it.

She could get help if he kicked her out. There were places she could go—as long as she didn't have to worry about him coming after her. As long as she was free from the lies, the threats. The violence. Loretta had a huge room. Jamie could probably stay there. She could finish school. Get a job. If he'd just let her go...

"But then, I wouldn't be the man I am if I tossed your little butt out in the gutter where it belongs, would I?" he asked.

Of course not. Jamie's heart sank. How stupid could she be? He wasn't ever going to let her go. Because he'd look bad if he did. He could explain away her tripping on the stairs, falling during a family hike or being thrown from a horse. He'd never be able to explain leaving his seventeen-year-old stepdaughter homeless.

His eyes were gleaming as he watched her squirm in the doorway. Why did it always have to come to this? Why did she always end up reacting just the way he wanted her to? Like…like a helpless bug at his mercy?

"So, my dear daughter, you're going to have to earn your keep."

So, what else is new? The words almost escaped. She'd been doing the majority of the housework for years.

He came closer, slowly, gaining on her inch by inch, his height throwing a shadow on her in the doorway. Jamie didn't want to shrink from him. She forbade herself to give him that satisfaction. Not anymore. Her mother had gone to her grave a beaten woman. Jamie wasn't going to do the same.

"I'm curious." He stopped, pinning her with his cold stare. "How does it feel knowing all of those people were crying today because of you?"

"What?" She shifted away from the door frame.

"You killed her," John said.

His expression had softened and he smiled sadly as he gazed at her. Jamie's heart began to thud so heavily in her chest it constricted her breathing. But she still didn't shrink from him.

"I didn't," she whispered. She wasn't going to let him convince her of something so horrible. She refused to accept any guilt. She'd risked her life for her mother—many times. Sadie Archer had been the one person in the world who loved her. Jamie would have killed herself before she ever did anything to hurt her mother.

"Of course you did," John whispered hoarsely. He'd stopped a couple of feet in front of her and stood with his hands in his pockets. "Won't do you any good to pretend, Jamie. You killed her as surely as if you'd put a gun to her head."

"No!" Jamie felt the tears start to flow, deep inside, where no one could see them.

"That night you called to ask permission to stay later at the library."

"You said I could." Jamie hadn't wanted to leave her mother alone with John, but he'd been in one of his nicer phases. And she'd needed to get a few more references for an English paper she was writing.

"Yes, well, unbeknownst to me, your mother had already left to get you."

He was a raving lunatic, his story so obviously unfounded. "She knew where I sat in the library. If she'd come, she would've found me."

"Her car broke down on the way."

Thinking back to that night a couple of weeks ago, Jamie remembered her mother and John picking her up when the library closed. They'd been in John's car.

She wasn't sure where this was leading, but she was suddenly scared. Too scared to run. Too scared to move when John took a step closer.

"It was raining that night," he said.

His voice was still soft, but Jamie trembled anew when she heard the lilt of victory in his tone. He advanced another step.

She was confused now, doubting herself. And if she'd had anything to do with the illness that had finally taken her mother's life, she didn't care if John hit her. She didn't care if he killed her.

"Your mother was exposed to that rain when she had to walk the half mile to a phone, then wait there for me to come bail her out of her troubles again," John said. His hands were still in his pockets, but the muscles in his forearms were bunched.

His dark hair left menacing shadows on his forehead.

"The next day, as you know, she came down with a cold that led quickly to the pneumonia that killed her."

Jamie stared at him. Horror made her sick, weak. Surely she couldn't be blamed for the rain! Or the run-down state of her mother's car.

"If you hadn't been at the library, forcing Sadie out in the first place, she'd never have been exposed to that rain at all."

"But..."

"Or if you'd found another way home, a friend maybe, like most teenagers do, rather than relying on your mother all the time, she wouldn't have been out in that rain."

"But..." Desperate to end this nightmare, to be certain she wasn't to blame for her beloved mother's death, Jamie meant to tell John that if he'd only kept her mother's car in better shape, Sadie wouldn't have had to worry about the rain. But she never got the chance.

"Or—" he took another step "—if you'd called sooner, before seven, when she left to pick you up, none of this would have happened."

He was right. Dammit, he was right. She'd been so caught up in her reading that she hadn't noticed the time. Her mother always got her from the library at 7:30; it was a standing arrangement. Jamie should have called earlier, saved her the trip.

John took another small step, pulling one hand slowly out of his pocket.

Jamie shrank back.

SHIVERING, Jamie clutched her stomach with both arms, her gaze darting frantically around her cheery kitchen, trying to connect with the present, to bring herself back. To hold on. But the memories just kept right on coming, right on hurting....

"YOU'RE LUCKY I'm willing to keep you, considering what you've done."

John's soft voice penetrated Jamie's numb mind. So filled with guilt was she that for a second or two she almost believed him.

She saw his hand coming toward her, braced herself for a blow to the side of her head.

And felt a gentle caress, instead. His hand stroked from the top of her bent head, moving slowly down to her chin, lifting her face to look at him. And suddenly Jamie knew fear like she'd never known before.

She couldn't breathe, couldn't stop trembling, couldn't stop the tears that ran down her cheeks when she encountered the hot fire of lust in her stepfather's eyes.

"You took my companion from me," John whispered. "A man has needs, natural, powerful needs."

Unable to make a sound, shaking convulsively, Jamie just stared at him in horror. *God. No. Not this. Let him beat me to death. Let him stick a gun to my head. But not this.*

"Wouldn't look right for me to search out another woman to take to my bed, not so soon after your mother." His caress continued slowly downward, along the length of her neck.

She stood frozen beneath his touch, completely unprepared.

"So you see how lucky it is that I don't have to search. You took her from me." His hand reached her collarbone, his fingers sliding inside the neckline of her sweatshirt.

Jamie flinched. And just that quickly, the caress became brutal, a vicelike grip bruising her collarbone as John pulled her closer.

"The very least you can do after depriving me of my wife is to take her place yourself."

"No!" Her scream tore past the constriction in her throat. She was burning up. Sick. And freezing, too.

"Yes." John bit the word out through clenched teeth as he planted his other hand firmly on her breast.

A part of Jamie just evaporated as her stepfather's

big hand kneaded her soft flesh roughly, touching her where she'd never been touched before. Where he should never have been touching.

His eyes gleamed, almost glassy with lust. Still holding her in a bruising grip, he moved his hand to her other breast. "Oh, yes, I'm going to like this," he murmured.

And almost before she knew it was happening, he'd pushed up the hem of her sweatshirt, ripping her bra in his hurry to get to her naked flesh.

"Nooooo!" Jamie screamed. She yanked away from him, not caring if he broke her neck with his violent grip.

"Get back here, you little bitch!" He grabbed her hair, his fingers tangling in the tightly wrapped curls, wrenching her back to him. "You owe me, and I'm going to have you."

Only if he killed her first.

Filled with a strength she wasn't aware she possessed, with a purpose that hadn't been there seconds before, Jamie suddenly knew exactly what to do. John was too busy groping her again, too caught up in his crazed lust, to be wary. With one perfectly aimed swipe she kneed him squarely between his legs.

And ran for her life.

CHAPTER THREE

LOOKING BACK, Jamie wasn't sure just when she'd made the wrong turn, which decision had been the one that catapulted her from a damaged childhood into a hellish life. Though she desperately didn't want it to be so, she couldn't help wondering if maybe she'd always been tainted; maybe there'd never been any question as to what course her life would take.

Lord knows, she'd tried to be moral, to do what was right. She'd tried to make the proper decisions, to search out the best choices available to her. There just hadn't seemed to be much to choose from.

Leaning her head against the kitchen cupboard, she closed her eyes, wishing that sleep would come. The night was already half over. And there she sat, a full nine years after she'd last seen John Archer, still alone, still frightened.

Had it been wrong to run? Slowly shaking her head, Jamie couldn't believe that running wasn't her only choice. She'd run to Las Vegas. Because it was close. And because she knew enough about the city to realize that if there was any place in the United States that she had a chance of not being found, it was in the city that never slept. Where "no questions asked" was an accepted standard.

She'd left her purse on the front table when she'd come in from the funeral that day and had grabbed it again on her way out. She had enough money for a couple of nights' cheap lodging, but other than that, she was broke. She'd tried to get a job immediately. Had spent two days answering every want ad she could find. She was a high-school dropout, though, and the most anyone offered her was a fast-food position that didn't pay enough to cover rent and expenses—let alone any extra to cover the education she'd need to better herself.

Jamie studied the uneven grain in the cupboard across from her. Maybe she should have known when she'd visited the community college, passed the entrance exams without her diploma and applied for scholarship money that she was reaching too high. The guidance counselor she'd seen had tried to tell her, suggesting Jamie go home to John, apologize, ask him to take her back until she finished high school. She was told to save her money and move out when she'd established herself, became "independent."

Maybe that was where she'd gone wrong, Jamie thought now. She hadn't listened.

But she couldn't possibly have returned home as the counselor had encouraged her to. Nor could she have begged her stepfather to take her back. What he'd asked of her had been wrong. Very, very wrong. And illegal.

The possibilities floundered in her weary mind, a

cacophony of might-have-beens and should-have-dones. Still, she'd known even then that she couldn't have gone to the authorities for help. After thirteen years of silence, of John's generous example to the community, of his breaking down her own credibility, who'd have believed her? And what if they had? Could she really have faced her stepfather across a courtroom? Could she have told a roomful of strangers, of reporters, what he'd done to her?

But more, could she have hidden herself from John? After thirteen years of living with the man, of witnessing his diabolical abilities, she knew that even the witness protection program wouldn't have been able to keep him from finding her if she'd turned traitor on him. And that was exactly how he'd see it; what was self-protection to her would seem betrayal to him.

So maybe her biggest mistake had been believing in fairy tales. Not running as fast and as far as she could when Prince Charming bowled her over in the lobby of his office building. Prince Charming, alias successful business entrepreneur Tom Webber. She'd been standing there looking at a watercolor she didn't understand, waiting to be interviewed for a job she knew she'd never get, and he'd knocked her right on her butt as he'd come barreling through the revolving door on his way up to the penthouse office.

He'd not only picked her up but insisted on buying her lunch. A meal she'd have turned down flat if she hadn't been so hungry. As it was, she'd needed the meal even more when she met him at the restaurant an hour later, as he'd instructed. She'd had her interview—and lost the job—in the interim. And over the first real meal she'd had in days, she'd told him the whole sorry tale. She hadn't been able to resist. He'd been kind, sympathetic, showing her more compassion during that long lunch than she'd known her entire life.

Maybe she should have said no when he'd offered to help her, no strings attached. But he'd said almost plaintively that he had more money than he knew what to do with. He'd offered to set her up in a small unit in one of his many apartment buildings, support her while she finished high school, send her to college. He'd begged her not to say no—and she hadn't. Should she have denied him the opportunity to be the Good Samaritan he wanted to be? Denied herself the miraculous help that had finally fallen her way?

After growing up under John's damaging influence, she'd soaked up Tom's kindness. And he had been kind, if not as altruistic as he'd seemed. He'd been true to his word, too. For a while. Long enough for her to grow fond of him, feel indebted to him. He'd helped her—no strings attached, just as he'd said—right up until she turned eighteen.

He'd been there at her high-school graduation. And had come immediately the day he'd received the news that John was dead. He'd apparently hired a detective agency to keep track of John and had told her as soon as he'd heard. John Archer had been killed by an unidentified hit-and-run driver.

John was dead. If there was anything in her life,

besides Ashley, for which Jamie was thankful, it was the death of her stepfather. Which was probably just another immoral decision she'd made. To be happy that a man had lost his life.

Jamie stood and took her exhausted body to bed, her mind finally quieting with fatigue. She had no more answers now than she'd ever had, and she was beginning to suspect that she'd never have them—that, in fact, her questions were unanswerable. Maybe it didn't matter *how* she'd become the woman she used to be, the woman she'd renounced.

Maybe there'd been choices and maybe there hadn't.

But she'd been wrong to think she could escape that woman.

"ASHLEY ASKED ME yesterday if her daddy died fighting for our country."

Jamie's stomach, already queasy, protested as she glanced across at Karen. The two were sharing a cup of coffee during Jamie's morning break before Karen left to get the girls from school.

She said the first thing that jumped into her mind. "Why didn't she come to me?"

Karen shrugged, paying unnecessary attention to the sugar she was stirring into her coffee. "I asked her the same thing."

"And?"

"She said you might get sadder at her."

"*Sadder* at her?"

Karen shrugged again. And continued to stir.

"She thinks she makes me sad?"

Karen glanced up, her blue eyes warm with compassion. "Kids are pretty perceptive."

"But Ashley hasn't made me sad a single day of her life!"

"Apparently, she doesn't think so."

"She hardly even makes me mad."

"You do have amazing patience with her."

Jamie pushed her coffee away, sick at the thought that Ashley might be growing up the way she had, shouldering the blame for everything that happened, or might happen, in the lives around her.

"Obviously I need to be more careful, as well." Jamie flipped the spoon she'd used to stir her abandoned coffee. "She must read my moods like a book."

"She's one smart little girl. Imagine, a four-year-old figuring that her father was a war hero."

And suddenly they were back to where the conversation had begun, Ashley inventing excuses for the absence of her father. And Karen wondering how true they were.

Funny how life had a way of regurgitating on you all at once. First yesterday's phone call. And now this.

"I thought I'd have a few more years before she started asking questions."

"Wished was more like it, huh?" Karen asked with understanding, in spite of the fact that Kayla's father was very much a part of their lives. A software consultant, he traveled frequently, but when he was home, he belonged one-hundred percent to Karen and Kayla.

"Ashley's father isn't dead."

The bald words fell into Karen's sunny kitchen to lie, completely exposed, on the table between them. Karen had never asked about Jamie's past. Jamie had never offered a word. This particular silence was an understood part of their friendship. A pact Jamie had needed in order for the friendship to exist—a pact she'd just broken.

And she had no idea why. She couldn't tell Karen about that time in her life. Not if she wanted to hang on to the life she'd made for herself since.

"He didn't want her?" Karen stirred furiously, staring at the coffee sloshing over her cup.

"He doesn't know about her."

"Oh."

"We were only...together...once."

Karen laid her spoon in her saucer and looked up at Jamie, her eyes still glowing with tenderness. Not with the condemnation Jamie knew she deserved.

"The baby that resulted simply wasn't an issue. Wasn't part of that night."

"How can you say that if he didn't have the opportunity to make her a part of that night?" Karen asked softly.

Jamie remembered, very clearly, the wad of bills on the nightstand.

"Let's just say it was an unspoken rule. Any consequences were mine alone."

"The bastard!"

"I went with him willingly."

"And I know you well enough to be absolutely sure that he'd touched your heart. You cared for him and thought he cared back. You never would've done it otherwise.''

Ironically, concerning that one time, Karen was right. But Karen's loving support was like bitter ashes in Jamie's mouth. Because there'd been other nights, lots of them, when Karen would have been dead wrong.

PUSHING his wire-rimmed glasses onto the bridge of his nose, Kyle Radcliff took the cement steps two at a time. The Archer woman was meeting him in his office in five minutes. And he wasn't there yet. The semester was just starting, and already his resolution to stay on top of things had vanished. The one thing he could never seem to get right was time management. He bought planners—every kind known to man—he made schedules, he wrote lists. And he still ended up chasing his tail.

But could he help it that a couple of his students got into a debate about Twain's obvious disdain for the pseudoaristocratic antebellum South, as demonstrated in the thoroughly adult classic, *Huckleberry Finn?* The relationship between biography and literature, between a writer's life and time and his or her work, had always fascinated him. Kyle could no more have walked out on that discussion than burned his original copy of the novel. Some things just took priority.

But he needed Jamie Archer's help. With the move to Larkspur and now into his new home, some numbers needed to be crunched. Fast. He certainly didn't have time for a battle with the IRS any time in the near future.

Practically skidding around the corner on the second floor of the English building, Kyle slowed when he noticed the empty hallway outside his locked office door. He'd beaten her there.

He was whistling as he juggled his leather briefcase, along with the couple of texts that hadn't fit inside, to unlock his door. If his luck held out, he'd even have time to check over the paperwork he'd thrown in a manila folder before he'd left home that morning. Just to make sure he hadn't forgotten anything. Now, where was the blasted thing?

Five minutes later, Ms. Archer still hadn't arrived, but neither had Kyle found the folder he was looking for.

"I know it's here," he mumbled, tossing aside the class planner he'd forgotten to take with him to his American lit class. Not that it mattered. He could conduct his classes blindfolded and textless if he had to.

Finding a couple more folders beneath his personal daily planner, he glanced through them. Nope. One was filled with maps of literary tourist spots on the East Coast. The other was his gas-receipt file. Or what would be his gas-receipt file, if he'd ever get around to putting them all in there. He really needed to stick labels on his folders. That'd save him a lot of time. If he could only *find* the time to do it.

He'd been through every folder on his desk twice, and none of them contained the tax receipts and

W-2 forms he needed to give his new accountant. Looking up at the clock on his office wall, he frowned. They'd said 9:30. It was almost 9:45. He wasn't going to be able to wait much longer.

"The satchel!" He practically sang the words as he remembered where he'd put the tax folder. He'd shoved it in his satchel on the way out to his garage that morning, then promptly forgotten about it when faced with the more important matter of whether or not he'd heard a forecast of snow. He hadn't driven his beloved mint-condition 1957 Thunderbird in more than a month. Not that he'd taken out the '64 T-Bird lately, either. No, he'd only risked the new and easily replaceable '98 Bird with the maniacal winter drivers of Larkspur Grove.

A quick search proved him correct—the tax papers were in his satchel—after which Kyle paced back and forth in front of his desk for another couple of minutes, waiting. Richard P. Adams. He was the critic who'd written so convincingly about Huck's moral growth. Two minutes later, Kyle was seated at his desk poring over a text, anxious to meet again with his debaters.

As he reached for a pen, Kyle's gaze fell on the corner of an envelope that had come in yesterday's mail. *Jamie Archer. Tomorrow, 10:00.*

He read the note a second time, and, of course, remembered that he'd called her and asked to change their meeting from 9:30 to 10:00 when he'd realized how close he'd be cutting it to get from class back across campus to his office. He just hadn't remembered to make a note of the time change on any of his calendars.

In an attempt to make being a slave to his planner a habit, Kyle dutifully zipped open the leather book and flipped to the tabbed page marking that week. He was immensely relieved to find that he *had* changed the time after all. Hey, maybe he was getting the hang of this time-management thing.

He'd covered a full sheet of the yellow legal pad on his lap, when he heard a light knock at his door.

"Come in," he called, his head bent as he hurriedly finished the note he'd been writing.

In his peripheral vision he saw a slim figure enter the room. Judging by the way she hovered on the threshold of his office, like an intimidated freshman, he quickly determined that Ms. Archer was the shyest accountant he'd ever met.

"Finished!" he said, looking up with a welcoming smile. He tossed the legal pad on his desk.

Half in and half out of his chair, intending to offer his hand in greeting, Kyle froze. And stared.

"I can't believe it." He didn't realize he'd said the words out loud until he heard his voice mirror his thoughts. "It's you...."

Based on the shock in her lovely gray eyes, she'd been no more prepared than he.

"You've changed." He said the first thing that came to mind. Her face was older, more mature, though beautifully so. She'd filled out a bit, but only in her breasts and hips. Her hair wasn't permed anymore, either, and it was a little darker, falling in soft curls down her back. She wasn't wearing near the amount of makeup she used to wear. And her clothes were completely different, merely hinting at the beautiful body beneath rather than broadcasting her assets. But he'd have known her anywhere. Those eyes had been haunting him for years.

Kyle came around the desk quickly, grabbing her arm as she turned to leave.

"You obviously aren't as pleased to see me as I am to have finally found you again," he said.

She still hadn't spoken a single word. Just stared at him like a trapped bird. Her reaction puzzled him—a lot. The last time he'd seen her had been in that Las Vegas hotel. She'd been sleeping in his bed, a half smile on her face.

What on earth had gone wrong?

"Do you have any idea how many Jamies I've chased down trying to find you?" he asked, smiling at her. Putting people at ease was something he did well. One of his few natural talents.

Had he suddenly lost his touch? She was still staring at him like he was a dead man come to life.

"Wouldn't you know it." He continued to hold her arm, though not so tightly that she couldn't get away from him if she wanted to. "The first time I hear the name and I don't wonder if just maybe... And it's the one time it turns out to really be you!"

Okay, so maybe he was rambling. But he couldn't believe he'd finally found her. The woman of his dreams. Literally.

"I—" She broke off, swallowed, tried again. "You looked for me?"

"Of course!" Kyle couldn't believe she had to

ask. They'd shared some pretty emotional moments, not to mention the best sex he'd ever had.

"Why?"

"Why what?" He was still holding her arm, but only because she felt so good. So warm.

"Why did you look for me?"

Kyle grinned at her, cocking his eyebrows a time or two. Trying desperately to find the warm, funny woman he'd spent the best night of his life with. "Need you ask?"

His answer must have disappointed her somehow. She looked away, down at the floor. He could almost feel her gathering her strength. He just had no idea why she felt she needed it.

"I'd never talked to a woman as openly as I talked to you that night," he said, forgoing light and easy for complete honesty.

That was better. She was looking up at him again, a question hovering over the panic in her gaze.

"I've never met anyone since then that I wanted to repeat the experience with."

"Talking, you mean?"

Well, the sex, too, but... "Yes."

Feeling the muscles beneath his hand relax, Kyle took his first full breath since he'd glanced up and seen her standing there. Phew. He'd finally said something right.

"I should probably go," she said, nodding toward the door. But she still didn't pull out of his light grasp. Kyle found her passivity rather odd.

"We haven't even discussed my records yet." He had to keep her there. At least long enough to be sure that he'd see her again. That she wasn't going to just disappear the way she had the last time he'd been with her.

"Surely you don't still want me to do your taxes."

He frowned, truly puzzled. "Why not?" He could understand a certain reluctance to follow him home and climb with him into his unmade bed—though there was nothing he'd like more at that moment. But what was so alarming—or intimate, for that matter—about taxes? IRS agents would be going over them pretty carefully and he'd never even *met* them. Not even once....

"Well...because...surely you don't."

Now probably wasn't the time to ask her out to dinner. "Of course I do. Dean Patterson says you're the best."

She took a full minute to digest that remark. Or at least Kyle figured that was what she was doing while she stood there silently gazing at him. During the brief time he'd known her, she'd been a woman of few words, a woman who kept most of herself locked away. But by the end of that night, he thought he'd been admitted inside—though just inside—the locked corridors of her mind. He'd been looking forward to exploring those corridors much more fully.

And then she'd vanished.

Jamie's next comment had nothing to do with taxes. "You cut your hair."

Ridiculously pleased that she'd given him that much notice, Kyle shrugged. "Made me look older.'' He'd worn a ponytail the night she'd met him.

"Looking older's important?"

"Maybe not, but when you're in the classroom and you want to discourage any interest from nubile college girls, it can't hurt."

Obviously uncomfortable with his vaguely sexual reference, Jamie simply looked away.

"It would have to be business only."

She'd said the words so softly he barely heard them, but his heart jumped with hope just the same. "Of course. If that's what you want."

Her gaze met his solidly then, filled with strength, with conviction. "That's the way it has to be."

He refused to be disappointed so quickly. "You're married?"

"No."

Then he could wait. "If you say it has to be just business, just business it is," he told her, forcing himself to release her arm as he headed back around his desk. So it was going to take longer than an hour or two to unlock her defenses this time around. He'd waited more than five years. He could be patient.

Holding out his tax file, he said, "It should all be in there. You can reach me here or at home if you have any questions. Both numbers are on the inside jacket."

Nodding, she took the file and flipped it open.

And for the first time since she'd walked back into his life, he caught a glimmer of a smile.

"What?" He was grinning from ear to ear. She'd almost smiled. He was climbing already.

"You want me to submit a bunch of maps to the IRS?"

He wouldn't bother telling her what he really wanted. Not yet. At least not until he got as far as a full smile. He handed her the correct folder, instead. And was still grinning as he hurried across campus to his next class. He'd just found the woman he was going to marry.

CHAPTER FOUR

KAREN SMITH LOVED her husband. But she didn't want to have his baby. Not again. Not alone.

She didn't think he wanted her to have his baby, either. Which made telling him that she might be pregnant almost impossible.

She paced her living room, where the girls sat watching cartoons, little legs straight out in front. Their closeness comforted her, even if the irritatingly high voices on the cartoons did not. Jamie was due any minute. Her appointment with the new client from the university had been more than an hour ago.

Jamie was so damn lucky. She had it all. A career. A home. And Ashley. Oh, and a planner with appointments and meetings written in for practically every day. Karen didn't have enough to keep track of to need a planner.

Jamie had a life. And probably because of that, she was the most unflappable, centered person Karen knew.

Karen, on the other hand, got up every morning, sent her baby off to school, cleaned, ironed and cooked, only to start all over again the next day. Cleaning the very same things. Ironing the very same clothes. Cooking the very same meals. No challenging decisions. No real thinking at all.

The fact that she loved doing household work made it even worse. That meant she really might be the boring, frumpy person her husband probably thought she was.

She ran her fingers through her short blond curls, the ones she'd styled so painstakingly that morning—as she did every morning—and her eye fell on the picture of Dennis perched among a collection of family portraits on the side table. God, she loved him. So much. He wanted her to spend more time with him. Maybe even travel with him a bit now that Kayla was getting older.

She'd love that.

Almost as much as she'd love a career. Something that was hers alone. Less because she actually needed to go out and do a job than because she wanted her husband to see her as a person, not just a housewife. She wanted to *feel* the way she was sure those women who worked with Dennis must feel. The way Jamie must feel. Confident. Intelligent. Important.

Though even the thought of having a career was laughable. What could she do? She'd married Dennis right out of high school. She had no skills, no training.

But she could change diapers. Oh, yeah, now there was something she could do....

The girls giggled and Karen nearly jumped out of her skin. They were so sweet, so innocent and precious, caught up in the ridiculously unbelievable antics of an animated cat and bird on the television screen. Her heart swelled with love as she watched their cheerful faces.

"You guys want some orange juice?" she asked.

"Yeah!" They chorused, never taking their eyes from the screen in front of them.

Glad of something to do, Karen headed for the kitchen to collect the two plastic cups with lids. Purple for Ashley. Yellow for Kayla. She filled them with juice, and while she was at it, she poured a glass of water for herself. Determined to be the type of wife a husband craved coming home to, she'd lost the weight quickly after Kayla's birth. Especially since coming home was something Dennis did so infrequently.

And now, no matter how much she dieted, she was going to get fat again. Panic returned in force and she carried the drinks back into the living room—to the two little girls who thought she was great just as she was.

"Thank you, Mama," Kayla said, sliding her chubby fingers into the handle of the cup.

"Thank you, Miss Karen."

Ashley's sweet smile almost brought tears to Karen's eyes. But as she stood she caught a glimpse of her svelte figure in the mirror above the fireplace. How could she hope to keep Dennis interested in her while she was at home swelling up like an elephant and he was out doing business with remarkable, fashionable, intelligent women like Jamie? How was she ever going to compete?

How was she going to make it through another

bout of midnight feedings, colicky crying and dirty diapers? Kayla meant the world to her; she'd give her life for her daughter in an instant. But she still felt trapped.

And might very well have another baby on the way. Washing down a sob with a sip of water, Karen turned back to the front window.

She just had to keep it together for a few more minutes. Then, once Jamie got there, maybe she could work up the courage to take the home pregnancy test she'd purchased that afternoon.

JAMIE STAYED UP late again that night. Doing Kyle Radcliff's taxes. She wanted him gone from her life as soon as possible. She didn't want to think about him. Didn't want to remember the hours they'd spent talking. And more.

And she couldn't think about Karen's news, either. Hated the insidious envy that had been eating at her all evening as she pictured, again and again, the color change in that little vial this afternoon. Her friend was going to have another baby. Another legitimate baby. A privilege Jamie could only imagine. An impossible dream.

The Karens of this world had husbands. Their children had fathers. Jamie had men like Kyle Radcliff.

She knew what he'd wanted from their association five years ago. What he eventually got. And paid for. Anything else was irrelevant.

''Mommy?''

Or was it?

"Ash?" Jamie pushed away from her desk as the little girl scurried into the office, rubbing her eyes with a pudgy fist. "What's wrong, baby?"

The footed bottoms of her pajamas scraping along the carpet, Ashley covered the distance between them and crawled onto her mother's lap. "I waked up."

Stifling the grin that rose easily to her lips as she gazed at the earnest face of her young daughter, Jamie gathered the child close and gently rocked her back to sleep. But, holding the tender weight against her heart, she couldn't help wondering if she was waking up, too. From the wonderful dream world she'd created—back into the nightmare that was her life.

She couldn't let that happen. Not at any cost.

And certainly not for a man who, with a look, a smile, a couple of eloquent words, could make her forget.

Especially not for him.

"PROFESSOR RADCLIFF? Jamie Archer here." The heavy beating of her heart was due to the speed with which she'd made it from the garage to her office after dropping the girls off at school. Nothing more. With Karen's news still fresh in her mind the next morning, Jamie was in a hurry to immerse herself in business. Or so she told herself.

"Jamie!" The pleasure in his voice was unmistakable. "I didn't expect to hear from you so soon." He paused. "And what's this 'Professor' bit? I'm 'Kyle,' remember?"

Yeah. She remembered. "I'm missing some receipts."

"Okay."

His voice cooled a bit. And Jamie hated herself for being disappointed.

"I'll see if I can find them. What do you need?"

Reading from the list she'd prepared before falling into bed early that morning, Jamie told him.

"I don't know if I even have all this stuff, but I can check this afternoon," he said. "Give me your address and I'll bring them by this evening."

"No!" Thinking only of Ashley, Jamie panicked. "I mean, um, I'll be out this evening." She paused. Swallowed. "Tomorrow's soon enough. I'll come to your office."

"Since you're going to be out, why don't you come here to pick up the receipts tonight?" he asked, sounding more cheerful. "I'll be home."

"That won't be necessary. Tomorrow at your office is fine."

"It's just that with some of this stuff, I'm not sure exactly what all you need. It might be better if you look things over yourself. It'll probably save you another trip."

Deforming a paper clip, Jamie blurted, "I might be out late."

"Doesn't matter. I'll be up grading essays, anyway."

It was hard to picture him as an English professor. She would have been much more comfortable if he'd turned out to be an ambulance-chasing lawyer or something.

"What kind of essays?" She didn't want to know.

"We're doing an in-depth study of Clemens, his political and religious views."

"Huckleberry Finn." She'd loved the American-literature class she'd taken on Samuel Clemens, alias Mark Twain.

"And 'The Celebrated Jumping Frog of Calaveras County.'"

"Tom Sawyer," she said, remembering.

"Yeah, what's with Aunt Polly? You think she's a woman ahead of her time—or a small-minded old bat?"

"She loved Tom."

"You go for small-minded, huh?"

Jamie picked up another paper clip. "She did her best. Life hadn't dealt her an easy hand, raising a hellion like Tom."

"You think the cards you're dealt are an excuse to be small-minded?"

"No!" Jamie almost laughed. And then caught herself. What was she doing? "And this has nothing to do with your taxes," she reminded them both.

"So you're coming by tonight?"

"I don't think that would be a good idea."

"Don't trust yourself?"

"Of course I trust myself." Jamie forced every bit of disapproving indignation she could muster into her reply.

"You don't trust me?"

"Why wouldn't I trust you?" Why, indeed? But that was something they weren't going to talk about.

He rattled off the directions to his house. "Come

anytime. I'll be up,'' he said. And then rang off before Jamie could tell him, in no uncertain terms, that she would not be stopping by his home that night, taxes or no.

When she rang back, she got his answering machine. Throughout the rest of that day, the man never answered his phone. Jamie didn't know if it was her imagination that had her thinking he was purposely avoiding her—or if she was just growing unnaturally paranoid. But because she couldn't get hold of him to make other arrangements and because she needed those receipts if she was going to get his taxes done and out of her life, she asked Karen to keep Ashley that evening.

IT HAD BEEN SO LONG since he'd cared enough to impress a woman that Kyle was a little unsure of himself as he unpacked enough stuff to make his house look like home. A home minus most of his furniture, of course. There'd been a little mix-up with that.

Give him a classroom full of know-it-all six-foot punks who hated English, and he was comfortable. But give him an hour to win over a 110-pound woman with a heart of gold, and he was at a complete loss.

In the first place, he didn't even know why he was having to win her over again. He thought he'd done that—quite thoroughly—five years before. He couldn't have imagined those phenomenal hours with her. Couldn't have imagined her response.

And couldn't understand why she'd disappeared.

But one thing he did know for sure: now that he'd found her, he wasn't letting her get away again.

"At least not without knowing why," he muttered. "Now, where are those damn files?"

Spying an unopened box across the kitchen, he grabbed his razor knife and headed over. The box was full of files. Surely the ones he needed were in there. Pulling off his glasses and tossing them on the counter, he crouched down to investigate.

"Oh, good, there you are," he said a few minutes later as he opened what was probably his twentieth manila folder to reveal the extra set of lesson plans he'd worked up for the semester. He'd had to turn in the set he'd brought with him in his briefcase and had forgotten to make a copy first. At least now he'd be spared the relatively humiliating experience of having to go ask the department secretary for a copy.

The doorbell rang just after eight. He'd finally found the travel receipts Jamie had requested—at the bottom of a box of socks and skivvies. They'd all been in a suitcase together, left over from his visit to New England, where he'd visited the homes and graves of most of his idols—Ralph Waldo Emerson, Henry David Thoreau, Nathaniel Hawthorne, Henry Wadsworth Longfellow, Louisa May Alcott.

"This isn't late," he said as he opened the door. He had to say something. Drooling over his reluctant accountant probably wasn't wise.

She shrugged her beautifully slim shoulders. "I finished earlier than I thought."

And what *he* thought was that she hadn't had anything to do that night to begin with. That she'd been making excuses. Which made him all the more curious. And determined.

"Here's my office, such as it is." He directed her to the little room off the entryway. His desk was there because he'd purchased a new one. And a sturdy box he was using as a chair. The filing cabinets hadn't made it yet.

"What on earth is in all those folders?" she asked, staring at the piles surrounding the room.

"Stuff." Kyle shrugged. He still hadn't found his folder of photos from Walden Pond. Maybe they were in the sock and skivvies box, too.

"So, you have the receipts?" she asked, standing just inside the door of his office.

Handing her the manila folder he'd unearthed, Kyle said, "You'd better take a glance at those, make sure everything you need is there."

And while she looked, he looked, too. Dressed in a pair of loose-fitting slacks and an equally loose cotton blouse, she could have been trying to hide her glorious body. But unfortunately Kyle found her modest clothes more of a turn-on than the form-fitting skimpy red dress she'd worn the night he met her.

She could wear a tent, and he'd be turned on. He knew what secrets the voluminous clothes hid. Knew them intimately. Every inch. Every taste. Every smell…

"These are all plane tickets and hotel receipts, but what about mileage, parking and meals?" she asked, frowning as she once again thumbed through the slips of paper.

Meal receipts? Who saved meal receipts? And where would he save them? His organizer was already bursting at the seams. "Surely they aren't going to amount to enough to matter."

"Of course they will." She glanced up—and then quickly back down. "They're one-hundred percent deductible as a business expense."

"What happens if I don't have them?"

"We can claim up to a certain amount without them. You lose the rest."

Her expression was so serious he couldn't help grinning. "Gosh, and I'm such a big eater, too."

Jamie's face was straight as she looked back up at him, taking him in from the glasses across the bridge of his nose to his jeans and bare feet. "I wouldn't know," she finally said.

"You would have, though, if you'd hung around long enough to find out," he said softly. He'd promised himself to move slowly, to stay away from accusation.

But patience wasn't one of his strong suits.

"Hung around?" Her blue eyes were confused. "Where?"

"In the hotel room."

Head bowed, she studied the receipts she held. "I did hang around. All the way till morning."

"Dawn was more like it."

"It was long enough." She raised a hand to lift the hair off her shoulders. He thought her fingers were shaking. "When I woke up, you were gone."

"Only to get breakfast." Kyle took her hand, held it as he stepped behind her. "I came back with two sacks of goodies and had no one to share them with.''

She *was* trembling. He could feel it as she turned slowly to face him. ''You came back?''

Gazing down into the only pair of eyes that had ever taken his breath away, he nodded. She thought he'd abandoned her? Was that why she'd run away? Was that *all* the past five years had been about?

''Why'd you come back?'' she asked.

''You had me under your spell.''

''The sex was good.''

So she'd felt it, too! Kyle breathed a huge sigh of relief. He'd nearly driven himself crazy the past twenty-four hours wondering what he'd done wrong, what he'd done to scare her away.

He moved closer to her, rubbing his thighs against hers. ''The sex was great.''

''What about electric and phone bills?''

''What?'' His body was on fire, his head filled with visions of...

She pulled away from him, flinging out her arm to encompass the room, her voice cold. ''You have a home office. Electricity and phone are deductible for that portion of your home.''

Kyle would have said goodbye and good riddance then and there if he hadn't noticed the slight trembling at the corners of her lips. She wanted to pretend that what they'd shared wasn't special. That it meant nothing. But it was; it did. Deny it all she wanted, she still felt the connection.

Somehow, somewhere, he had to come up with the patience to wait for her to be as happy about that fact as he was. But first, he was going to find out why she was so adamantly against taking up where they'd left off. She'd given herself to him that night five years before. Not just her body, but the person she was inside.

Their conversation had been unusually frank. He'd attended Tom Webber's party at the invitation of an old college buddy, to avoid thinking about the woman he'd buried that day. The mother he'd never loved. More emotionally vulnerable than he'd realized, he'd told Jamie things he'd never told anyone before—or since. Dreams, hopes, emotional stuff a man spent most of his life avoiding. He'd told her how lonely and empty his childhood had been. Without needing any of the details, details he'd been loath to give, she'd known exactly how he felt—because she'd grown up lonely, too. Was still alone, inside, where life really happened. He'd always loved reading, had always escaped into books. So had she. She wanted to be a mother—and have a house with a white picket fence. He hoped to write a classic someday.

But more than the words they'd said were the things they'd understood without words. They'd connected in a way he'd never known was possible, an intimate, intuitive way.

The sex had been an unexpected bonus. She'd given herself to him joyfully. Willingly.

And Kyle didn't turn his back on what was his.

THE NOTE FROM Ashley's teacher was a total shock. It came home with Ashley two days later, just after

Jamie had hung up the phone from leaving a message for Kyle Radcliff. His taxes were done. All she needed was his signature in the appropriate places and she could mail them—and him—right out of her life.

"Miss Peters wants you to have this," Ashley said, running into the house. Karen and Kayla were right behind her.

Jamie's eyes met Karen's over the girls' heads. Opening the envelope, she frowned; Karen just shrugged and mouthed the words, "Don't know."

Ms. Archer, Jamie's hand trembled as she tried to read the letter she held.

> *I'm sorry to have to report that your daughter, Ashley, had some trouble at school today involving one of her classmates. Please call me at your earliest convenience to discuss...*

"Ash?"

"Yes, Mommy?" The little girl left the toy she'd been showing Kayla and came over to Jamie's desk.

"You have some trouble at school today?"

Ashley shook her head, auburn curls bouncing with the force of her denial.

"Miss Peters said you did."

"Pro'bly means that dumb Nathan," Kayla muttered, not looking up from the different-sized squares she was fitting one into the other.

Karen's raised eyebrows and shake of her head were the only help Jamie got from that direction.

"What happened with Nathan?" Jamie asked her daughter, taking Ashley's hands in her own.

"He says dumb stuff 'cause he's dumb."

"That's not a nice word to use, Ash, especially when you're talking about someone else."

"But it's true, Mommy, he *is* dumb." Ashley's pretty gray eyes were somber yet completely sincere.

"And I'll bet you told him so, didn't you, Ash?" Karen asked, still standing in the doorway. Her gaze was compassionate.

Ashley nodded and Jamie let the little girl go. Ashley's thumb promptly found her mouth.

Jamie would have her talk with Miss Peters first, and then, when she had the full story, she'd have a heart-to-heart talk with her daughter. Ashley needed to learn to be a little more accepting of other people's shortcomings.

"How about some lunch?" she asked.

Karen nodded, but her smile was forced. "I made some chicken salad this morning," she said. "How's that sound?"

"Great." Standing, Jamie ushered the two energetic children next door.

But as she helped Karen make sandwiches and pour juice, Jamie felt increasingly worried about her friend. Karen had been looking a little lost ever since she'd taken the pregnancy test. She wasn't bubbling with excitement yet. Not the way Jamie would be if she were in her shoes. She decided Karen was probably just anxious for Dennis to come home so she could share her news. He was going to be thrilled.

Of that Jamie was certain.

CHAPTER FIVE

"WE'D LIKE YOU to make things a little easier on him."

Pulling off his glasses, Kyle peered up at the coach standing in the doorway of his office. For a Monday, the day was going stereotypically true to form.

"You want me to doctor his grade."

Coach Lippert, the head coach of Gunnison's football team, slipped his bulky frame into the room and closed the door.

"Brad Miller's good. Better than good."

Kyle nodded. He could appreciate that. Talent was a valuable commodity. As was integrity.

"He's star material. Scouts are already looking at him. Another year at the university and he's sure to get the offer of a lifetime." Coach Lippert came closer, leaning his beefy hands on Kyle's desk.

"I hope he gets it."

"He's already on academic probation. If he doesn't pass your lit class, he's out."

"I've offered to tutor him."

"Come on, Professor." Coach Lippert pushed away from the desk. "The boy shows up for every class. He attempts all the homework. And he's still failing. You really think a little tutoring's gonna help?''

Kyle shrugged. ''I can only give him the grade he earns.''

''That's bullshit and we both know it.'' The coach paced in front of Kyle's desk, his shoulders bunched until his neck disappeared beneath a face getting redder by the minute. ''Your tests are mostly essay questions, they're subjective. You control the grades.''

''On the basis of preset criteria.''

''But it's *your* opinion as to whether or not he meets those criteria.''

''To date, Brad Miller hasn't met any of them. If he reads this stuff at all—'' Kyle held up a copy of Twain's *Huckleberry Finn* ''—he doesn't comprehend a single sentence.''

''It's a little late in the boy's life to be diagnosing reading disorders, Professor. All he needs is one more semester. Two at the most, and he's home free. Without football he doesn't have a hope in hell of making something of himself.''

''Most of the essay questions are also discussed in class. If he can't figure out what a novel or a poem's about, he could learn it in class.''

The coach slammed his palm against Kyle's desk. ''You're not going to budge on this, are you?''

''I'll tutor him. Every afternoon if you like.''

''He's got a workout schedule!''

''I guess he needs to decide what's most important.''

''To Brad Miller, football is the most important.

It's all he knows. And that's what bugs you, isn't it?'' There was a sneer on Coach Lippert's face as he headed for the door. ''You're so caught up in your fairy tales you can't stand it that someone else doesn't love your imaginary people as much as you do.''

Steepling his fingers across his chest, Kyle half smiled. ''I can't stand it that a poor boy has an opportunity to get a fully funded college education and is gaining nothing more than what he knew before he came here—football.''

With a few choice words, Coach Lippert wrenched open the door, then slammed it behind him.

Kyle picked up his glasses and carefully positioned them across the bridge of his nose, glad no one could see how his hands were trembling.

NERVOUS, JAMIE knocked on the door of Ashley's classroom early Monday morning. The kids were all in another room for story time, and Miss Peters had suggested this might be a good moment for her and Jamie to talk.

''Come in, Ms. Archer.'' A warm smile on her face, Miss Peters ushered Jamie over to the art center. ''Hope you don't mind sitting on a table,'' she said, perching on the corner of one herself. ''The chairs are all a bit small in here.''

Attempting a grin, Jamie sat. Even at table level, her knees were hugging her chest.

''Ashley told me about Nathan,'' she said in a rush, determined to meet the situation head-on.

"And I'm really sorry she's so rigid in her expectations. But I'll work with her."

"So you know she slapped him?" The compassion on Miss Peters's face was the only thing that kept Jamie from sliding right off her seat.

"Slapped him?" she squeaked out. "You mean as in hitting another little child?"

Jamie's heart caught in her throat as Miss Peters nodded.

"Is he hurt?"

"Not really," the preschool teacher said. "She hit him hard enough to leave red fingerprints on his face, but they were gone by lunchtime."

"I can't believe it!" Jamie felt light-headed, confused. Scared. "I've never hit Ashley in her life."

"I wasn't sure…"

Eyes open wide, Jamie stared at the other woman. "Never!" After the way she'd grown up, Jamie could hardly bear to speak harshly to her daughter, let alone spank her. Had never needed to. "Ashley's been a model child," she added. "Loving. Almost too good."

"I must say I was quite surprised."

"What'd you do to her?"

"Put her in time-out down in the office to begin with. That's procedure."

Jamie hated to think of her daughter sitting all alone in that dreaded corner. Could just picture Ashley's forlorn little face, her feet dangling above the ground as she swung them in her chair.

But she hated even more the thought that her daughter had struck another person.

"Why'd she hit him?" she asked softly. Perplexed.

"Probably because he deserved it."

Miss Peters's dry reply surprised Jamie. She looked at the other woman with new respect. "What did he do?"

"Nathan's not the most likable kid at the best of times," Miss Peters said. "Having met his mother, I think he comes by it naturally."

"But that doesn't give Ashley any reason to hit him."

"Of course not," the teacher agreed. "Ordinarily she just ignores him when he gets mouthy, but yesterday he was teasing her about her father."

"Her...father?"

Miss Peters nodded. "He wouldn't believe that Ashley's father was a war hero who died in battle."

Not that again.

"Apparently, the more Ashley insisted he was, the more outrageous Nathan got, until he was suggesting some pretty terrible things about Ashley's dad." The teacher went on to repeat just what those things had been.

Livid, burning up on behalf of her innocent little girl, Jamie had to take a deep breath before she spoke. "How would a four-year-old kid even *know* to say something like that?"

The teacher shrugged. "I can only assume he learned it at home. Most likely on television, or some conversation he overheard." She paused, looking at Jamie apologetically. "When I questioned him about it, it was clear he had no real understanding of what he'd said."

"And Ashley?" Jamie asked, feeling the tears start deep inside. "How much do you think she understood?"

Why hadn't her daughter shared any of this with *her?*

Laying a hand on Jamie's, tangled together in her lap, Miss Peters squeezed gently. "Don't worry," she said. "I don't think she was aware of much more than the derision. That and the fact that he wouldn't believe her in the first place."

"This father thing must really be getting huge in her mind for her to have exploded like that," Jamie murmured, thinking out loud.

Miss Peters stood, then moved behind her desk. "You know how kids are...."

Not really, she didn't. "What do we do now?"

"My suggestion is to get everything out in the open so Ashley doesn't have to keep defending herself."

The teacher's words brought panic, sheer and terrible.

"Give Ashley her legitimacy instead of forcing her to fight for it...."

Jamie barely heard. The air in the room was warm, foggy, closing in on her.

"So I'd suggest, assuming it wouldn't be too painful for you, that the two of you put together some kind of presentation, you know with history, pictures—"

"What?"

"For show and tell," Miss Peters said as though she'd just explained. Which she probably had. "We can turn it into a history lesson." She paused. Smiled. Seemed satisfied that her plan had been met with the approval she'd expected.

"Did you lose him in an overseas military action?" The teacher's eyes were brimming with compassion.

Trapped, Jamie shook her head. She had no idea what to say. What to do. How to control the panic.

But instead of raising Miss Peters's suspicions, Jamie's lack of response seemed only to confirm what the teacher already believed. That Jamie had lost her husband tragically, and that the wounds were still raw.

As Jamie left, still with no resolution, she couldn't help imagining how the conversation would have gone if she'd confessed the truth. That she'd never been married in her life. That her precious Ashley was exactly what four-year-old Nathan had so cruelly claimed. A bastard.

THE NIGHT WAS bitterly cold. Forecasters predicted that temperatures would reach record lows for Denver—and nearby Larkspur Grove. Weather that seemed fitting as Jamie sat alone, huddled in front of a blazing fire in the living room of the quaint little house she was so proud of. Her furnace had chosen that night, of all nights, to be temperamental. A night when repairmen were overbooked and the best anyone could promise was to make it out by the next afternoon. Karen was looking after Ashley next door. She'd offered to put up Jamie, as well, but Jamie hadn't been at all confident in her ability to keep up appearances and opted for a cold night on the living-room floor, instead.

But at just past eight o'clock, she wondered if maybe this latest decision was another bit of idiocy. Dressed in leggings, jeans, a flannel shirt, sweatshirt and two pairs of socks, she was warm enough—as long as she didn't leave the five-foot range of the roaring flames. She'd trapped herself again.

Papers lined the hardwood floor around her and were neatly piled on the colorfully braided rug that covered most of the floor. Papers, work, that should've absorbed all of her attention. Except that they didn't. Nothing did. Except Ashley. And Ashley's father.

If the little girl only knew how much hell there'd be to pay—for both of them—if her father's name was revealed. But a four-year-old couldn't possibly know. Or understand. Not in a million years. Jamie was an adult and *she* didn't understand. And she'd been there.

So what was she going to do?

She'd been handling crises all her life; surely she'd find a solution to this one.

She wrapped her favorite blue blanket—soft and worn from its many washings—around her and huddled inside, searching not so much for warmth but for comfort.

Fifteen minutes later, the doorbell rang. The blanket fell off her shoulders and puddled at her waist.

"Who on earth..." Grabbing up the blanket, she

headed for the door, wrapping it once again securely around her. Had the furnace guy found himself with a free minute? Maybe someone else had canceled, or he'd finished a job earlier than he'd thought.

She could always hope.

On tiptoe, she peered through the peephole in her front door.

And began to tremble again. Softly.

Kyle Radcliff, handsome, confident and slightly disheveled-looking, stood on her front porch. What did he want? And what were her chances of pretending she wasn't home?

What were the chances he'd go next door and ask Karen if she knew where Jamie was? Or that Karen would see him standing out here?

As she opened the heavy wooden door, she let in a blast of cold.

"I saw your car," Kyle said before she could get out so much as a hello. Or a "go away," for that matter. "And the house lights were on, so I decided to stop by."

Jamie frowned. What did he want? Calculating how long Ashley had been at Karen's, the extended bath time necessary with two of them in there playing, she figured it was still a good bet that Ashley was safely tucked in bed, sound asleep. Not likely the child would come tearing across the yard in sub-zero temperatures to kiss her mother good-night.

"May I come in?"

Stepping back, Jamie allowed him inside. Only because she was still afraid Karen might peer outside and see him standing on her doorstep. And because she was freezing.

"What do you want?" she asked through teeth that were practically chattering, though from cold or nerves she wasn't sure.

"You said you had papers for me to sign."

"I said I'd bring them to your office."

"I thought I'd save you a trip." His words were easy enough; the challenge in his warm brown eyes was not.

"That wasn't necessary." She felt ridiculous all trussed up in several outfits, with stocking feet that looked big enough to belong to a bear.

Hands in his jeans pockets, he asked, "You conserving electricity?"

He was wearing a corduroy jacket much like the one he'd had on in his office that day but no overcoat. He must be as cold as she was.

"My furnace is on the fritz." Damn her chattering teeth.

"You're going to catch pneumonia if you stand around shivering much longer," he said, grinning at her. "I know a motel that's only a couple of miles from here...."

His comment was so outrageously out of line, the laughter in his eyes so blatant, Jamie couldn't help but smile right back at him. "I have a perfectly good fire going in the next room," she told him. "I didn't want to leave in case the repair guy has a chance to get here any earlier than tomorrow afternoon."

Kyle rocked back and forth on his feet, his jeans fitting his lean legs to perfection, as he watched her.

"What?" she asked, exasperated at the half grin lifting the corners of his mouth. What was it about this man that made him so different from any other man she'd ever known? She'd certainly known enough of them.

"I'm just wondering how long it's going to take you to work up the courage to invite me to that fire."

"I'm not intending to invite you at all." Jamie couldn't remember if Ashley had left any toys lying around the living room. "I-I'll just get the forms for you," she stammered. "Wait right here."

Hurrying back to her office, Jamie stopped only long enough to close Ashley's bedroom door. She was probably being irrational, but she didn't want him touching Ashley's life in any way. Not even by knowing of her existence.

He was adding a log to the fire when she returned to the living room. His thick leather driving gloves lay on top of the mantel.

"I heard the fire hiss and checked to make sure a log hadn't fallen. Could've been dangerous," he said, brushing his hands together as he stepped back from the fire.

Her favorite picture of Ashley—the one where her two-year-old chubby cheeks were surrounded by a halo of riotous curls—was on the mantel. The little girl was wearing her most impish grin.

"Must be a relative," Kyle said, following her gaze. "She looks like you."

Her throat was so tight she couldn't have spoken if she'd had to save her life. Jamie nodded.

"Looks too young to be a sister," he observed. "She your niece?"

She'd had sex with this man. Which made it almost impossible to understand why she still found him so damned attractive.

He seemed not to notice her silence as his gaze moved slowly around the room. Jamie's accompanied it. And landed on the pile of children's books under the coffee table at exactly the same time. Her eyes reached the baby doll tucked so carefully into the rocker before his. But only just.

It didn't take him long to put two and two together, college professor that he was.

"She's yours."

She'd always thought that when the world came to an end, it would do so with a lot of clanging noises and blurs of action. But then, that would be the whole world ending; this was only hers.

Kyle's gaze took another stroll around the room before coming back to rest on her.

"You have a daughter."

Crushing his envelope of papers between her fists, Jamie nodded again. *He knows nothing. He knows nothing....*

She repeated the words, like a catchy tune, over and over in her mind.

Relentless, watching her with his hard brown stare, he finally spoke. "You said you weren't married."

"I'm not."

"Where's her father?"

"Gone."

"You loved him?"

"I thought I did."

He moved closer to the photo on the mantel, studying it—and her. "She must be about two."

And because he'd just given her an out, because she was desperate and didn't know what else to do, Jamie stood there, mute. Ashley *had* been two in that picture.

Her knees almost collapsed as he approached, his eyes warmer now. He reached out and brushed her cheek. "She looks very much like you—beautiful."

"Thank you." She forced herself not to flinch from his touch. Nor to press her face into it. She had to stay calm, satisfy his curiosity and get rid of him. Once and for all.

Glancing from the blanket she still clutched around her, to the cold hallway behind her, he said, "Where is she?"

"Away for the night." With the irrational thought that he might ask to see Ashley if he knew she was sleeping right next door, she scrambled for something else to say. "Visiting friends," she added.

He nodded, apparently satisfied, and Jamie relaxed just a little, giving herself a huge, if imaginary, pat on the back for an acting ability she'd forgotten she possessed.

"Here." She shoved the crumpled envelope at him. "Your completed forms."

If he thought it odd to have his accountant handing him his tax forms in a less-than-pristine condition, he was gentleman enough not to say so.

He also didn't seem particularly interested in opening the manila envelope to examine them.

"I've x'd all the places you need to sign. If you have any questions just call."

He continued to stand there, assessing her. Making her nervous as hell.

"I'll be happy to mail them for you as soon as they're ready."

"Have dinner with me."

"I already ate."

"Won't you have to do so again sometime?"

Of course. In the morning. And at noon. And tomorrow night. With Ashley. "I don't date."

His eyes narrowed. "He burned you that badly?"

She couldn't have this conversation. Not with him. "I have different priorities now."

"You're no longer a woman?"

"I don't have to date to be a woman."

"Ah," he said, running his hand lightly through her hair. "But you're forgetting that I know how passionate you really are."

"That was a long time ago."

"Not so long, Jamie." The pad of his thumb brushed her lip. "See?" he asked, meeting her eyes with his own. "You still tremble for me."

"No, I don't." She pulled away from him. He couldn't be right. She couldn't let him be right. She had to remember the money. "I'm just cold."

"One dinner, Jamie," he said softly, all teasing gone. "One meal together, and if we don't find the conversation as stimulating as it was five years ago, if we find that we are indeed two different people now, then I won't bother you again.''

"Not ever?" she whispered. Dear God, could she do it? Could she control her odd connection with this man for one evening?

"Never," he said. "You have my word."

Thinking of the little girl tucked securely in bed next door, of her daughter's quest to know her father, Jamie had no choice but to do whatever she had to do to protect Ashley's future. Including going to dinner with the one man who'd made her forget all the rules. Who'd made her forget, for a few short hours, that she was a woman men paid to take to bed, not a woman they gave their hearts to.

"How about Friday?" she whispered.

CHAPTER SIX

OVER THE YEARS Jamie had perfected the art of coping. Of shutting down enough of her mind to get her through one day after another. Surviving. And so it was the rest of that week. She got through each day by concentrating on small moments, not big pictures.

The repairman came to fix her furnace, to the tune of only a couple of hundred dollars instead of the many hundreds she'd envisioned. That was a good thing. A small moment that got her through Wednesday.

On Wednesday night, after Ashley's bath and her bedtime story, Jamie gathered her daughter on her lap and plopped down on the floor beside Ashley's bed.

"We need to talk, punkin," she said softly. How to correct her child while at the same time making sure she understood that she wasn't to blame? To be honest with her without telling her the truth?

"What, Mommy?" Ashley's thumb went straight to her mouth.

"I guess most of the other kids at school have daddies, huh?"

Leaning sideways to look at Jamie with big earnest eyes, Ashley pulled her thumb from her mouth and shook her head. "No. Brent doesn't. And neither do Debbie and Dana. They're twins."

Jamie knew all about the identical twins in Ashley's class. They had fascinated Ashley and Kayla since the twins had first joined their class the previous October.

"And do you know where their daddies are?"

Slumping back against Jamie, Ashley spoke around the thumb once again in her mouth. "Brent's daddy lives in Cali…Cali…"

"California?"

Ashley nodded. "Mmm-hmm."

"And what about Debbie and Dana? Where's their daddy?"

"Their mommy divorced him. But he still comes to school and gets them sometimes. He's really tall. Kayla says he's big enough for his head to touch the ceiling, but I don't think so. Men can't get big enough to touch the ceiling, can they, Mommy?"

"Not usually, sweetie." Jamie brushed at curls, still damp from the bath, on her daughter's brow.

"Mommy, if a tall man jumps really, really hard and even jumps from a tall, tall ladder, could he at least peek into heaven?"

Afraid she knew right where this was going, pained that her daughter found it necessary to struggle so adamantly for her identity, Jamie slowly shook her head. "I'm afraid not, honey."

"Don't cry, Mommy."

"I'm not crying, Ash."

"But if I ask about my daddy, you'll cry, huh?"

"No, honey. We can always talk about anything, you and I. I thought you knew that."

"'Cept my daddy. We never, ever talk about him."

"You never asked."

"Miss Karen has pictures of Kayla's daddy. Where are my daddy's pictures?"

"I don't have any." The words almost choked her.

"Did my daddy die fighting for our country before you could take pictures?"

Hugging the child against her, Jamie forged on. She'd have prayed for guidance if she'd thought there was any chance her prayers would be heard. But the only God she'd ever learned about couldn't hear people like Jamie Archer.

"No, sweetie, I just didn't have a camera."

"'Cause you were poor?"

She hadn't been rich. But she'd had enough money. She'd worked hard for it. Sold her soul for it. "'Cause I didn't think there'd be anyone I wanted to take pictures of."

Wriggling closer, sliding her pudgy little arms around Jamie's neck, Ashley said, "But now you gots me for pictures, huh?"

"Yep." Jamie smiled. "Now I do. As soon as I knew you were on the way, I went out and bought a camera."

"That's when I was in your tummy?"

"Mmm-hmm."

Ashley was quiet for so long Jamie assumed she'd fallen asleep. And though they hadn't resolved a darn thing, Jamie was relieved. She just didn't know where to go with this one. And was finding herself damn stupid for not foreseeing this eventuality. When she'd let the town think what they wanted about her husband, she'd never thought about this tiny baby of hers growing up. Hadn't considered the fact that while she could ignore the curiosity of a town, she couldn't refuse to answer her own child.

"Where was my daddy when you bought my cam'ra?"

Damn. So much for sleeping. "He was, um, already gone."

"Gone away forever?"

"Yes, honey, forever."

"To heaven?"

"No."

"Then he was gone 'cause he getted mad and didn't want a baby girl?"

"Is that what Nathan told you?"

Ashley's nod against Jamie's chest hurt worse than a lot of the things she'd endured in her lifetime.

Jamie sat the child upright and gazed into Ashley's eyes. "That's not true, Ash. It's just not true. You understand?"

Never breaking contact with her mother's gaze, Ashley nodded. But Jamie knew that Ashley didn't understand at all.

"Your father never even knew I was pregnant, honey. He didn't know he *had* a baby girl to love."

"'Cause he died fighting for our country before you could tell him?"

The little girl's earnestness almost broke Jamie's

heart. "No, baby. He didn't die fighting for our country. But he'd already left before I knew I was pregnant with you and so I couldn't tell him. I didn't know where he was."

"But is he died now?"

Frozen to the core, Jamie stilled, no longer holding Ashley, barely supporting the child's weight against her body.

"No, Ashley, he isn't."

Wincing as the little girl scrambled around so fast she bruised her in the process, Jamie waited almost with equanimity. What was to be, was to be. She couldn't lie. Not to Ashley.

"Miss Karen said he's died," the little girl said.

"When she told you that, she thought he was and I hadn't told her he wasn't."

"Why, Mommy?"

"Because that was my secret," Jamie said, choosing her words carefully. "And now it's your secret, too."

"I can too keep secrets, can't I, Mommy?" the child asked solemnly.

"Of course you can, darling. Did someone tell you that you couldn't?"

"Kayla," Ashley said. "Her mommy has a secret and Kayla says she won't tell us 'cause we don't keep secrets good."

"But you'll keep this secret, won't you, Ash?" The words stuck in her throat, burning her even as she uttered them. They were wrong. She was wrong to ask such a thing of her child. But what was her alternative? What would Ashley's life become if the truth were revealed?

Ashley nodded. "It's our secret, huh, Mommy?" the little girl asked. "Just you and me?"

Gathering the child close once again, Jamie hid the tears brimming in her eyes. "Just you and me, Ash, and that's okay, isn't it?"

"Mmm-hmm." Ashley's thumb was obviously back in her mouth. The guilt in Jamie's gut grew a little bigger, singeing her a little more.

And as she tucked her sleeping daughter into bed half an hour later, Jamie knew she'd accomplished nothing. In trying to protect the innocence and sweetness of Ashley's life, the security, she'd done nothing to alleviate the child's doubts about herself. About the man who'd fathered her and then disappeared. She'd given Ashley nothing to take to school with her, nothing to help her face a world full of curiosity and nastiness and children with cruel tongues.

Because, when it came to Ashley's father, Jamie had absolutely nothing to give her daughter. Except the truth. And that would hurt Ashley far worse than all the accusations the Nathans of this world could ever conjure up.

JAMIE SENT Ashley to school with a note for Miss Peters the next morning. She thanked the teacher for her kind offer to help with Ashley's problem, but added that she and Ashley had talked and she'd decided just to let things lie for a while. She ended the note with a request that Miss Peters call her immediately if she became aware of any further altercations on the subject of Ashley's father.

Small moments. Not big pictures.

And the next small moment was getting Kyle Radcliff out of her life. Her fascination with him didn't matter. The fact that he seemed able to reach something in her that nobody else could—that didn't matter. The money mattered. All she had to remember was the wad of bills he'd left her five years before. And get rid of him.

"BRAD, CAN I see you a second?" Kyle called out after dismissing class five minutes late on Friday afternoon.

"Sure, Professor Radcliff, wha's up?" The bulky linebacker lumbered up to Kyle's lectern.

Kyle waited until all the other students had vacated the classroom. "Coach Lippert tells me it's really important that you pass this course."

"Yessir, it is."

"We're almost four weeks into the semester and I'm rather concerned about your chances of doing that."

Brad shuffled his feet, looking like a little boy in spite of his imposing size. "Me, too, sir."

"So what do you think's the problem?"

"I don't know, sir." The young man shrugged, his face contorted in a serious frown. "I just don't get this stuff. A boy breaking rules, an old black slave running from the law. Just don't seem like no heroes to me. And the rest, I don't see it at all. You say it's got undercurrents, that it means stuff, but it ain't like no politics or religion talk I ever heard.''

So the boy *was* listening. Kyle just wasn't reaching him.

"Okay," Kyle said, straightening his notes and placing them in the open folder on the lectern. "That's fair."

Brad grinned, looking immensely relieved.

"But I still can't pass you," Kyle added. "Not unless we find a way for you to learn about American literature."

"But I'm never going to use this stuff!" Brad said, his voice raised. He tossed his book bag on the desk behind him. "I just want to play football! Why do I need to know stories about fake people written by dead guys to do that?"

Kyle removed his glasses and set them down on top of his folder on the lectern. "A college degree stands for something," he replied slowly. "It's the assurance to anyone who asks that the person holding the degree has been given a well-rounded body of knowledge. That this person can think logically about a problem or situation and come to an informed conclusion. That he or she can join in various conversations and actually have something to contribute."

The frown was back on Brad's face. But the momentary anger had abated.

"Let's say you're at a party sometime," Kyle continued. "Let's say some franchise owner's daughter's there."

"What she look like?"

"She's a beaut. Great legs. Terrific body."

"Big breasts?"

"Sure, if that's what you like."

"Okay," Brad said. "So?"

"Well, she's looking for some fun, but she's bored by all her daddy's brute guys who have no brains. Nothing to talk about but football."

"Why would we need to talk?" Brad asked, his grin cocky. "I can make sure she ain't bored without ever saying a thing."

"But, you see, that's just it, Brad." Kyle leaned his forearms on the edge of the lectern, the way he always did when he was driving home a particularly important point. "She can have her pick of a roomful of men who've had lots of practice pleasing a woman. She's got so much money she can't be swayed in that direction. She wants…conversation. Somebody who can talk about something besides football."

Brad plopped his big body down into the chair. His bulky frame barely fit between the chair and the regulation college-classroom desk.

"You sure about this girl, Professor?" he asked. He didn't seem at all convinced, but he was studying Kyle.

"I'm sure that sometime in your life, whether it be at the doctor's office, the bargaining table or when you're out with a beautiful woman, you're going to need to be able to think. To reason. To know something besides football."

"And you ain't gonna pass me, are you?"

"Sure." Kyle put his glasses back on. "If you do passing work."

"An' how'm I gonna do that?" The linebacker was getting angry again.

Kyle couldn't lie to the kid. "I don't know for sure if there's time, Brad, but I'm willing to tutor you—no charge—and see where that gets us."

"Tutor me."

Kyle grinned. The idea seemed so foreign to someone who needed the service so desperately. "Yeah. Like private coaching to help you learn the right plays."

"When you gonna tutor me?"

Reaching for his planner, Kyle gave the kid a pained look. "Hey, don't make it sound like I just shot your grandma."

With a sheepish smile, Brad said, "She'd shoot you dead 'fore you even had a chance to pull your gun, Professor."

Kyle might have continued that conversation if he hadn't suddenly discovered that he had the wrong planner. He'd opened the book to the day's date to find only three words scribbled there. *Dinner with Jamie.* He'd been in such a hurry to get to class he'd grabbed his personal planner. Not the one he used for school.

Damn.

"How about Mondays, Wednesdays and Fridays right after class?" he ad-libbed, hoping he was free then. After having gotten this far with his most re-calcitrant and neediest student, he wasn't about to lose credibility by admitting he couldn't even bring the right calendar to class.

"I got gym time then."

"Can you make gym time an hour later?"

"Maybe." Brad's face was blank. "I'm not sure."

Kyle grabbed up his folder, the planner and the text he'd brought to class, and slid them all back inside the leather satchel that went everywhere with him. "It's your choice, Brad. Either you make passing this class a priority or you don't."

"I'll be here," Brad grumbled as he followed Kyle out of the classroom. "Thanks a lot."

Kyle ignored the sarcasm.

KAREN GLANCED around critically, although she already knew what she'd find. The house was spotless. There were fresh flowers in the foyer and on the kitchen table. Kayla and Ashley were upstairs in the playroom doing puzzles and listening to Disney songs. The girls had had an early bath and dinner and were ready for bed. And the best news was, in return for Karen's keeping Ashley that night while Jamie met with a client, Jamie was going to keep both girls the following day and night so Karen and Dennis could have some time alone.

Karen had been to the hairdresser while the girls were in school that morning and had treated herself to a manicure as well as a trim. She'd even thought about highlights, but Dennis loved the color of her hair.

She'd bought a new outfit, too. A black, long-sleeved dress that reached only enough past her thighs to be decent. And she'd made reservations at Dennis's favorite ski resort. The weekend package included dinner and dancing the following evening, as well as champagne and a whirlpool bath in their room. She and Dennis had gone to the resort only a couple of months before. It had been the best weekend of her life.

Even if the consequences were disastrous.

Dennis was due home any minute. The table was set with candles, flowers and their best china. The makings of a steak dinner waited for him in the kitchen. On the counter, his favorite dessert, blueberry buckle, was still warm from the oven. Fresh sheets adorned the king-sized bed upstairs in their room. His robe lay across the bed, ready for him to get comfortable and relax.

She couldn't wait to see him after their long week apart.

And she'd made up her mind. She wasn't going to tell him about the baby. Not yet. Not until she was better prepared to handle the news herself. She couldn't bear it if his reaction confirmed what she already suspected. That the pregnancy would turn him off, make him not want her anymore. Throwing up and pregnant, she'd never be able to compete with his savvy business associates.

Walking around with spit-up scented clothes and leaking breasts—yeah, that would impress him.

Not only would she lose her husband's interest, she'd lose her chance to be something more than a wife and mother. Any hopes she'd had of starting college in the fall when Kayla started school full-time were smashed before they'd ever been born. She could hardly put her own needs before that of a baby. Couldn't even contemplate giving her children over to strangers to raise while she gallivanted like some immature kid around a college campus.

Jamie had been so smart. As usual. She'd gone to college *first* and then started her family. Karen wished, not for the first time, that she had half the sense her friend had. Jamie always made the right decisions. If Karen didn't love her friend so much, she'd have to hate her for being perfect.

Too tense to sit and wait any longer, and loath to peek through the living-room curtains one more time, Karen slowly climbed the stairs. Lured by the sweet voices coming from the room at the end of the hall, she sought solace from the two little girls, who always managed to make life seem bearable.

REFUSING TO THINK of her dinner with Kyle as anything other than a business meeting, Jamie dressed accordingly. After donning one of her simplest one-piece skirt outfits from her "accountant attire" wardrobe, she even closed the top button she normally left open. Navy and white, with a white collar and a navy belt that cinched at the waist, the outfit screamed business. Not woman.

She hoped.

Her hair was halfway up in a professional-looking chignon when she remembered that was exactly how she'd been wearing it when she'd first met Kyle. She had, after all, been working that night, too.

She could still remember his fingers pulling the pins from her hair, one by one, his smoky brown eyes devouring every inch of her face, his lips alternating between kissing her and telling her how beautiful—how perfect—she was.

The most amazing thing of all was that she'd believed him. She, who'd heard every compliment in the book, who got paid to take compliments while she let men touch her body, had actually believed a john.

The money. She just had to remember the money he'd left on the bedside table—and then she'd be rid of him. Free to get back to the long lonely chore of trying to forget.

What did it matter if he'd come back with breakfast that morning, as he claimed? He'd still paid for her.

She left her hair down, held back from her face with a couple of combs. And wore a minimum of makeup. She'd have put on a pair of glasses if she'd had them. Men weren't turned on by schoolmarms.

At least Kyle wasn't; she knew that much. His tastes ran to the more exotic—enough makeup to disguise even the most distinguishable features, breasts falling from skimpy clothes. Oh, yeah, and young. He definitely liked them young. Jamie had barely been old enough to drink the champagne he'd poured for her the last time—the only other time— she'd spent an evening with him.

Reaching for a bottle of perfume, she stopped. She didn't need to adorn herself. She wasn't going on a date. Hadn't been on a date since she'd slept with Ashley's father. Hadn't slept with a man since that night, either.

There was no man alive who could ever love the woman that Jamie had been. The woman she still was, deep inside where the memories lurked. Those memories were always there in the background, vivid reminders of things she'd done.

And there was no reason for Jamie to date a man except for love. Because she was never going to return to the life she'd known. She'd had no choice then. But she had a choice now. And she'd rather die than live one minute of that life again.

Damn Tom Webber and his generosity. Damn his friends. Damn his lies, his choices, the choices he'd left her. Damn him for taking her youth, her innocence, and making her a whore without her even knowing what he was doing. But most of all, damn him for making it so easy to fall into a life she'd never wanted. For making it almost impossible, and completely stupid, for her to walk away.

Minutes later, Kyle's knock on the door reverberated through her small house. Jamie wasn't sure what he'd see as she opened her door to him. She'd been unable to meet her reflection in the mirror before she'd left the bedroom, couldn't stand to see the woman who would've been staring back at her.

The money. She just had to remember that last hateful wad of bills. They'd changed her life forever.

CHAPTER SEVEN

SHE WAS SO BEAUTIFUL she took his breath away. He'd carried an image of her for five long years— Jamie in the skintight red dress, so short he'd caught glimpses of her fanny every time she'd bent over, her lush breasts tumbling out at the neckline. The image paled in comparison to how she appeared now, standing in her doorway in that prim little suit thing, as though she were off to do battle in a court-room. Or a library.

Back then, the tight dress had been appropriate. There'd been outfits at that party that had made Ja-mie's look modest. Not that he'd been surprised. He'd grown up in Las Vegas. And one party in the town that never sleeps was much like the rest.

He much preferred the subtle taunting of tonight's outfit to that other, blatantly sexual display.

"Do I pass?" she asked, an edge to her voice.

Taking her arm to lead her out to his car, Kyle grinned. "Sorry," he said sheepishly. "And yes, you most definitely pass. You're a beautiful woman."

"You're late."

"I know. I'm sorry." He'd actually been pissed

as hell at himself. "I was grading papers and lost track of the time."

"Good papers?"

Kyle shrugged. "Thought-provoking," he said, remembering that last one. It had had him so engrossed he'd never even heard the alarm on his watch go off to tell him it was time to get showered. "Not that I agree with all of them."

"And do your students lose points for daring to have alternative opinions?"

"Nope." Kyle grinned at her. "Alternative opinions are always graciously accepted."

"Always?"

"As long as they have a valid argument to back them up."

"Nice car," she said, admiring his metallic-blue Ford Thunderbird.

"Thanks." Odd, as forcefully as she affected him, there were so many things she didn't know. Like the fact that he had a passion for Thunderbirds. Owned three of them. From three different decades. He'd brought the brand-new one tonight. For her. Had wanted her to travel in luxury as well as style.

"Where's your daughter?"

She shot him a startled glance, almost as though she'd forgotten he knew about the child, and then seemed to relax a bit.

"Actually, she's spending the night next door," she said, climbing into the T-Bird.

Kyle looked at the two-story next to Jamie's smaller house. "Friends of yours?"

She waited until he'd rounded the car and gotten

in. "Good friends," she said then. "They have a daughter Ashley's age."

"Ashley," he said, trying out the name. Liked it. "That's your daughter's name?"

A little jolt again, barely perceptible except that Kyle was in tune to every breath she took. "Yes," she said. "Ashley Mariah."

"It's a nice name."

He wanted to ask about the child's father. To know if he was the reason Jamie had erected such walls around herself.

And he would. When he was more certain she'd answer him.

"SO WHAT'S YOUR aversion to compliments?" He'd chosen the restaurant carefully. One of his favorite places, Gulliver's not only served superb steak but offered warmth and intimacy. Each table was set off in its own alcove, and every alcove gave the appearance of being its own private den—complete with bookshelves built into the walls.

"I don't have an aversion to compliments." She was smiling, but the smile didn't reach her eyes, and her eyes didn't quite meet his.

"Sure you do." Kyle grinned at her across their table for two.

He expected her to brush him off, as was her wont, and was surprised when she suddenly met his gaze head-on.

"I guess I'd just rather people appreciate *me*, inside," she said. "The person they can't see."

"He really did a number on you, didn't he?"

"Who?" She withdrew from him again.

"Ashley's father."

"No!" She looked around the room, at the other tables, a waiter passing by. "What do you know about him?"

"Absolutely nothing," he admitted. "But I can't help wondering if maybe he isn't at least part of the reason I'm having to scale mountains to find the woman I spent such an incredible night with five years ago."

She fiddled with the straw in the diet soda she'd ordered. "He has nothing to do with it."

The waiter approached, pad in hand, ready to take their dinner order, Kyle asked him to come back later. "So you do at least admit I'm having to scale mountains."

Jamie frowned at him, not at all pleased that she'd fallen into his trap, but her shrug acknowledged that she had indeed fallen. For one brief second, as their eyes met, Kyle felt a spark of the nonverbal connection he'd shared with her across the crowded, noisy room the night of his mother's death.

"If it's not him, what is it?" he asked softly.

Her eyes revealed nothing. "You really want to know?"

More than anything. He inclined his head.

"The money." She held his gaze for a second longer, then glanced down, drawing shapes on the white linen tablecloth with her finger.

The money? What? He didn't make enough of it? She'd just done his taxes. She knew exactly what he was worth....

A lot.

"The money," he finally repeated, more confused than ever.

"Sure, it might have been expected, but the way you just left it there, without a word..." Her voice trailed off and Kyle just stared at her.

Her face was flushed, a muscle twitching at one corner of her mouth. She was really upset.

And he was completely lost.

"I'm sorry, Jamie." She glanced up then, as if the apology meant much more to her than he'd intended. "I'm afraid I have no idea what you're talking about."

"You're telling me you aren't the one who put the wad of bills on my dress?" she asked sarcastically. "I know—housekeeping came in before dawn and left me a tip to clean the room myself, right?"

"The dress!" When he'd gotten up that next morning, after an embarrassing amount of time staring at the woman asleep in his bed, reliving the incredible hours he'd spent with her there, he'd noticed the dress he'd ruined the night before when he'd spilled champagne on it.

"I see you remember." Her tone was dry, but at least she was looking at him.

"Of course I remember." What he didn't get was why such a small thing was such a big problem. "Like an idiot, I'd ruined what appeared to be an expensive piece of designer clothing. Paying for it was the least I could do."

Brows raised, she froze, staring at him. "That money was supposed to pay for the dress?"

Kyle could feel the heat rising up his face. "It wasn't enough, was it?" he muttered. "I knew I should have left more."

"No!" she said loudly. And then, with a glance at their fellow diners, she continued more quietly. "It was plenty to pay for the dress."

So what was the problem— Oh. God. Kyle felt sick to his stomach. "You thought..."

She looked away, her auburn hair hiding her face.

"You thought I'd left that money to pay for something else, didn't you?" The thought filled him with horror.

Her silence kept the horror flowing.

"You did." He couldn't believe it.

With only her hair visible to him, he couldn't read the thoughts in her eyes. Couldn't connect with her.

How could she have thought that poorly of him? And yet, considering the night from her point of view, given the fact that she'd woken up all alone in a hotel room with a wad of bills lying on top of the dress she'd taken off at his instigation...could he blame her for jumping to conclusions?

"Jamie?" She didn't move, didn't appear to have heard him.

"Please look at me."

Still no response.

The waiter was approaching again. Wordlessly Kyle sent him away a second time. Then he reached across the table, taking Jamie's chin gently between his fingers and turning her toward him.

"I wouldn't have hurt you for the world, Jamie," he said, willing her to hear the truth in his heart.

"Don't you know," he continued as she remained silent, "I've never talked to another woman—another person—the way I talked to you that night. Never shared those things with anyone."

His mother had died the day he'd met Jamie. The mother he'd hated. She'd paraded more men than he could count through Kyle's life; she'd been a whore and he'd detested her. Not that he'd told Jamie the details—only that he'd hated the woman.

And that on her deathbed his mother had said she loved him. Even then, he hadn't been able to muster up enough compassion, enough affection, to let her die in peace. Even then, he'd gone on hating her.

That night, drowning his grief in the cacophony of Tom Webber's party, Kyle had begun to hate himself.

"You saved me from hell that night, Jamie," he said. "Your eyes met mine and something happened." He paused, took her hand in both of his, held on. "It was like you were speaking to me, telling me everything was going to be okay...."

She almost smiled. He could see that she was remembering, too.

"I never intended anything to happen, never for one second thought about wanting to, um, score."

She opened her mouth, but he cut her off before she could speak. "It's the truth," he said. "Yeah, I noticed you were gorgeous," he admitted. "I'd have had to be dead below the neck not to, but that wasn't what compelled me to get up and walk across that room."

She pulled her hand from his, saying, "I might have believed that." Her voice was thick. "Once."

He had a hell of a lot of damage to undo. "You might as well believe it—" he reached for her hand again "—because it's true. If I hadn't humiliated myself by spilling that champagne down the front of your dress like some kind of bumbling idiot, I would never have rented a room that night. I just wanted you to have a chance to rinse off, a chance for the dress to dry."

He saw the sudden warmth in her eyes, her need to believe him. And he saw the doubts. At the moment, her doubts were stronger than her ability to believe. He'd hurt her. Before he'd left the money, he'd hurt her by making love to her at all. It had been too soon, the night too emotionally charged. He'd done the inexcusable—taken advantage of a sweet, innocent woman.

"You know, Jamie, you weren't the only beautiful woman in the room that night," he said. "If I'd just wanted to get laid, I'd have chosen someone forgettable, not a woman who's haunted my dreams ever since."

THE NIGHT WAS HARDER than Jamie could ever have imagined. Somehow she got through dinner, though she didn't eat more than a spoonful or two of her potato-and-broccoli soup. Kyle was a perfect companion, charming, funny. And after those few intense minutes, he steered clear of loaded topics.

They discussed literature, recent movies they'd seen, who they'd voted for. They talked about everything from the economy to their shared passion for plain old-fashioned Hershey bars. She'd never enjoyed the company of an adult more—except maybe his, the first night she'd met him.

And on the way home, she felt again the frightening sensations she'd felt that first night. Something she'd never experienced before—or since. The stirrings of desire.

"So, you're going to be stranded on a desert island and you can take one video, one CD and one book with you. What would they be?" Kyle asked as they cruised through the streets of Denver on their way back to Larkspur Grove.

Books. CDs. Videos. Anything but him. "The book would have to be the Bible," she said, thinking carefully. She'd never been more thankful for a diversion in her life. "CD would be the soundtrack from *Phantom of the Opera* and the video would be *Annie.*"

Kyle nodded, glanced briefly over and smiled. "Okay, why?"

"The Bible because it's one-stop shopping—mystery, suspense, action, romance, history and self-help."

He nodded again, and Jamie felt inordinately pleased with his approval. "Why *Phantom?*"

"It's incredible singing, there's lots of variety, a story to follow, and it's filled with passion."

"Passion's good."

There was that feeling again, sliding insidiously through her belly, making her far too aware of his thigh resting so close to her own.

"So why *Annie?*"

"It's about hope. Endurance."

"How so?"

"'The sun'll come out tomorrow,'" she quoted from the song the orphan sings with such gusto. "I figure if a little girl can endure, I can, too."

"I wouldn't have chosen the Bible, but after hearing your justification, I can't think of any other book that beats it," Kyle said, entering into his own game. She'd been afraid to ask, afraid to get that close.

"I'd choose one of those greatest hits CDs they offer on late-night TV for $19.95," he said, frowning as he considered. "Most variety."

"And a video?" she prompted. She had no business getting to know this man.

"One of the *Raiders of the Lost Ark* series."

Jamie smiled. "Why?"

"Because they make you laugh, for one."

"Superficial." She heard herself digging at him playfully.

"Nah, filled with all kinds of inventive ways to do things. I figure if I'm stranded I'll need all the ideas I can get."

Jamie was almost comfortable as silence fell around them.

After a few minutes he broke the silence. "What I'm not taking are planners of any kind." His tone was boyishly defensive.

Bursting into laughter, Jamie asked, "Whyever not?"

"They intimidate me, and if I have to be stranded, I'm not going to be intimidated, too."

"But what if there are lions or bears on the island? Wouldn't *they* intimidate you?"

"Nope." He shrugged. "I've got *Raiders* to help me beat those."

"What about typhoons, spiders, poisonous plants?"

"I'm a man—I'll handle them."

"So it's just planners you find intimidating?" she asked, grinning.

He glanced over at her, suddenly serious. "And you."

She got that frightening feeling all over again.

LYING ON HER living-room floor, Jamie gazed into the flames flickering in front of her. She'd given up on sleep. It just wasn't going to come. Not with so many memories pounding in her head. Kyle had left her at her door, without even so much as an attempted kiss good-night, hours ago. But he hadn't left without reminding her of their deal—if they spent an entire evening together without connecting, he'd go away forever. And then he'd looked her straight in the eye. Even in the dim moonlight, she'd seen the man who'd once touched her so deeply. The man who lived all alone inside and wanted to write a classic someday. And she knew he'd seen a small piece of her—the piece that was lonely, too.

She was just going to have to find a way to convince him he hadn't. Because there was too much at stake. Ashley's entire future rested on the death of her past. She couldn't resurrect it—not for anything.

And there was something else to consider, as well. Something new.

A log splintered, spraying ashes as it fell from the grate to the fireplace floor. Jamie watched the orange-red glow of the ashes, mesmerized.

There was no point in resurrecting her past, even if doing so wouldn't destroy Ashley's safe, secure world. There was no point because Kyle was infatuated with a woman who didn't exist. When she'd talked to him tonight about the money he'd left, she thought they'd both known why he'd left it. And why she'd been hurt but not surprised.

He'd never suspected. Not even when it became obvious that she'd believed the money was in payment for services rendered. Even then, he'd never suspected why she'd jumped so quickly to that conclusion. He had no idea why she'd been at that party, dressed like a whore. Had no idea that was exactly what she'd been.

Looking back, she should have known. She'd been certain, after his desertion, that Kyle had chosen her on purpose. That he'd merely been using her to lay his ghosts to rest. But when she'd spent those hours talking with him, when she'd *made love* for the first time in her life, she'd known he was different. That *they* were different.

And if he ever found out that he'd actually been with a woman who regularly sold what favors she'd given him that night, anything special they'd shared would be gone as if it had never existed. He'd never believe that with him it *had* been different....

As the fire dwindled before her eyes and the room

cooled, Jamie slipped back to those cold, lonely years....

Desperate, frightened, alone, the young Jamie had soaked up Tom Webber's kindness, studying hard to make him proud of her. The months passed and she began to gain some confidence, but she'd felt worse and worse about being his charity case. She'd insisted over and over again that she wanted to be able to do something for him, something to earn her keep.

And he'd insisted that all he wanted from her was her time. He lived alone. He'd be thrilled to have a companion for dinner. Someone to see now and then—take to the symphony, the theater—without messy entanglements. Good, intelligent conversation that wasn't accompanied by the need to watch for hidden agendas and innuendos.

And a year later, when she was a legal adult and things started to slip naturally into something more, Jamie was happy to follow his lead. He'd saved her life. And if she wasn't in love with him, she did love him. He made her feel safe.

Until the next year, when an unknown but perfectly manicured woman came knocking at her door. Tom's wife had called her horrible things, her view of Jamie so completely opposite to the modest, moral way Jamie had seen herself. She'd thought Tom was only waiting until she was a little older before he married her. She'd thought he'd been waiting to propose for her sake, so his business associates wouldn't say he was robbing the cradle.

She'd thought that was why he'd kept her a secret from all his acquaintances.

But that day, she'd had a horrifying look at the person she'd become without even knowing it. She saw herself through the eyes of a woman who'd had every reason to hate her. This revelation was so much worse than anything she'd ever suffered at John's hands. Because Tom had destroyed her trust, but worse, her self-respect. Just nineteen years old, she was an old man's whore.

Tom came to her that evening, full of contriteness, but Jamie didn't even get the satisfaction of telling him he could never touch her again. He didn't want her forgiveness. He was there to end their association. Not only wasn't he trying to get in her pants, he wasn't going to be financing her education any longer. If he did, his wife was going to sue him for divorce.

For Jamie, the worst part was that Tom was only contrite for breaking off their relationship. He apparently felt no compunction about deceiving her in the first place, for making her the "other woman" without even giving her the opportunity to decide on that role for herself. And he wasn't the least bit sorry for choosing his wife over Jamie. Seemed to think that was a foregone conclusion. Jamie wasn't worth a messy divorce. Wasn't worth the public humiliation and censure divorce might have brought. When all was said and done, she wasn't worth anything at all.

He'd left her shaking and alone, with nowhere to turn, nowhere to live when her lease was up at the end of the month. By the time Tom called, after midnight that same night, she'd been so frightened, so desperate, she'd talked to him.

She'd cried with relief when he'd told her he still wanted to help her. Gradually she'd understood what he meant, but by then she was too needy not to listen. He'd told her he had friends, professional classy men, who'd be willing to pay her well for just a little of her time, men who traveled often, who usually came to town for only a day or two. Powerful men who took care of their own.

It was too late to be anything other than what she was, so when the powerful businessmen called her, Jamie accepted the money they offered. But the one constant that allowed her to do so was the affection each man, without fail, lavished on her. God help her, she was starved for affection, for approval, and being with men who were kind to her, who appreciated her, who *wanted* her, went a long way toward mending the emotional damage her stepfather had caused.

Her clients were all referrals from Tom. And if she received a phone call from one she didn't immediately like, she was too busy to see him. She played games with herself. She told herself that as long as she didn't enjoy the physical ministrations of the men she was with, as long as she never shared a climax with them, she wasn't selling anything that mattered. She had her rules. She always, always, insisted that the man she was with be sober and that he use protection. She abided nothing rough, nothing kinky, and never, ever consorted with more than one man at a time. She'd take a repeat client only if she wasn't currently seeing another.

And before she knew it, she was in her junior year at the university, an honor student, a favorite with all her teachers, popular with other students. And no one there knew that for a few hours a couple of evenings a week, she was a very expensive, high-class prostitute.

Wrapping her arms around herself on the cold living-room floor, Jamie stared at the dead embers in her fireplace and cried. She'd had one goal back then: to finish school, get a decent job and never have to be dependent on anyone for the rest of her life. The only thing she'd lived for was the day she could own her life, her body, for the first time since she was four years old.

And then she'd met Kyle Radcliff.

Shuddering, trapped, Jamie didn't know where to go from there. Kyle was a time bomb slowly ticking. If she didn't get rid of him, her life was going to explode right before her eyes.

But as she contemplated lying to the man, or better yet, running again, something frightening held her back. Her conscience. She'd worked so hard to become the respectable, honorable woman she'd always known she could be. The woman she really was. And now her respectable, honorable conscience wouldn't let her just take Ashley and vanish.

Because with Kyle Radcliff in town, with her discovery that he might, after all, be an honest decent man, she had one powerful reason to stay. Ashley.

CHAPTER EIGHT

"Miss Karen's mad at me." Ashley moved the queen's boat across the ocean, 'cept the queen wasn't in the boat; the king was.

"No, she isn't, honey," Mommy said. "Why would you think she's mad at you?"

"When I slept there, she didn't talk to me."

"But she talked to you this afternoon when she came over to pick up Kayla."

Ashley pondered that for a minute. She dumped the king from the queen's ship and put the queen in. And then ran the ship through a big cloud that was really a big pile of bubbles. But that was okay because the ocean was really just in the bathtub with Ashley.

"Miss Karen's got a lot on her mind right now," Mommy said. She was the lighthouse, even though she was just a person sitting on the closed lid of the toilet and didn't have a light at all.

And Mommy always said that about people having things on their minds when she wanted Ashley to stop asking questions.

Somehow, Ashley knew she'd made Miss Karen sad with her and she didn't know how, but she didn't want Mommy sad with her, too, so she'd quit asking questions just like Mommy wanted. Just like she wasn't asking questions about her daddy, either.

They'd made Mommy really sad with her, those questions. Ashley thought she knew why, and she didn't want Mommy to tell her, so she didn't ask about her daddy anymore for that reason, too. Mommy was sad about Ashley's daddy because of Ashley. Because he'd made Mommy have Ashley. Maybe Mommy didn't want that. Which was something Ashley couldn't stand to think about.

She just wished her daddy didn't keep jumping into her stories and her school time, and even when she was playing with Kayla.

"You ready to get out, punkin?" Mommy stood up and held up a big, big towel for her. One that would make Ashley feel all warm and happy inside. "Tomorrow's Monday and you have school."

"Okay." Letting the queen sail away, Ashley stood up, really careful 'bout not slipping, like Mommy always told her.

"I love you, baby," Mommy said, snuggling Ashley up against her as she rubbed her hands along the outside of the huge towel.

And Ashley felt all warm inside, exactly like she was s'posed to. "I love you more than you love me," she said, and giggled.

"No, you don't, buster." Mommy picked Ashley up and carried her to her bedroom. "I'm bigger so I get to love more."

Ashley was counting on that.

A PARTY. Kyle had to plan a party. Yeah, right. In the first place, the only thing he knew about food was how to order it—or nuke it. And that occasionally he needed some. But his stomach wasn't finicky, didn't demand things in a certain sequence or combination. Like when he had cereal and a cucumber for breakfast, there were no complaints.

But a party. Now, there people expected particular kinds of food. Not only did they want those foods, they wanted them to go together somehow. Of course, nobody at the grocery store bothered to put signs on things to tell a guy what went with what. No color coding there. Nope, people just seemed to be born knowing that green beans didn't go on hamburgers. That lettuce was for salads. That pancakes weren't for making turkey sandwiches. Or maybe their mothers taught them.

Which would explain Kyle's ignorance.

Tossing his glasses down on the piles of folders hiding his desk, Kyle read again the memo he'd just received. He was in charge of the reception for the local chapter of the National English Honor Society. He'd been given a budget to provide a generous spread of hors d'oeuvres, decorations, a program. Faculty heads and dignitaries had been invited to attend, not only to welcome new and current honor society members, but also to be introduced to Kyle, the new head of the English department.

And how impressed they'd be when the food showed up a week early. And the decorations a day late.

And what about decorations? Had the dean seen Kyle's house? Other than his bed and desk, he used cardboard boxes for furniture. Okay, maybe only until his shipment of chairs, sofas and tables arrived. But still, he knew less about decor than he knew about food. He didn't need decor to live.

And he was virtually color-blind.

Unburying his phone from beneath a stack of essays, Kyle dialed a number without looking it up.

"Hello?"

Just hearing her voice made him smile. "Jamie?" He had the perfect plan. If it worked, and he'd somehow make sure it did, he'd get his party *and* an excuse to see Jamie.

"Kyle?"

"See, you know my voice already."

"Don't flatter yourself," she said dryly, but he heard a hint of laughter. "I just can't think of any other man who'd be calling me at seven o'clock on a Monday morning."

"Oops." He grimaced as he verified the accuracy of her words. Yup, his office clock said three minutes past seven. "I was out running at four," he explained, "and I've been at my desk since five— kind of seems like midmorning to me."

"You're at work already?"

"I had some things to get through. Like last week's mail, for one."

"I sure hope there wasn't anything too pressing in it."

Not unless you counted the honor society reception that was due to happen in less than a month.

"I put my bills on automatic payment as soon as the technology was invented."

She did laugh then. "So I suppose there was a reason for your call? You didn't just dial the wrong number."

This was going almost too well. He'd known, after Friday night, that Jamie wouldn't be able to deny there was something special between them. But dared he hope that he wouldn't have to spend months undoing the damage he'd done by making love to her so prematurely five years before?

"I have a favor to ask."

"You need more accounting done?"

"I need a party."

"What?"

Picking up the memo he'd found that morning, Kyle read it aloud. Every word.

"So what's the problem?"

"Wait until you've known me longer. You won't have to ask."

Her laugh was a little less natural, and Kyle's guard went back up. So she could handle a friendly phone conversation. She wasn't yet ready to talk about a relationship or even, apparently, getting to know each other.

Fine. They wouldn't talk about it. They'd just do it. And maybe his prickly angel of mercy wouldn't notice.

"Please, will you plan my party for me, Jamie?" he asked, injecting just enough little-boy earnestness to make her laugh. If she had any idea how badly he really needed her help—or how determined he was to spend time with her for any reason—she'd probably hang up on him.

"It's three weeks from this Friday?" she inquired.

Kyle nodded. And then realized she couldn't see him. "Yes."

"Where?"

"My house."

"You'll have furniture by then?"

He would've had it already if he hadn't told the company February 1 instead of January 1. Somehow, he'd thought the interim furnished apartment he'd rented was for sixteen weeks instead of twelve. "Yes."

"Do you have any idea what kind of theme you want?"

He opened his mouth to say no. To tell her he'd leave it completely up to her.

But... "I figured we could come up with something together." Where did one shop for themes?

"If I do this, there can't be any, um, funny business."

"I'm wounded," Kyle said, allowing himself a victorious grin since she wasn't there to see. "What kind of man do you take me for?"

"I mean it, Kyle." There was no laughter in her tone now. "If I help you, it has to be on strictly a friendship basis."

"Fine." If she needed time, he'd give it to her. He was too damn relieved that she was willing to see him at all to worry about the small stuff.

"Okay, then."

"Okay."

"Well, maybe we should meet one day this week to decide on a theme?"

"How about dinner?" he asked, both his planners in front of him. "Tonight?"

"I can't."

"Lunch tomorrow?"

"Ashley's only at preschool in the morning."

"A late breakfast on Wednesday?"

"Do you ever think about anything but eating?"

Yeah. He thought about her. A lot. Way more than he thought about food. All the time. "Nope. That's about it."

"Okay." She was laughing again. "I'll see you Wednesday morning."

Kyle set a time, writing it down in both his personal and school planners, just to be sure he didn't miss it, and rang off.

But not before he'd heard the sleepy little voice in the background calling for Mommy. The jolt that shot through him just before he put the phone back in its cradle shocked him. Until that second, Jamie's daughter had been little more than a picture, a fact from her past. Suddenly the child was real—a living, breathing part of Jamie. Kyle felt a strong desire to meet her. And to know what had happened to her father.

"So, HOW'D DENNIS take the news of his impending fatherhood?" Jamie asked her friend later that morning. Dennis had just left for Lake Tahoe, where he'd be making calls for the next couple of days.

Because she jumped up from the kitchen table to

take the coffee grounds from the filter of her automatic coffeemaker and throw them away, Karen's reply was muffled. "I didn't tell him."

"You didn't?" Jamie frowned. She'd been envisioning the scene all weekend. Had played it out in a variety of different ways—all ending with an ecstatic Dennis taking Karen in his arms. "Why not?"

Karen shrugged, wiping off not only the coffeemaker but the kitchen counters. "I lost a baby before Kayla—did I tell you that?"

"No!"

"Well, I did." Karen topped their cups of coffee. "It was hard."

"I can imagine." Jamie bit her lip. "What happened?"

"Doctor said it was just one of those things."

Jamie couldn't even imagine how she would've felt if she'd lost Ashley. In spite of the circumstances surrounding Ashley's conception, she'd been elated the second she'd known she was pregnant. She'd been completely in love with her baby.

"Did you have problems with Kayla?"

Shaking her head, Karen stood by the table, sipping her coffee.

"Should you be having that?" Suddenly Jamie was afraid for Karen, for the baby she carried.

"It's decaf," Karen said. "Anyway, I just want to be a little further along before I tell Dennis about this new baby."

Jamie didn't agree with her friend. In her view, it made sense for Karen to share her burden, her fears, with the man who had as much at stake as she did;

that was what love, marriage and family were all about. But she was the last person who could call herself an expert on any of those subjects.

As Karen busied herself with early lunch preparations, Jamie couldn't help wondering if there was more on her friend's mind than a miscarriage that had happened five or six years ago. If maybe there was some other reason Karen wasn't telling Dennis about the baby. Could there be trouble in paradise? Were her friends having problems with their marriage?

The thought discomfited her. Karen and Dennis were perfect together; they complemented each other. When one was discouraged, the other was uplifting; when one had a thought, the other completed it. Jamie lived every dream she'd ever had of love and marriage vicariously through her friends. She couldn't bear it if they weren't happy together.

"You know that new client from the university I was working for last week?"

"The great-looking guy who came by your house?" Karen turned around and grinned, more her old self.

Flushed, Jamie looked away. "His name's Kyle Radcliff. He's the new head of the English department."

"Yeah. So, do I detect interest here?"

"No!" Jamie made sure Karen got that picture loud and clear. It was precisely because she hated the idea of her friend jumping to conclusions that she was saying anything at all. "But he's new in town and has to host some honor society gathering. I said I'd help him.''

Karen stared at her. "You *are* interested in him."

Shaking her head, Jamie joined her at the counter, took up a knife and started chopping vegetables for the soup Karen had started. "Not in the way you mean, I'm not," she said. Absolutely certain on that count. Even if she *were* interested, there was no point. "But he's kind of endearing, in a friends sort of way, and seems to be completely hopeless when it comes to ordinary, everyday things." Jamie smiled, thinking of his cardboard-box furniture. "He asked if I'd help, since I'm about the only person he knows except for his students and Dean Patterson. I didn't have the heart to refuse."

In actuality, Jamie had seen the party as just the opportunity she needed to get to know Kyle, to determine her next course of action. The *right* course of action. Whatever that might be.

"Is he interested in you?" Karen dumped a bowl of sliced potatoes into a dutch oven.

"It doesn't matter if he is. I'm not going out with him." Jamie was adamant.

Karen stopped, a cup of diced onions suspended over the pan. "I don't see why not," she said, her tone exasperated. "In all the years I've known you, you've never had a date." She continued to pin Jamie with her gaze. "You're young, beautiful, a great person. It's not natural for you to be alone."

The knife in Jamie's hand slipped, slicing the tip of her finger instead of the carrot she'd been aiming for. "I'm not alone," she said, her injured finger in her mouth. "I have Ash."

With an inelegant snort, Karen let Jamie know what she thought of that. "Have you been out on a date, even once, since you had her?"

"Not…really." Last Friday didn't count.

"Don't you think five years is long enough to grieve?"

If she only knew. "I'm not grieving." Had Karen forgotten she wasn't a widow?

"Aren't you?" Potatoes and onions in the pan, Karen started scooping up the carrots Jamie had managed to cut. "Seems to me you got burned and you're grieving for the dreams you lost."

Jamie was so busy convincing herself that she knew exactly what she wanted—or didn't want— that it took a minute for Karen's words to sink in. For the truth to hit her.

Maybe she *was* grieving. Not for lost dreams; she'd given up on them the day she'd met Tom Webber's chic and "out of her league" wife. But the more time she spent with Kyle, the more she suspected that the night they'd shared all those years ago had been as special as she'd first thought—and the harder it was for her to forget, to be happy only with what she had.

It seemed there were some dreams that didn't die. No matter how hopeless they might be.

KYLE WAS ON his third cup of coffee by the time Jamie arrived at the campus deli they'd decided on for their breakfast Wednesday morning. And because he was sure she was the punctual sort, he figured he'd arrive half an hour or so early. He couldn't be positive, of course, as he'd left both his planners at home that morning, so couldn't confirm the exact time they'd agreed on. Nine-thirty, he thought. He'd slept through his alarm and been pushed just to make it to his 8 a.m. class before everyone figured him for a no-show and cut out. Under the circumstances, he could hardly be blamed for forgetting a thing or two. Anyway, better to get there early.

"Hi, sorry I'm late," she said, out of breath as she slid into the booth across from him. "Ashley's school called. She fell and they thought it might be more serious than it was."

"She's okay?"

"Fine." Jamie smiled, shrugging her overcoat off her shoulders. "A bruised chin, but with all the attention she's getting, I'll bet she thinks a bruise is a small price to pay."

"You've seen her?" He didn't even need to ask. Jamie was that kind of person, would be that kind of mother. Her kid would never have to wonder if there was going to be dinner on the table or clean clothes for school. Jamie's daughter would never go without a warm hug when the boogeyman reared his ugly head.

"Just came from her preschool." She glanced at her watch. "It's after ten—I'm sorry. But that's why I'm almost half an hour late. I didn't think you'd still be here."

Kyle shrugged. "Shows you how desperate I am." Looking his fill, loving the rosy flush on her cheeks, the slight tilt of her lips, the way her bulky sweater all but hid her generous breasts, Kyle knew there was more truth than he'd like in that remark.

After they decided what they wanted to eat, Kyle went up to the counter and bought breakfast. And then, without even trying, he spent the next half hour showing her what a complete ignoramus he was when it came to party planning. But he was great at taking suggestions, and they soon had a basic plan for the reception.

Because it was scheduled for mid-February, she was going to build it around Valentine's Day, using romantic literature as a theme for the evening. She suggested they blow up book covers—classics like *Jane Eyre, Wuthering Heights, Pride and Prejudice.* They'd attach the covers to Styrofoam and use them for wall decorations. She discussed renting additional tables and chairs, tablecloths, dishes. They'd need floral arrangements and candles. And what about a basket of books on each table? Her thoughts flowed so fast Kyle couldn't keep up with them. But he enjoyed listening to her just the same.

"We can use the books for food ideas," she said, finishing off the last of her cheddar-cheese bagel.

"Okay." Whatever.

"If we do Brontë, we can serve English tea cakes, maybe miniature shepherd's pie pastries, stuff like that."

Fine. If she thought cakes and pastries went together, then he was sure they did. "I'd like to meet your daughter."

Her face froze. "Why?"

He probably shouldn't have pushed. But the woman was driving him crazy. When she smiled at him, she touched parts of him no one else had ever touched, and yet at other times, like now, she held him at arm's length, as if he were a complete stranger.

"She's obviously an important part of your life."

"Of course she is."

She wasn't going to make this *friendship,* as she'd called it, easy—for either of them. "So I'd like to meet her."

Jamie looked away, completely separated from him. "I don't think that's a good idea."

"Why not? I don't bite."

"No, but you're a man."

"Last time I checked." He shrugged lightly. "But I don't see the crime in that."

"Ashley's obsessing about her father right now. I don't think it would be wise to bring home a man."

There he was again. This mystery man Jamie had known, intimately, since that incredible night Kyle had made her his. Kyle was really starting to hate the guy. "Where is her father?"

"Out of her life." Jamie wouldn't look at him. "That's all that matters."

"Is he out of your life, too?"

Her gaze flew back to him, her eyes pleading for—he didn't know what. And then she nodded. "In any way that matters, he's more lost to me now than ever."

"The guy's a jerk."

Through the pain in her eyes, Kyle saw the beginnings of a smile. ''How could you possibly be in a position to know that?''

''First, because he left you.''

''Maybe I left him.''

''Second, because he left his daughter.''

''Not all men want to be fathers.''

''Like I said, he's a jerk.''

''What about you?'' she asked, searching his eyes. ''How would you feel if you suddenly found out you were going to be a father?''

''It would depend on how I felt about the mother.''

''You'd judge a child based on her mother?''

''Of course not,'' he said, staring into the most beautifully expressive eyes he'd ever seen. ''My delight would only intensify if I happened to love the mother, as well.''

He wasn't sure of her reaction to his answer. She continued to speak to him with her eyes, but there were so many messages—mixed messages—he couldn't decipher what she meant. And she wasn't saying a word.

''You remember me telling you about my lack of closeness to my mother?'' he asked, waiting for her confirmation before he went on.

''When I was growing up, there were many nights she didn't come home, and I used to lie in my bed and dream about the family I'd be part of someday.'' Her eyes filled with the same compassion that had attracted him the night of his mother's death. ''From the time I was a very young child, I knew what kind of parent I wanted to be, what kind of parent I *will* be if I ever get the opportunity.''

She blinked. And looked away. He couldn't figure her out at all. Why did he get the feeling that his wanting to be a good parent was a bad thing? ''I will never have a child of mine wondering who his or her father is, and never will he or she have one second's doubt about how much I love him.'' He paused, took a breath. ''Or her.''

Jamie remained silent. Studying the napkin she was folding neatly in front of her.

''And why is it that you have such an intense effect on me?'' he asked, only half joking. ''I go thirty-two years without spilling my guts to anyone...except once.''

She glanced up.

''With you, five years ago.''

Pushing her napkin aside, she continued to watch him. ''So why have you never married if children mean so much to you?''

''I couldn't find you,'' Kyle said, more serious than she'd ever know.

''What's the real reason?''

He'd just given it to her. ''I never met a woman I was thrilled about spending the rest of my life with.''

''So you're looking for a big thrill, huh?'' She smiled at him, teasing, but the glow was gone from her eyes.

''Sure. Aren't you?''

''I'm not looking.''

The words were meant as a warning. A warning

Kyle had no intention of heeding. Not because he was some kind of stalker jerk, set on pursuing a woman who didn't want him. But because he had a very strong suspicion, an intuition that wouldn't be ignored, that she needed him, maybe even more than he needed her. He couldn't explain the feeling. He just knew there was something very special between him and Jamie. Something he couldn't walk away from.

CHAPTER NINE

IGNORING HER CONSCIENCE wasn't something Jamie did well, but she was giving it her best shot. Still busy with her extra tax clients, plus all her year-round accounts, trying to take on a little extra where the care of the girls was concerned, she'd also signed Ashley up for dance lessons. The child was to have her first class that next week and was so excited she could hardly fall asleep at night.

And whenever Jamie's conscience managed to yell loudly enough to be heard through all that ruckus, she muffled it by immersing herself in plans for Kyle's party. The dean and his wife were going to be there. Some of her other tax clients were going to be there, too. She wanted them all to be very impressed.

Of course, it wasn't as if they were going to know about her part in the shindig. Or as if she'd even be attending. Still, she didn't want the people she was fond of not to have a good time. Or so she kept telling herself as she ran around town shopping and looking for ideas. She'd hired the caterer—one of her clients—chosen the menus, been to the florist and visited the craft store more times than she could count. Her desk was currently sharing space with piles of books and various Styrofoam-backed posters of blown-up covers. By Wednesday afternoon, the only thing left to plan was the program. And for that, unfortunately, she needed Kyle's help. He should've been out of class almost half an hour earlier and hadn't yet returned to his office, where she'd been waiting for him. Jamie had finally asked the division secretary where Kyle's class was held and, having trekked across campus, was just reaching the room. Sure enough, just as she'd suspected, he was still there. She recognized his voice, despite the closed door.

Slowing her approach, she listened to determine whether it would be appropriate to interrupt. To see whether they were discussing Poe or basketball scores.

"So you've got this linebacker..." Okay, so she'd had the wrong sport. Jamie headed toward the classroom door. "What's his name?" Kyle asked, but he didn't sound nearly as casual as his words implied.

"Number eighty-five. Jim, just Jim, no last name."

Whoever he was talking to didn't sound casual, either. Was this some kind of test?

Stopping just short of the door, Jamie leaned against the wall and listened a little longer.

"Right," Kyle said. "What else can you tell me?"

The question was met with total silence.

"Jim's got this manager..." Kyle prompted.

"Uh, right, a manager, and she's a woman."

"What's her name?"

"Miss Watson." The answers were flowing a little faster.

"What do you know about her?"

"She's like this Bible-totin' do-gooder broad who's always goin' around preachin' about doin' right."

Didn't sound like any sports manager Jamie had ever heard of.

"Okay."

"Except she ain't so right 'cause Jim's good— best linebacker anybody's ever seen. He's got the chance to make something of himself, and she won't let him."

"Why not?"

"She's a two-faced bitch."

"Maybe so." Kyle didn't seem put out by the reply. "But there's more to it. Why doesn't she want to sign Jim to a contract?"

"'Cause he's black. She makes deals for the white boys."

"Is that fair?"

"Hell no, it ain't fair!"

"Why not?"

Mesmerized, Jamie continued to listen. She didn't recognize the other male voice at all, but there was no mistaking the seriousness of this odd conversation.

"'Cause Jim's a guy just like the rest. What matters ain't the color of his skin but how many guys he can cremate so they don't score."

"So why doesn't somebody can her?"

"'Cause the people where she lives feel just like she does. They think blacks are lesser citizens."

"Where do these people live?"

"In the South?"

"Yes. When?"

"Jim, linebacker, number eighty-five," the student recited so quietly Jamie hardly heard him. "In 19...no, 1885?"

"Right." Kyle obviously meant business. "And does Jim have a particular team he wants to play for?"

"This is a dumb one, Professor."

"Who cares. You're learning, aren't you?"

"He plays for the Huckleberry Finns. Ain't no football team ever going to call themselves 'the Huckleberry Finns.'"

Jamie grinned. She had to agree with the guy.

"Who's the owner?" Kyle wasn't lightening up a bit.

"Mark Twain?"

"And how does Mr. Twain feel about Jim's plight?"

Sliding down to sit on the floor, Jamie listened intently, waiting to hear the student's response.

"He knows it ain't right, that those people are evil for wanting to keep the blacks down that way, but the people are his fans who pay for tickets and if they don't want to see Jim, he can't make them."

"So how does he view those people?"

"As hypocrites."

"And?"

"They're filled with lovelessness." The word was

said so slowly Jamie could almost have spelled it as it was being said.

"Okay." Kyle sounded relieved. "Do we know anything else about Jim?"

"Yeah, he ain't givin' up."

"Anything else?"

Silence.

"Think, Brad," Kyle encouraged. "What's the name of the team?"

"Oh, yeah," Brad said, sounding as if he were really expending some mental energy. "Jim's got one friend, a white boy, Huck," he said. "The team's named after him."

"And?"

"Huck helps Jim get free from his old biddy manager. He gets to play ball, but then they can't be friends no more 'cause the fans just ain't ready for that."

"And that, my boy, is the story of Huckleberry Finn." Kyle sounded inordinately pleased.

"You're somethin' else, Professor," Brad said. "The guys are never going to believe this—the Huckleberry Finns."

"What matters is that you remember this stuff for the next essay quiz."

"Right."

Jamie heard books and papers rustling, zippers zipping and stood up.

"Oh, and Brad?"

"Yeah?"

"Be sure you drop the football stuff when you write your answers."

"Will do, sir, and thanks."

"No problem," Kyle said, his voice coming closer. "As long as you're willing to try, I'm happy to do everything I can to help."

If Jamie hadn't already been half in love with the guy, she'd have fallen hard right then. He was a good man. A caring, giving man. A man who'd make a wonderful father.

Suddenly she had to hide, get away before Kyle saw her. There was no way she could discuss the reception with him right now. Or anything else for that matter.

Her conscience gave an uncomfortable tug, but she had to fight it. And keep fighting it. Or lose everything that had ever mattered.

Spying a women's rest room across the hall, she ducked in just before Kyle and his student reached the classroom door.

"GOOD NIGHT, Mommy. I love you."

Ashley's little voice washed over Jamie as she bent down to kiss her daughter good-night that same evening. Even through the angora sweater she wore with her jeans, she could feel Ashley's little hands clutching her.

"I love you, too, Ash, so much," she said. God help her, she couldn't do it. Couldn't risk losing this. Ashley was all zipped up in her *Little Mermaid* blanket sleeper, tucked under her *Little Mermaid* quilt. The picture of sweet innocence.

"I know, Mommy. You love me enough for a mommy *and* a daddy, huh?"

"That's right, baby." But the words stuck in her throat. What was she doing to this child?

Standing in Ashley's doorway as she watched the little girl snuggle down to sleep, Jamie had never hated herself more.

Ten minutes later, buried in her office in an attempt to find a moment's rest from her tortured thoughts, Jamie heard a knock on the front door.

It was Kyle.

"My secretary told me you'd stopped by earlier today," he said, stepping into her small foyer before she could invite him in.

Dressed in what she'd come to recognize as his usual work uniform of faded jeans, long-sleeved shirt and corduroy jacket—didn't the man ever wear an overcoat?—he looked wonderful to her. Reassuring.

Yet his presence there scared her to death.

"You could have called instead of coming all the way over."

"So could you." He had her there. He was looking past her into the living room.

"I, uh, just wanted to discuss the program for the reception, but we can do it another time."

"Why not now?" he asked with his hands in his pockets, the very picture of an innocent bystander. "I'm already here."

Jamie had a feeling he knew just how uncomfortable he was making her. Just as he probably knew how glad a very contrary part of her was to see him.

Far too aware of Ashley sleeping right down the

hall, she stared at him. "Well, then—" she crossed her arms in front of her "—come on into the living room."

NEEDING NO second bidding, Kyle quickly settled himself in the middle of her couch. "Where's Ashley?" He was disappointed to see that the room was empty.

Stiff and unyielding, Jamie stood in front of the fireplace. "In bed asleep."

"At 7:30? Isn't that a little early?"

"Not when she's up at six."

"I remember you telling me that you're a night person."

"I used to be."

Kyle grinned, picturing an irritable and oh-so-lovely Jamie up at the crack of dawn with a two-year-old dynamo.

She shifted from one stocking foot to the other, looking toward the door.

"So what ideas do you have for the program?" he asked. He wasn't about to be dismissed when he'd just gotten inside.

"I don't."

A moment's panic ensued. "You don't?" Was she ditching him? He couldn't believe it. Jamie wouldn't do that.

"You're the English guy, Professor, and this is a meeting for the National *English* Honor Society. I figure you're just the person to hit up for ideas."

Kyle tried. He really did. But all he could think about was hauling Jamie into his arms and kissing her until she remembered, in complete detail, how close they'd once been.

"We could do a fashion show," she finally said, frowning.

A fashion show. Kyle blinked. He wasn't sure how impressed the dean would be with designer fashions taking the stage at an honor society meeting.

"There are groups who specialize in period costuming," she explained while he was trying to figure out a way to tell her he didn't much want a fashion show at his reception.

"We could have male and female models dressed as characters from some of the novels," she said, coming closer as she grew more excited about her idea. "You know," she said, "Scarlett O'Hara could appear in one of her famous gowns."

More in love with her enthusiasm than the idea, Kyle gave it some thought. "They actually have an authentic dress somewhere like the ones she would've worn?"

"Absolutely." Jamie perched on the edge of the couch beside him. "If not authentic, it'll be a perfect replica." She smiled. "They'll even go so far as to model the dressing process, showing the various stages of undergarments and how they're put on."

Kyle liked that idea a lot. As long as Jamie was the model and he was the only other person in the room. But with the dean there?

"I don't know…"

"They're completely decent, Kyle." Jamie laughed, patting his arm reassuringly. "These are

educational shows that are entertaining, not entertainment shows with little or no education. Really.''
Her eyes met his, connected.

He didn't know whether it was Jamie's reassurances or her proximity, but suddenly the idea didn't
sound half-bad. At any rate, it was better than a
bunch of boring speeches, which was all he'd have
been able to come up with.

''Can we have Rhett, too?''

''Of course.'' Jamie laughed and jumped up from
the couch, reaching into a side table for paper and
pencil. ''We can write some kind of script, setting
the scenes that anyone who's read the novels will
immediately recognize. You know—Cathy and
Heathcliff on the moors, Scarlett and Rhett at Tara,
and so on.''

He liked the sound of that. Live literature. Yeah.
He liked it a lot.

''Tell me the characters you want and I'll see
what we can do.'' She was sitting beside him again.
For the first time in his life, Kyle had to force himself to think about the work he loved.

''As soon as I find out which of these costumes
are available, I'll let you know,'' Jamie said twenty
minutes later. Somehow they'd come up with an entire list. ''I'll need you to write a script.''

''That I can do.'' Finally, something about this
get-together he could feel confident about.

''Mommy?'' The voice was faint, sleepy-
sounding, coming from somewhere down the hall.

Jerking upright, Jamie called out, ''I'll be there in

a second!'' The change in her was immediate, and a little confusing in its intensity.

''I, uh…'' She looked from the hallway to Kyle.

''Go ahead. I'll be here when you get back.'' Not sure what was causing her so much distress, Kyle tried to be comforting.

''Well, I…''

''Mommy!'' The voice was stronger, tearful now. With one last worried glance at Kyle, Jamie ran.

''I'm here, baby…'' Kyle heard the soft words, a door close, then nothing more.

But he thought plenty. And by the time she returned, more than fifteen minutes later, he figured he'd drawn some pretty logical conclusions.

''She okay?'' he asked, standing as Jamie came slowly back into the room.

''Fine. She just needed a drink.'' She moved to the fireplace, not a relaxed muscle in her body.

''It makes you uncomfortable, my knowing about your daughter, doesn't it?''

''No!'' She was lying, and she knew he knew it. ''Why should it?''

''Because what we shared that night was pretty incredible… Wait,'' he said, holding her off as she would have argued with him. ''And now, having met each other again, we've discovered that some of what we shared is still there.''

''How can you be so sure?'' she whispered, her beautiful face marked with something akin to fear.

Kyle spread his arms. ''Can you deny it?''

She couldn't. He knew she couldn't. Even if she wouldn't say so.

"What does any of this have to do with Ashley?" she asked defensively.

"Only that it's a little awkward, perhaps, to find these feelings again with another man's child between us."

The explanation must have been more on target than he'd guessed, based on the rapid way her brow softened, her eyes cleared.

Kyle moved slowly, until he was standing in front of her. He reached out a hand, drawing it softly down the side of her cheek. "It doesn't matter, Jamie." His finger stopped at her lips, tracing them. "She's a part of you and that makes her special. The rest just doesn't matter."

And then he bent his head, tasting those lips for the first time in more than five years.

"Mmm," Jamie whimpered against him, her lips warm, soft—and welcoming.

Desire raged through him, but Kyle promised himself he wasn't going to blow this chance. He'd hurt Jamie once. He wasn't going to hurt her again.

SHOCKED AT the instant response racing through her body, Jamie opened her lips to Kyle almost before she knew what she was doing. The power of his kiss controlled her, taking her back to that one night of ecstasy, back to the only fairy tale she'd ever lived.

Her tongue met his eagerly, understanding exactly how to respond. She'd known him this way only once, for a very few hours, and yet his taste was as familiar as if she'd spent the past five years loving him. As familiar. And as welcome.

Her arms stole around his neck, her body sliding into his as he pulled her close. Feeling his strong arms around her, Jamie gave in to the unfamiliar security. The feeling of home.

She'd known when Kyle had taken her in his arms the first time that she'd belonged there. She felt as sure now, giving him kiss for kiss. As eager as he for the loving to continue.

"You taste so good," he murmured against her lips. "So right."

He ran his lips along her cheek, down to her neck, and Jamie accommodated him, lifting her chin, allowing him to rediscover places he'd visited before. And when one of his hands moved up to splay across her breast, she allowed that, too. Reveling in the rediscovery, in the confirmation that she hadn't dreamed the magic they'd shared so long ago, Jamie couldn't think at all. Could only feel.

"You are so beautiful, so perfect." Kyle's hushed words were a balm to her injured spirit, a solace she soaked up greedily.

As she drew her hands along his spine, down to gently grasp his hips, the words were torn from her. "I remembered this," she cried. All those nights when she'd lain alone, hating herself. "I remembered."

"It makes no sense, this connection we share...." His thumb teased her nipple through the thickness of her sweater.

"I thought I'd imagined it, made it all up."

Kyle's lips captured hers again. Lingering. "Never," he assured her and kissed her once more.

"Nothing else matters, Jamie," he said, gazing into her eyes as his arms slid around her again, pulling her close enough to feel the hardness in his groin. "Nothing."

Reality, worse than the most vicious physical blow, hit Jamie, rendering her incapable of feeling anything but pain.

"You have to go," she whispered, stricken, backing out of his arms.

"Jamie?"

"Shh," she said, tears brimming in her eyes as she silenced him with one finger against his lips. "You have to go. Please."

And that was when Jamie knew how special this man was, how incredibly attuned to her. Because he let her go.

"Call if you need me," he said.

And with one last kiss on her brow, a tender, non-sexual kiss, he left.

Taking her heart with him.

CHAPTER TEN

"SOUNDS LIKE your party was a rousing success."
Karen glanced over at her friend, then returned her
eyes to the road. Jamie looked great, her auburn hair
such a perfect color, her makeup just right. She was
wearing the cashmere overcoat Karen just loved.
And a pair of overalls. On Jamie they were chic. On
Karen they'd look frumpy.

"It wasn't my party," Jamie pointed out, "but
yeah, Kyle said everyone had a great time."

Glancing in her rearview mirror, Karen merged
onto the freeway. They were on their way to the
shared flute lessons Dennis had bought them for
Christmas. During a barbecue last summer, they'd
been talking about things they'd always wanted to
do as kids but never had the chance. As it turned
out, Karen and Jamie had both wanted to take flute.
Dennis had remembered and arranged for the lessons—another sign, as Jamie told her frequently, of
what a wonderful guy Dennis was, what a good husband and good friend.

"The food at the party was okay?" Karen asked.

"Great! Everyone ate a ton." Jamie laughed.
"Kyle said he got so many compliments he lost
count of them."

"Kyle said." "Kyle said." Karen wondered if Jamie realized how many times she uttered those words. Or how hard she was falling for the new English professor. Karen hoped not. She wanted Jamie to be too much in love to fight the inevitable, as she knew her friend *would* fight once her mind caught up with her heart.

"He said the fashion show was a real success," Jamie continued. "I guess Dean Patterson was more than impressed."

"That must have scored you a few points with Kyle."

Jamie shook her head. "Kyle's not like that." She paused. "And besides, I'm not looking to score points." She was staring out the front window of the minivan, her face expressionless. Karen had never known anyone who could hide emotion as well as Jamie could.

Much as she envied Jamie her nearly ideal life, Karen felt a deep sadness for her friend. If Jamie could only allow herself to love a good man, she'd have it all.

"Have you told Dennis about the baby yet?"

Karen shook her head. No matter how hard she tried not to, she felt a sadness for herself, too. She'd already started to feel heavy and unattractive because of this pregnancy. She was still uncertain about her husband's reaction—not to the baby but to *her*. Worst of all, she felt trapped. And guilty for resenting this baby. Yet at the same time, she looked forward to the child's birth. She sighed, frustrated by her contradictory emotions.

Glancing from Karen's stomach to her face, Jamie asked, "Don't you think it's about time?"

Of course it was. Past time. "I've tried to tell him on a couple of occasions, but...the words just won't come."

"You're three months now!" Jamie said. Though she didn't take her eyes from the road, Karen could feel her friend's gaze. "Surely you aren't worried about a miscarriage anymore."

Karen shrugged. She was so confused, worried about so many difficult things. "It could still happen."

And there were lots of gorgeous, young, businesswomen on the road, too—possibly setting a snare for Dennis that very moment.

"Kar, are you unhappy about this baby?"

"No!" Karen surprised herself with the vehemence of her reply. Except that she knew it wasn't really the baby that upset her. She loved babies. She'd just wanted to be more than a wife and mother—and she was desperately afraid that, compared to the career women with whom Dennis spent his days, he'd find her boring.

"Do you think Dennis will be unhappy about the baby?" Jamie asked hesitantly.

"Of course not. He'll love him just because he's ours." Which was true. It was just Karen he might not love anymore.

"And you're feeling okay?"

"Fine." Karen grinned at her friend. "With you mothering me so much this past couple of weeks, I'm feeling downright slothful."

"No more morning sickness?"

A car cut in front of them and Karen put on the brakes, then changed lanes to let the faster traffic go by. "An occasional bout. Nothing like I had with Kayla."

"Have you made an appointment yet to see your doctor?"

Karen nodded. And she'd cried for an hour afterward, too. "I go in next week."

"So, you gonna tell Dennis this weekend?"

Karen looked at Jamie, wishing she had her friend's strength, her confidence. Her life. "I guess I kind of have to, huh?"

"Unless you want him guessing first."

No, she didn't want that. She wanted to be the one to break it to him, to see his expression the exact second he heard. She could read Dennis like a book, and that instant expression would tell her what she needed to know. She was just scared to death to see it. Signaling their exit, she steered the van down the ramp.

"I'm going to tell Ashley's father about her."

Swerving, Karen pulled into the gas station at the corner of the exit ramp. "What?" She stared at Jamie. "When? Where is he?"

Jamie tried to grin, but her lips were quivering.

"*Who* is he?" Karen asked.

"It doesn't matter who he is," Jamie whispered, gazing out the windshield again. "I don't expect anything from him." She took a deep breath. "But he has a right to know."

Frowning, wishing she could read Jamie's mind, Karen asked, "Why now? Ashley's four years old."

Jamie glanced over, and then away again, shrugging. "Because she needs to know who he is."

"Do you think that's wise?" Karen certainly didn't. "I mean, if he doesn't want her, wouldn't she be better off not knowing?"

"He'll want her."

"I thought he didn't." Karen wasn't getting this at all. And hoped Jamie wasn't letting misplaced guilt open up a Pandora's box she'd never be able to close.

"I thought so, too."

Karen's heart thudded. "You've heard something different?"

Jamie nodded, sucked in her lips and took another deep breath, her face still expressionless. "I've done some...checking."

"And?"

"He's a good man." Karen saw just the hint of tears in Jamie's eyes, tears she was sure would never be shed when anyone else could witness them. She wanted to haul Jamie into her arms and never let go.

"That doesn't mean he'd want a daughter sprung on him." Then something else occurred to Karen. "Did you find out if he's married? If he has other children?"

She just didn't see any sense in upsetting the nearly perfect life Jamie had created for herself. And where would the handsome professor fit in all of this?

"He's not married, doesn't have any other children." Jamie sighed and squeezed Karen's hand. "He's an honorable man, Kar. He deserves to know."

"So why didn't you tell him before?"

Releasing Karen's hand, Jamie looked away. "I just didn't... There were circumstances—" She broke off.

"Hey." Karen reached for Jamie's hand again. "It's okay. You don't need to tell me any more." Jamie gave her a tremulous smile, those tears almost brimming over. "I just want you to know I'm here for you, okay?" Karen said.

Jamie nodded but still couldn't speak.

"Anytime, day or night, if you need me, you just call, got it?"

Jamie nodded again, gratitude shining from her eyes.

Karen gave her hand one last squeeze and put the van in drive. She pulled out into the Denver suburb toward the little music shop she and Jamie had been visiting every Thursday morning for the past six weeks.

"When're you gonna tell him?" She finally broke the silence that had filled the van.

"I don't know." Jamie was staring out at the rows of middle-class houses with their nicely manicured lawns—as nicely manicured as they could be with an inch of snow still covering them. She looked at the toys and sleds littering the shoveled walks. "Soon."

Making a mental note to keep close tabs on Jamie

in case, when the time came, her friend needed her, Karen drove the last few blocks without speaking.

Denver was such a beautiful city, a combination of big city and natural wonders. The trees were still bare, but they'd be getting their buds and blossoms soon, their leaves and flowers. She wondered where her life and Jamie's would be by then.

"Did you practice this week?" Jamie asked, grabbing her rented flute from the car floor as they parked in front of the shop.

"A little. How about you?"

Jamie grinned. "Not quite that much."

"Think he'll notice?"

"Maybe not."

"Ready to go get yelled at?"

"I guess."

The two women were giggling as, flutes in hand, they strolled to the door of the music shop.

"HI."

Recognizing the voice on the other end of the line that Friday morning in early March, Kyle felt a grin spread from the inside out. "Hi." He dropped his glasses onto his desk in front of him.

His times with Jamie had been somewhat limited over the past few weeks, but they'd talked almost every day. And each day he was more convinced that their fate had been sealed years before and there was nothing either of them could do about it. She needed time. Had established a hands-off policy as far as any physical relationship went. After the way he'd jumped her bones the first time they'd met, he figured he owed her that much.

"How were classes today?"

"Lively," he said, leaning back in his desk. "We've moved on to Edgar Allan Poe."

"The poet who killed himself?"

"That's debatable."

"That he's a poet or that he killed himself?"

"That he killed himself. He was poverty-stricken. His wife died first and illness took him two years later."

"I heard he was an alcoholic. That he died in a gutter."

"That doesn't prove suicide, does it?"

"Let me guess. You spent the past hour debating it, right?" She sounded just a little too sure of herself. Of him. Just as she had that day his furniture had arrived and she'd insisted he needed her help deciding where things should go. As if he hadn't been living alone most of his life. And who cared if he kept his dresser in his office? He was usually returning phone calls when he got dressed in the morning.

"Maybe." He was grinning, but only because she couldn't see.

"And you lost."

He tried to keep the smile out of his voice. "Maybe."

"So, which side were you on?"

"I happen to know, Miss Smarty Pants, that the man did not commit suicide."

"Oh, you were a friend of his? You witnessed the death?"

"How was your flute lesson?"

"After he yelled at me for not practicing, you mean?"

"Okay."

"It went fine. There wasn't much time left." He could tell she was grinning, too.

Kyle swung around, glancing out his second-floor window to the quad below. Students laden with backpacks were heading to and from class, on foot, on bicycles and even on in-line skates. "Why are you taking the lessons if the guy gives you such a hard time?"

"Because I love them. But learning the flute just isn't as much of a priority as paying the bills—or playing with Ashley."

He couldn't argue there.

"How'd she do at dance class yesterday?"

"She didn't cry."

"That's an improvement. Did she participate?" Kyle couldn't understand why, after the first futile attempt when Ashley had refused to go into the class without her mother, Jamie insisted on taking Ashley back. Two years old was obviously a little young for dance lessons.

"You should've seen her, Kyle."

The enthusiasm in Jamie's voice got to him, as it always did when she forgot herself enough to go on about her daughter. The love she had for the child was unmistakable. Kyle had very mixed feelings about that. While he fell deeper in love with her every time he heard it, he was also just a little jealous. If she'd hung around five years before, that child would very likely have been his. He could've been sharing these moments with her instead of just hearing about them.

Spending the next five minutes hearing about every move Ashley made in dance class, right up to the star sticker she got at the end, Kyle could only blame himself for being on the outside looking in. If he hadn't been such an ass, hadn't taken advantage of an emotionally charged situation five years before, Jamie wouldn't have thought, even for a second, that he'd left her high and dry the next morning.

"Sounds like she had a great time," he said, when she finally took a breath.

"She loved it, Kyle."

"Margot Fonteyn better watch out, eh?" These conversations with Jamie had quickly become the favorite part of his day. Talking with her about every little happening in their lives was an intimacy he'd hardly dared hoped for six weeks ago.

"Margot Fonteyn has nothing to worry about," Jamie was saying, laughing. "For one thing, she's dead. For another, Ashley's a horrible dancer. She's got two left feet."

"But you said she did so well!"

"I said she loved it, and she tried," Jamie told him, laughter still in her tone. "But she couldn't step to the beat if her life depended on it."

"No future in ballet, huh? When you going to break the news to her?" he asked solemnly.

"I'm not." Jamie didn't surprise him. "As long as she's enjoying herself, I'll take her to class."

"Good for you."

"You'd do the same, wouldn't you?" she asked.

Those were the times Kyle liked best. When she included him, when she asked his opinion. Especially about Ashley. "I would."

"You busy tonight?" Her tone was different somehow.

"Just grading papers."

"Brad's essay?"

"Among others." She'd finally confessed to him that she'd overheard the conversation between him and Brad about *Huckleberry Finn.* The only thing he'd never understood was why she'd left without letting him know she was there.

"How do you think he did?"

"I don't know. Haven't looked at it yet." But he was afraid the boy still hadn't passed.

"Can you spare an hour tonight?"

"Of course," he said, sitting forward, pulling his calendars out of his briefcase. He had a faculty meeting in—he glanced at his watch—five minutes, but other than that, he was free for the rest of the day.

"Say around eight? It'll give me time to get Ashley to bed."

Disappointed that he still wasn't going to be allowed to meet the child, Kyle agreed to be at her house at eight.

"Is something up?" he asked, suddenly uncomfortable. It wasn't like Jamie to invite him over for no reason.

"No!" she said.

And he knew instantly that there was.

Ringing off with one minute to spare before his meeting, Kyle was no longer in a good mood. In fact, his whole being was filled with dread.

Whatever Jamie had to tell him, the news was going to be bad. And the only thing that could come between them was Ashley's father. If the man had come back, if Jamie still loved him, there was nothing Kyle could do. Except hurt.

PROBABLY BECAUSE he was driving himself crazy with worry, Kyle was right on time that night. He'd stayed on campus all evening, not wanting to face the loneliness of his empty house, and his corduroy jacket was showing the day's wear. At least it was one of his newer ones and didn't have patches on the elbows. His blue jeans were fairly new, too. He might not have been at his best, but if he had to measure up to another guy, he wasn't at his worst, either. Not wanting to rush things, Kyle stood on the doorstep, waiting for the minute hand on his watch to reach the twelve. He brushed his hand through his thick mop of hair and wondered if he'd made an appointment to get it cut. If not, he needed to.

"Were you ever going to knock?" Jamie threw open the front door.

"Eventually." She looked beautiful. Her black slacks molded her hips and thighs before flaring down to the floor, and the blousy thing she was wearing tucked in at the waist showed off her pro-portions to perfection.

She motioned him in and shut the door behind him. "Why were you standing out there in the cold?"

Kyle shrugged, his unusual lack of confidence discomfiting. "It wasn't quite eight."

Jamie's smile seemed forced. "Since when has a minute here or there been a big consideration with you?"

He couldn't work up any humor. "I wasn't sure whether or not you were alone."

"Why wouldn't I be alone? I asked *you* over." She was frowning—and obviously nervous.

Which only increased Kyle's anxiety. If he hadn't been so certain they were meant to be together, he'd have given up on her long ago—and he wouldn't have been here tonight. As it was, her tension made him feel as though he'd been transported to the world of Poe's story, "The Cask of Amontillado." He didn't figure being trapped in a tomb could be any worse.

There was a fire in the fireplace. A couple of wineglasses sat on the coffee table with a chilled bottle of wine in a cooler beside them.

"What's up?" he asked. He was too tense to sit. Too wary to take hope from those wineglasses.

She sat, if you could call it sitting, perched on the very edge of the couch. "Come sit down." She picked up a little pillow, playing with the lacy edge, and laughed nervously.

It occurred to Kyle that this could simply be a

poorly executed seduction scene. His blood thrumming through his veins, his eyes met Jamie's—and he saw the fear. This was no seduction scene. Jamie knew full well she had no reason to be afraid on that score.

"Mommy?"

Kyle wasn't sure who reacted first as they heard the voice accompanied by little footsteps pattering down the hall. Jamie's eyes filled with horror at the same time Kyle turned in anticipation.

"I'm not asleep, Mommy," the child called just before she came tumbling into the room.

Rushing for the door, blocking his view of the child, Jamie cried sharply, "Ashley! No! Go!"

Kyle was shocked at her tone. So, it seemed, was Ashley. She stood frozen in the doorway and burst into tears.

"Oh, baby, I'm sorry," Jamie said, instantly contrite. "Mommy didn't mean to yell at you." She bent, pulled Ashley into her arms—and that was when Kyle got his first look at the child he'd been so eager to meet.

Something wasn't right. He stood there in a fog, staring at the little girl. She looked just like her mother, only in miniature. Her wavy auburn hair was Jamie's, though the way hers fell over Jamie's arms, he figured it must hang all the way down to her waist. Her eyes were like her mother's, too. Big and gray. Kyle had to think, had to figure out what was wrong.

"She doesn't look two." *That* was it.

Ashley pulled her thumb from her mouth, all trace of tears gone. "I'm not. I'm four."

Four? But he'd thought… He glanced at the picture on the end table. Considered the conclusion he'd drawn. Jamie had done nothing to dispel his assumption that the picture was recent. Why would she want him to think…

Jamie's back was stiff, her head held at an unnatural angle as though awaiting a blow. She didn't turn around.

"You're four?" Kyle asked, because the child was looking at him, not because he hadn't understood her the first time.

"Yes—but I'm a little more than four because my birthday came by a while ago."

If he hadn't been so numb, he'd have smiled at that. He was sure he would have. Now all he could manage was a nod.

"Do you have a birthday month?" she asked him, apparently not at all daunted to have a strange man in her mother's living room. "Mommy says everyone has a birthday month."

"I do," Kyle said. Though at the moment, he couldn't recall what it was.

"Mine's 'vember."

"November?" he asked.

Still crouching, holding the child, Jamie hadn't moved.

Ashley nodded, slid her thumb back in her mouth and stared at him. Apparently she'd said all she was going to say.

But it had been enough. Kyle was sure it had. He

wasn't completely sure *why*. Couldn't even begin to contemplate the significance of the last minutes.

"Let's get you back to bed, okay, punkin?" He barely heard the hoarse words through the roaring in his ears.

And did absolutely nothing when Jamie took the child from the room. He just let her go. Though a part of him knew he shouldn't have. That he needed that little girl right there with him. But the other part, the part that was strangling the air from his lungs, the thoughts from his brain, had too much control of him. Holding him senseless. In shock.

He had no idea how long he stood there, how long Jamie hid out in her daughter's room—away from him. But slowly, insidiously, awareness came to him. The room. The fire. The wineglasses.

The truth.

CHAPTER ELEVEN

OUT OF BREATH, every nerve in his body singed, Kyle sank to the couch. But he couldn't stay there. Driven by the emotions raging through him, he jumped up almost immediately and paced the small room.

He'd never been so angry, so excited, so scared in his life. He'd never hated, or loved, so intensely. And he had no clue how to handle any of it. Adrenaline pushed him, forcing activity, yet he had nothing to do. Couldn't have left that room, that house, if he'd tried.

So agitated he probably wouldn't have noticed an earthquake, he missed Jamie's reappearance. He turned from the fireplace and she was there, perched on the couch again, pillow in hand, picking at the lace edging.

She looked terrible, her eyes dry but red, no trace of makeup. Hair hung in her face with no apparent discipline whatsoever. And she'd pulled an old gray sweater over her blouse.

The seduction, such as it was, was over.

Tenderness welled up inside him, prompting him to take her in his arms, assure her that everything was going to be okay.

Except that he couldn't. And it wasn't. Tumbling through his mind were a thousand angry words. A blast of accusation, of blame.

And he couldn't say them. Because she was Jamie. His chin trembled with the effort it cost to restrain himself.

"She's mine." The words were torn from him.

Jamie looked up at him silently, neither denying nor confirming his bold claim. But her eyes told him the truth.

He shoved trembling hands into the pockets of his jeans. "When were you going to tell me?"

"Tonight." The word was strong, sure.

Kyle swore. "You expect me to believe that?"

"It's true."

He didn't know if it was or not, and he had too much else to think about. Whether or not she'd really meant to tell him this evening—did it matter?

"She's mine." He came closer to her, figuring in some illogical way that if he concentrated on the mother, the daughter's existence wouldn't torment him. "Say it." He lifted her chin, forcing her to look at him. "I want to hear you say the words."

He wanted to hurt her.

"She's your daughter," Jamie whispered. There was fear in her eyes—and more. Her pain tore at him and he turned away.

He needed to yell. Long and loud.

"Why?" The one word was all he dared.

"The way you left—"

She broke off, and Kyle suddenly understood.

Knew he was partially to blame. But the pain, the sense of betrayal, was stronger.

"You knew my name."

"And I thought you'd paid for your *entertainment*."

Again, he silently acknowledged her point. "How could you think that after the night we shared?" he demanded, facing her.

She looked down, but not before he'd seen the shame in her eyes. And wanted to shoot himself. He'd done this to her. Used her. He'd left her with no choice but to feel cheap, ashamed. Abandoned. Left her alone to handle the consequences.

He should be praising the woman, blessing her, thanking her until he was old and gray. She'd made a good life for her daughter. Taken full responsibility and done an incredible job. He couldn't have done better himself.

Except that he should have had the chance to try.

Ashley was his daughter, too.

As he thought of all he'd missed, the first smile, midnight feedings, the pain of loss was almost unbearable. He'd never see the trusting eyes of his newborn daughter gazing up at him. He'd never hear her first words, witness her first steps. He'd missed dirty diapers and doctor's visits. Discoveries. Guidance.

He had to get out.

Ignoring the woman watching him, Kyle strode from the room. But he didn't leave the way he'd come. Instead, he followed his instincts and walked quietly down the short hallway.

Her room was the first one he saw. He stepped inside...and found himself in fantasyland. Magic and dreams. Everywhere he looked happy eyes gazed back at him—and down on the sleeping child. Fish and crabs. A dozen mermaids. A merman. A seagull. Even a handsome young sailor. All keeping his daughter safe and protected in Kyle's absence.

His daughter. She was that bundle over there, all curled up and sound asleep in her bed. Completely unaware that he was there. That she belonged to him.

He crept closer. Scared witless. And yet compelled.

An unfamiliar moistness gathered in the corners of his eyes as he finally stood beside her, within touching distance, and faced all that he'd lost. He couldn't ever remember crying before. Hadn't thought he was capable. Until he felt the first tear slide down his cheek.

His baby girl didn't know him. She thought her daddy had deserted her. That he didn't want her. The one thing he'd always promised himself would never happen had happened without his even knowing it. His own daughter knew the same neglect he'd grown up with.

He didn't think it was possible for his heart to ache any more.

As he stood there, full of emotion and yet so alone, a hand stole into Kyle's. Soft, cool, reassuring. Silently, Jamie slid her fingers between his and held on. He couldn't look at her. Couldn't take on her pain, too. Not then. Not yet. He was still too angry. Too filled with both love and hate. But he took the comfort she offered. Squeezing her hand, he just stood there, all the while making silent apologies to the little girl he'd hurt with his negligence. And making silent promises, as well.

He was her father. For the rest of her life, she'd not only know that, she'd *feel* it, too. From that day forward, Kyle was going to help raise his daughter.

UNTIL THAT MOMENT, Jamie thought she'd already traveled the depths of despair, known fear in its highest form. If asked, she could have named the times: the night of her mother's funeral when John had almost raped her; the day Tom's wife had come to her; the same day, when Tom had shown her just how little she was worth; and the morning she'd awakened in Kyle Radcliff's hotel room to find that wad of bills. The morning she'd discovered she'd truly sold everything she had to give. The morning after the first climax she'd ever had.

But none of that compared to the debilitating terror she knew as she followed Kyle from Ashley's room. He had confrontation written all over him. She had things she could never tell him.

His eyelashes were moist, his eyes red-rimmed. Jamie's heart lurched as she witnessed the evidence of what she'd done. She wanted to apologize, to take away the pain, to promise to make things up to him.

She couldn't do any of it. How could she give him back the years he'd lost?

"I'm going to be an active part of her life," he said in a firm, clear voice.

Not trusting herself to speak, Jamie nodded. She'd expected nothing less.

"She's to be told immediately."

Again, Jamie nodded.

"I intend to be there when we tell her, even if it means I don't leave this house until morning."

Jamie swallowed, loving him even while she hated what he was doing to her life. "You're welcome to stay." She paused, holding back tears. "But it won't be necessary."

He glanced sideways then, studying her, as if measuring her trustworthiness. It hurt that he even had to wonder.

She'd known this was going to happen, had prepared herself all along. She'd always realized there was no chance of a future for the two of them. So why was the pain so intense? Why now, when only Ashley mattered, was she suddenly losing her ability to cope?

"We need to figure out what we're going to say." Kyle's tone left no room for argument. "We're going to start out as we must go on—united."

Jamie's eyes flew to his, her foolish heart taking hope for the brief second before reality intruded.

"For the child's sake," he added, obviously reading the question in her eyes.

Jamie nodded. Of course. She hadn't really thought he'd meant anything else.

"She's to know complete security," he said, pacing slowly as he spoke. "Never are we going to speak ill of each other in her presence."

He stopped, glanced at Jamie, his eyes full of the steadfastness of his purpose.

She nodded. Though he might not be aware of it, he had the power to destroy her. But she acquiesced to his demands because she agreed with them.

Turning, hands in the pockets of his jeans, he continued pacing. "She's never to feel guilty for loving both of us."

He stopped then, shoulders hunched as he gazed into the dying embers of a fire long forgotten. Without will of her own, Jamie went to him, sliding her hand gently across the back of his neck, into his hair.

"She'll love you with all her heart, Kyle."

He said nothing, but the tension in his neck told her what she'd already known. He was worried Ashley wouldn't like him. Wouldn't want him.

She owed it to him to make certain that his advent into their daughter's life was everything he hoped it would be.

"She's still so young, her emotions so close to the surface." Jamie heard herself introducing their child to him and almost cried. "She wants her father so badly," she forced herself to continue. "She'll love you instantly, just because you're her dad."

It was all too evident that he didn't completely believe her, but she could sense she'd relieved him at least a little.

He pulled away from her and resumed his wearing down of her carpet. And her composure. "We have to tell her I didn't know about her."

Which placed the blame squarely on her shoulders. Jamie hated this, hated what was happening between them, but she knew that his request was not only fair, it was necessary. Anything else would leave Ashley feeling he'd deserted her.

"We can't tell her the truth." Jamie was thinking out loud. She'd accepted all his demands thus far, and would continue to do so as long as she could. She owed him that. Maybe owed Ashley, too. But she wouldn't tell her daughter about the money—or the conclusions Jamie had drawn.

"She's only four." Kyle stopped pacing, faced Jamie. "We'll simply tell her we had a misunderstanding before we knew she was coming. That you didn't know where to find me."

Her gaze captive, Jamie held on to her composure with help from the strength she saw in his eyes. "Okay." She licked suddenly dry lips.

"We'll also tell her that I've been looking for you ever since."

That made him out to be a knight in shining armor. But it was also true.

"The problem is she'll think we're going to be a couple. She'll have us married and living together by tomorrow night."

"She'll think what we tell her to think," Kyle said, and then, for the first time that evening, he grinned. The grin was weak, definitely un-Kyle-like, but it was there.

"Until she's five or six, anyway," he added.

"We'll need to be very clear about our own relationship." Jamie was fighting for her daughter's emotional health now. "It would be cruel to raise false hopes."

Kyle's eyes softened, speaking to her in the way she'd grown to need.

"*Are* we clear about our relationship?" he asked.

Too confused to consider anything but co-parenting, Jamie nodded.

"When did that happen?"

Desperate, Jamie reminded him, "I robbed you of the first four years of your daughter's life."

He acknowledged the truth of her words with a nod.

"You hate me for that." The connection he kept talking about, the one that drew them inexplicably together, was as strong as ever.

"I admit I'm pretty angry with you."

"You'll never be able to forgive me." She didn't know which of the two of them she was warning.

"Never's a long time."

She was finding it harder and harder to breathe. "I think we need to stick to just being parents." She put the distance of the entire room between them. "At least for the next couple of years."

He followed her. "I can't agree to that."

Swinging around, she found him closer than she'd thought. But she refused to back away. Or to back down. "What's the point, Kyle? There's too much history between us. And if we hurt each other again, as we seem to keep doing, Ashley's going to be hurt, too."

Hands still in his pockets, he didn't back down, either. "It's precisely because of the history between us that I can't accept a platonic relationship forever."

Her heart lurched, her nerves fluttering with excitement. He still wanted her. She hadn't completely killed his affection.

"Our daughter is evidence of the bond between us. Whatever it is that binds us was so powerful it created Ashley. And then kept me looking for you for five long years. I can't turn my back on that, Jamie."

"I can't handle a physical relationship right now." She'd made that very clear to him the first time he'd called her after the explosive kiss they'd shared. The *only* kiss they'd shared this time around.

Tears burned the backs of her eyelids. She wanted to hope, to try to believe what he was telling her. But she had another secret. One she could never share. One that would always come between them…that wouldn't allow her to be a decent wife to a decent man.

And Kyle was the most decent man she'd ever met.

"Promise me that, aside from Ashley, we'll continue to explore this thing between us. We'll take it slowly, just as we've been doing," Kyle whispered. Pulling a hand free from his pocket, he reached out to her, brushing his fingers down the side of her cheek.

A lone tear followed his hand. He caught it, taking it to his lips.

"Promise me?"

Hating herself for her weakness, Jamie nodded.

THOUGH HE WENT home, Kyle didn't make it to bed that night. He knew he wouldn't sleep. Wasn't even tired. There were too many thoughts to think, too much emotion to assimilate. Aside from being a little angry, a bit sad, he was just too excited. As soon as daybreak arrived, he was going to meet his daughter.

He wondered if this was how Ashley felt on Christmas Eve awaiting Santa's arrival. He'd never had a visit from Santa Claus himself, but he was certain Ashley had. Four times already.

Next Christmas, *he'd* be her Santa.

He forced himself to wait until seven o'clock before he got in the shower. He took extra care shaving, not wanting to appear at all gruff to his sensitive four-year-old. Studying the thick hair that fell over his ears, he worried for a moment that she'd think he was some kind of bum and cursed himself for not paying more attention to scheduling his haircuts.

Next he slid on his glasses, but thought they might make him look too severe. Then he decided he had to wear them when he noticed how they lifted his hair above the tops of his ears. Besides, Santa wore glasses.

His closet was filled with jeans and shirts and corduroy jackets, a single suit, some shoes. Kyle considered the display with a frown. What kind of clothes would impress a four-year-old?

The suit beckoned him. And then not. He didn't want her thinking he was a doctor or lawyer or minister or something. A man in a dark suit might be intimidating to a young child. He reached for the usual, until he realized kids didn't usually want teachers showing up at their homes, either.

In the end, the jeans and jacket won out. But only because he remembered he had a Looney Toons tie he could wear with them. His students had given him the tie for Christmas one year and he'd yet to try it out. Now seemed like an appropriate time. Surely a little girl couldn't reject a guy with Tweetie on his chest.

Jogging out to his T-Bird, he realized that the long night had accomplished something besides ensuring that he was ready on time. He'd probably always hurt for the years he'd lost, but he couldn't stay angry with Jamie. Under the circumstances, he saw that what she'd done had been remarkable. Finding herself used, deserted, paid-off and pregnant, she'd taken what seemed to be a rotten situation and made a wonderful life. He hadn't meant any of it to happen, but it had. That was an unchangeable reality. A reality she'd coped with, made the best of.

He also believed that she *was* going to tell him the truth last night, just like she'd said. And he fully applauded the way she'd protected their daughter until she'd known she could trust him.

That hadn't been a seduction she'd tried to stage the night before. It had been a confession. Ashley had just beaten her to the punch.

JAMIE HAD obviously been up a while, too, waiting for him. She flung open her front door before he'd even put his Thunderbird in park. It suddenly occurred to him that he was going to have to get a toddler seat.

Walking up to that door, Kyle felt like a giant, growing by the second. He was going to dwarf this family, this house. Scare his daughter to death. And then Jamie smiled at him, almost as though, in spite of her own tension, she knew exactly how he was feeling. He was in control again. For a second or two, anyway.

"You look beautiful," he told the mother of his child. He liked Jamie just the way the Good Lord had made her. The more natural the better.

She glanced away with an embarrassed shrug. "I'm wearing sweats and I don't have any makeup on."

"I'd noticed." He grinned at her. "Did you go to all this effort in my honor?"

"Ashley would have been suspicious if I'd done anything else. I always look like this in the morning."

Kyle figured that was something to look forward to. Someday. Maybe.

He stepped into the house slowly, immediately tense again, on guard.

"She's in the kitchen." Jamie led the way.

Kyle stopped, no longer sure this was the best plan. Maybe he should have let Jamie break the news to Ashley alone. After all, the child knew her mother.

"You said she's a morning person, right?" he whispered. He'd never been as scared of anything in his life as he was of this four-year-old child.

"She's cheerful most of the time," Jamie whispered back, grabbing his arm. "Now, come on, you're making me a nervous wreck."

Still, he hesitated. "Maybe we shouldn't tell her so soon." He couldn't believe he was saying this. Not after the night he'd just spent, anticipating this moment. He *had* to meet his daughter, if for no other reason than the fact that he'd need to sleep again...someday.

"So soon?" Jamie was no longer whispering. "You call four years soon?"

She was right. He was making a complete fool of himself. He had to get a grip. His daughter deserved better than a blithering idiot for a father.

"Mommy?" Ashley yelled from what Kyle presumed was the kitchen. "Who you talking to, Mommy? I want to talk, too."

"I'm surprised she hasn't already run out to investigate," Kyle said, thinking of the night before, the glimpse he'd had of his little dynamo.

"She's eating," Jamie explained.

Ah. A captive audience. Kyle didn't know if that was good news or bad. He just knew he had to get this over with. As he followed Jamie into the kitchen, he issued one last silent prayer that Ashley wouldn't be disappointed with the talking she got.

THE NICE MAN was back. Ashley smiled at him when he came into the room with Mommy. Just to see if he'd smile back. She couldn't remember for sure if he'd smiled at her before.

He did smile. Really big. And she knew then he

hadn't smiled at her before or she would've remembered. She liked big smiles.

"Who's he?" she asked Mommy. He had a birthday month and he smiled and Mommy let him in their house, so he was good. Even if he did think she was only two. Two was baby, but maybe he didn't know that.

"My name's Kyle Radcliff."

The man answered instead of Mommy. Ashley giggled. He had a funny name. It reminded her of the story Mommy read her about the doggie that saved a kitten from falling down down down a cliff.

"Ash?"

Mommy sat down at the table.

"You remember when you were asking me about your daddy?"

Mommy's eyes were all serious. They scared Ashley so much she could hardly concentrate on Mommy's words.

Mommy was watching her, not talking anymore, so Ashley nodded.

"Well, he found us, sweetie."

Mommy's mouth started to move funny, in kind of a wobbly way.

"Your daddy found us."

Ashley stared at Mommy's lips for long enough that she wasn't sure what words Mommy had said.

So when Mommy started to talk again Ashley listened carefully.

"Your daddy found us, honey."

Her daddy! "Daddy!" she hollered, jumping up

till she almost fell out of her chair. She'd known her daddy would come someday. She'd known it!

The nice man moved closer to the table. Ashley was so happy she wanted him to be happy, too. "You know my daddy?" she asked him.

He came right up to Ashley's chair and bent way down until he was shorter than she was. "I'm your daddy, Ashley," he said, so soft she didn't think she'd heard all his words, either. Besides, she was too busy looking at the picture of herself in his glasses. She hoped her daddy had good glasses like that.

"Did you hear me, sweetie?" he asked her, his eyebrows coming together.

Hoping he wasn't going to be mad, Ashley did what Mommy always said was right. She told the truth. Shaking her head, she whispered, "No."

"I said I *am* your daddy."

Ashley froze. Her whole body felt like wiggling and she had to go potty really bad and she was afraid if she made a noise the nice man would disappear, just like in her dreams when her daddy came. She stared at him and stared at him and he didn't go away. He smiled, instead.

"You...you're my daddy?" she finally got brave enough to ask, but then covered her ears really quick in case he changed his mind.

It didn't matter that she couldn't hear him. He nodded yes.

Ashley wanted him to hug her up really big, just like Kayla's daddy did when he came home. She'd just known that when God finally heard her and brought her a daddy, he'd hug her up big like that. But he didn't, and that made her afraid.

"Do you love me like Kayla's daddy loves her?"

Daddy's eyes got really big and Ashley felt all better inside.

"Oh, yes, sweetheart. Maybe even more."

Of course more, Ashley thought. Just like God gave her the best mommy, He'd given her the best daddy, too. She just knew it.

And because he was a new daddy and maybe didn't know all about it yet, Ashley wrapped her arms around his big old neck to teach him what daddies did. He was really smart, because he picked her right up and squeezed her so tight she just about couldn't breathe.

Ashley was so excited she did a horrible, horrible thing. She wet her pants. And started to cry.

Daddy didn't get mad, though. He just hugged her more. And then helped her play with the queen and king and their boat the whole time Ashley was in her bath getting cleaned. He made up the best stories Ashley had ever heard.

She listened to every word, except when she took a time-out to thank God for hearing her and sending such a good daddy. Even if it took Him a while.

CHAPTER TWELVE

KAREN WAS SO ENVIOUS she wanted to die. Yet she couldn't help smiling every time she thought of Jamie's good fortune. She'd been a little hurt that Jamie hadn't told her right away that the new English professor was Ashley's father, but she understood, too. Kyle Radcliff had the right to know first.

And now they were living a fairy-tale ending. One Karen couldn't even hope to emulate. She still hadn't told Dennis about the baby. He probably just thought she was getting fat, becoming a dull, frumpy housewife. For all she knew, he could already be falling out of love with her. And how could she blame him? What did she have that could possibly hold him?

Holding her man was not a problem Jamie would ever experience. Not only was Kyle obviously besotted with her, she was beautiful, smart, successful. She was a fantastic mother, a loyal friend.

The only thing Jamie had in common with Karen these days, besides their daughters, was something Karen couldn't figure out. Jamie wasn't happy. As a matter of fact, there were times Karen would swear that Jamie needed a friend even more than she did.

Which made no sense at all.

SPRING WAS TEASING Larkspur Grove. March brought days that began with tantalizing sunshine and warmth, to be followed only hours later by a severe snowstorm. Three times that month Jamie sent Ashley to school wearing only a sweater and had to pack her winter coat in the car to bring her home.

The weather seemed to reflect her relationship with Kyle. Though, in all honesty, she had to admit the fault was hers. She was as inconsistent as the month of March, wanting to believe that what she'd once been didn't matter, that the woman she'd become was the only woman Kyle needed to know about. And acknowledging, the next instant, that she was, by omission, lying to him. Acknowledging, too, that a relationship built on lies would never survive.

She couldn't blame him for getting a little impatient with her, a little frustrated with the mixed messages she was sending. But neither could she quit sending them. She was in an untenable situation. For Ashley's sake and in fairness to Kyle, she had to facilitate meetings between them, all the while knowing their easy contentment existed on borrowed time.

They played the happy family so often during the weeks following that Friday night Jamie occasionally found herself believing the fantasy they were creating. They ate together a couple of evenings a week, went to movies, played in the park, visited the ice-cream shop, even went grocery-shopping once when Kyle stopped by as Jamie and Ashley were on their way to do that weekly chore.

There'd been a bit of gossip about town when word got out that Ashley's father wasn't dead after all. But Kyle covered up any awkwardness with his five-long-years-of-searching story—and a refusal to answer any other questions. Even Dean Patterson was left to draw his own conclusions. None of which seemed to hurt the way any of Jamie's acquaintances felt about her. She'd been prepared for cold shoulders and averted eyes, but none of them treated her any differently. Except maybe to smile at her more. Everyone liked being in on the happy ending.

Ashley was acting like a little imp these days, exploring her boundaries with her daddy, seeing what rules she could circumvent with him as an ally. And soon discovered that she couldn't get around any of them. In fact, the more time they spent with Kyle, the more rules tended to appear.

As Jamie had known he'd be, Kyle was a wonderful daddy, warm and loving, yet firm. Ashley adored him.

When she let herself, Ashley's mother adored him, too.

Spring break came the third week in March. Kyle had really pushed for a family vacation, four days in the mountains, and though she knew the forced intimacy would be dangerous, Jamie had finally let him talk her into it. He was so excited about the idea, so anxious to get away someplace where no one knew anything about them, she hadn't had the heart to turn him down.

But as they drove up into the mountains north of Denver, to the resort where Kyle had made reservations, Jamie couldn't help wondering if this break was going to become a breakup, too.

Kyle had told her that morning when he'd picked them up that he'd reserved a one-bedroom suite for the three of them. She'd been on edge ever since. Was he telling her that he was done waiting? That her hands-off policy was no longer in effect?

Not even for Kyle could she take pretending any further than they'd already taken it. She wasn't his wife. With her past, she wasn't ever going to be. And she wasn't going to sleep with him as if she were.

"You cold?" he asked, adjusting the T-Bird's thermostat.

"I'm fine." Jamie shook her head. The cold she was feeling came from inside—nothing a thermostat was going to help.

Kyle glanced in his rearview mirror, grinning at Ashley hunched over the padded safety bar of her new booster seat. "She always sleep like that in the car?"

After a quick peek, Jamie smiled, too. "Any time we drive more than twenty minutes."

"Is she a grouch when you wake her up?"

Watching her daughter, Jamie shrugged. "Sometimes. Not usually."

"Must be rough when you have to go into Denver."

Denver wasn't a trip Jamie made often. She liked the suburbs. "Actually, it was a blessing when she was little," she told him, eager to share—as had become habit whenever they were together now—everything he'd missed in the first four years of Ashley's life. "She was colicky for a while and when nothing I tried seemed to calm her down, I'd take her out for a drive. That always did the trick."

"Where'd you go?"

"Anywhere, nowhere, around in circles."

"That's what I'd call dedication."

"You telling me you wouldn't have done the same?"

"No." He glanced into the back seat again. "I'd have done it."

Jamie smiled at him. "I thought so."

"You said she was colicky. Did you breast-feed her?" He looked over at her and Jamie heated up instantly. She'd never forget how enamored he'd been of her breasts that long-ago night, the loving attention he'd given them.

"I did."

"For how long?"

"Almost eighteen months."

Kyle whistled. "That's a long time." He peered back at Ashley, as if there'd be some visible consequence of having nursed so long.

"Actually, my pediatrician said that the longer she breast-fed, the healthier she'd be," Jamie reported. "He said it was best, emotionally and physically, for Ashley to wean herself. And that she'd do it when she was ready."

"Did she?" He looked over intently, soaking up, as always, every tidbit she gave him.

"Yes, and what he said about its being better for her health must have been right, too. Ashley's never even had an ear infection."

They were on the highway, traveling a desolate piece of land, a few road signs their only companions. Kyle glanced at Jamie again, that particular light in his eyes.

"How'd it feel?" he asked. "Nursing her?"

Jamie supposed she should've been embarrassed at the intimate question, but she wasn't. "Incredible, weird, wonderful," she said, remembering those first few times she'd held her daughter to her breast. The experience was incomparable.

"Did it hurt?"

"Only after she started getting teeth." Jamie's nipples tightened. She was glad of the bulky sweater she'd pulled on over her jeans that morning, hoping the faded beige garment hid her reaction.

"She bit you?"

"Once or twice." Jamie grinned at his horrified expression. "She quickly learned that if she tried to chew, she didn't get her dinner."

"Well, I should think so."

THE REST OF THE TRIP passed uneventfully. Kyle was full of questions Jamie was happy to answer—all concerning the child they shared. Kyle was a mother's delight, someone to brag to who wanted to listen. Someone else who thought the child was the greatest kid ever to grace the earth.

Once she awakened, Ashley was her usual cheerful self. She wanted to choose her own order when

Kyle pulled into a drive-through at a fast-food hamburger place about half an hour from the resort.

"An' I'll have a chocolate shake, okay, Daddy?" she asked, ignoring her mother.

"Does your mother let you have chocolate shakes for lunch, Ash?" Kyle asked, meeting his daughter's gaze in the mirror.

"Uh-uh." Ashley shook her head.

"Then I guess it'll be milk, eh, squirt?"

"Okay, but can't I have some cookies for dessert?" The little girl grinned at her father. "Please, Daddy?"

Looking over at Jamie, catching her nod, Kyle ordered the cookies.

THOUGH THEY'D DROPPED their bags in the suite when they first arrived, they were so busy they didn't even unpack. Ashley dragged them all over the resort, insisting on trying every game in the game room, walking the trails, eating at the restaurant that opened out over the canyon. She even talked Kyle into renting her a pair of baby skis and agreeing to her first ski lesson. Kyle and Jamie clutched each other's hands, holding their breath every time Ashley fell during the half-hour lesson. Ashley fell a lot. And had a ball.

"That was the best ever, Mommy," the little girl claimed, slouched against her daddy's shoulder as they rode upstairs in the elevator later. "When I get big at it, I can fly right down the mountain!" Kyle and Jamie exchanged a delighted grin.

It was hard to say who was more exhausted as

Kyle unlocked the door of their suite. Unfortunately, however, Jamie wasn't too exhausted to be nervous. She brought her night things into the bathroom when she took Ashley in to wash her up. She'd brought a pair of sweats and a T-shirt to sleep in—nothing like the shorty pajamas she slept in at home—and padded out behind Ashley, climbing into one of the two double beds beside her daughter.

Kyle glanced pointedly at the beds when he came in from the living room a few moments later, but other than a raised brow, he seemed to have no other reaction to the silent statement she'd made.

In spite of the things that had changed over the past weeks, the rules remained the same. There was to be no sex between them.

PROBABLY BECAUSE of the full days she'd spent, Ashley fell asleep by six o'clock their last night at the resort as they were having hot chocolate in the dining room. Jamie racked her brains trying to think of something they could do while she held a sleeping child in her arms, but knew she had to follow Kyle up to the suite whether she liked the idea or not. Ashley didn't need to be in her arms. She needed to be in bed.

The only problem was, Jamie and Kyle needed to be as far away from bed as possible. Sharing a bathroom with Kyle, stepping into a shower that was still wet from his having stood there before her, seeing his razor on the counter beside her makeup, his toothbrush lined up with hers, his damp towels hanging beside her own—it all made her have thoughts she had no business having.

Thoughts she knew he was having, too.

"I've ordered up dinner," he told her as she shut the bedroom door quietly behind her. "Prime rib for two and a bottle of wine." He was sitting in the middle of the couch. Which left her the armchair across from him or one of the two cushions on either side of him.

"How about a game of cards?" She chose the chair.

"How about you sitting over here with me?"

"You don't want to play cards?" She wished she had that glass of wine already. She needed to relax.

"Not especially."

"We could watch a movie. They've got some good selections."

"I've seen them all." His gaze was pinning her to the chair, and she could feel it penetrating her blouse. Moving. Touching.

She wet her lips. "How long till dinner?"

"An hour."

She thought she heard Ashley in the other room and jumped up to check. The little girl was sleeping soundly.

She turned from the bedroom door and ran smack into Kyle. She hadn't heard him come up behind her.

His arms were around her instantly, steadying her. But it was only seconds before they were roaming. Before she was melting into him. And all thought was lost.

She wasn't even sure whose lips took whose, who led and who followed. She just knew that Kyle's kisses were like a drug she couldn't do without. She was addicted to the incredible feeling only he could arouse, the tension, the delicious excitement. And oddly enough, the security. He made her feel cherished. Cared for.

He made her feel like she'd never felt before in her life.

She welcomed the touch of his hands, eagerly explored his strong, hard body. He slid one hand beneath her sweater, touching the bare skin at her waist.

And scaring her to death. Remembering the other time Kyle had undressed her, the wantonness he'd aroused, her complete loss of control, she panicked.

A picture of Ashley popped into her mind, the little girl sleeping so innocently in the next room. She thought of the life she'd made for herself, and started to gasp for breath. She couldn't do this. She couldn't be that woman again.

"No." She pushed Kyle away. And prepared herself for his anger.

THE PHYSICAL LONGING was intense those first few seconds. It took all of Kyle's control to ride the waves of unsatisfied desire. And then his mind cleared enough for him to think. Or try to.

"What happened?" He was drawing a blank here.

Jamie turned away from him, standing by the couch with her back to the room. "I'm sorry."

"For what?"

Things had been going along so well. She'd even started the whole thing and he was sure she'd been enjoying the kiss as much as he had. What had he done wrong?

When he asked, she answered his question with a shrug, looking small and alone as she huddled in on herself. He wanted to go to her, but not knowing what had upset her, he didn't dare get close. Instead, he stood there, waiting.

"I don't blame you for being angry," she finally said.

Taking off his glasses, Kyle rubbed the bridge of his nose. "Okay, that's good to know," he said. "Now, do you mind telling me what I'm angry about?"

Jamie turned, glanced at him hesitantly, then sank on one arm of the couch. "You know—" she gestured between them. "That—stopping—wasn't very…nice."

"I'd hoped there was a lot more than 'nice' going on between us." Kyle moved over to her slowly, took her hand, led her to a seat beside him on the couch. "I think it's time we talked, don't you?"

Her gaze flew to his, her eyes filled with fear. Kyle bit back a groan of frustration. What had he done to bring that look to her face?

In that instant, another, horrifying, thought occurred to him. Could her reaction be something unrelated to him altogether? Had someone forced her—

"Talk about what?" Her voice sounded strained.

"About why you don't want to share any kind of physical intimacy."

She'd been wearing jeans and sweaters all week. Today's jeans were black, the sweater a striking shade of gray that matched her eyes almost perfectly. He'd been fantasizing about getting his hands under that sweater the entire day. He almost wished he hadn't tried.

"We need to talk about it, Jamie," he said gently when she remained silent and still beside him.

"I...can't."

He hoped his suspicion was completely ludicrous. "I'll help you, honey, but we have to get this out."

Again she answered him silently, this time with an adamant shake of her head.

Dropping his glasses on the coffee table, Kyle continued to hold her hand. His mind continued to process possibilities—all of them untenable.

"Did something happen to you after I knew you five years ago?" he asked carefully. "Something to make you afraid of sexual relationships?" He strained to keep his voice calm as he asked the question; he could do nothing to control the churning inside him.

"No."

Thank God. He almost fainted with relief.

"Then does it have anything to do with that time we were together?"

She didn't respond. Just sat there. He took that for a yes. Okay, so he'd narrowed down the problem. It was *him*.

"Because we slept together the first night we

met?'' He'd known all along he'd made a mistake there.

"Sort of." Her voice was barely more than a whisper.

He'd do whatever was necessary to take that trapped, frightened expression off her face. Except walk away. He just didn't believe that was the answer. For any of them.

"But we've done it right this time, Jamie." He couldn't undo the past; he could only spend the rest of his life trying to make it up to her. "We've taken the time to get to know each other, to be sure that what we feel is more than passing lust."

She nodded agreement. But the haunted look in her eyes hadn't dimmed.

Kyle could feel the promise of their future slipping away and didn't know how to hang on, what to grab hold of. "Can you tell me what you're feeling?"

She laughed bitterly. "Like I'd give anything for a little dose of self-respect."

Stabbed by her words, Kyle had nothing to say. He'd been an idiot not to realize the far-reaching consequences of what he'd done that night. How humiliating Jamie must have found those ensuing months, pregnant, unmarried, alone. Thinking that he'd used her and then cavalierly paid for the privilege.

"I'm sorry isn't enough," he told her. He didn't know what was, but honesty was all he had. "What I did five years ago, making love to you, it wasn't premeditated. I wasn't using you, Jamie. Or if I was,

I didn't do it on purpose." He stopped, remembering. "I—I thought we were starting a relationship."

He couldn't tolerate her silence. "I'd never have touched you if I'd realized I was stripping you of your self-respect."

"*You* didn't do that, Kyle." Her words were hard, uttered in a voice he hardly recognized. "I did."

"No." He knew the kind of woman who destroyed her own self-respect. Jamie wasn't that kind of woman. "I took advantage of the situation."

"And I enjoyed it."

Although he wished she sounded a little happier about that, Kyle's heart still gave a pleased little lift. He'd begun to think he was the only one with incredible memories of their night together. Memories that meant nothing if she didn't share them.

So he'd just have to help her see that night as it had been. And he knew right where to start. By telling her what she wasn't. What their lovemaking wasn't. He was an authority on both.

"You remember my telling you about my mother?"

Jamie nodded, giving his hand a little squeeze. "She'd just died. And you hated yourself for not being able to love her."

Kyle nodded, bile rising in his throat as the memories overwhelmed him. He'd never told her exactly why he hated his mother. He'd never told anyone....

"My first experience with sex..." He paused, wondering if he really wanted to do this. "I walked in on my mother—stark naked on my bed—with two men doing her."

He couldn't look at Jamie. Couldn't stand to see the horror—or the pity—in her eyes. Couldn't stand the fact that he'd come from such a woman. That he might very well be the product of an act like the one he'd just described.

The hand in his tightened, offering compassion.

"I was seven years old."

Jamie swore softly. Was silent. Then swore again.

Kyle's feelings exactly.

"Did she know you were there?"

Kyle shook his head. As far as he was aware, she'd never known. "Guess she was having too damn much fun."

"Did she look like she was having fun?"

It was Kyle's turn to swear. "How the hell should I know?" he asked, staring at her. "I was just a kid."

She hung her head. "Sorry."

"Besides," he continued, wishing he'd never started, "she would hardly have invited them in if she hadn't been planning to have fun, now would she?"

"Maybe."

Kyle frowned. "Whose side are you on?"

Jamie let go of his hand. "I didn't know there were sides here," she told him. "I just wonder if maybe she was being paid for what she was doing."

"Of course she was being paid." There. He'd admitted the rest. The pièce de résistance. The most damning part of all.

How could Jamie help but be disgusted by him? The son of a whore?

"So maybe she was providing for you in the only way she knew how."

With no idea how this conversation had gotten so out of hand, he wanted it over.

"She was a two-bit whore, Jamie. Don't make her out to be some kind of saint."

"But you told me the night she died that she loved you, that when she was around, she was good to you."

"You call humping two guys in my bed being good to me?"

"I call it very sad," Jamie said softly. "And maybe a little desperate."

Uncomfortable with her assessment, Kyle stood up. "The point I'm trying to make here is that women like my mother sell their self-respect. They deserve to live in the hell of their own making. You don't.

"What you and I shared five years ago was the furthest cry from the carnal degradation that robs women of their self-respect. It wasn't dirty. Or wrong."

"You don't know, Kyle—"

"I do know, Jamie." He pulled her up, held her gaze with his own. "And it's because I'm so sure that what we have is special, that it's beautiful and right, that I want to give you all the time you need to resolve this."

"But..."

He silenced her with a finger on her lips. "If I have to, I'll wait until I'm a hundred for you to come to me. And not regret the waiting."

She studied him, questions in her eyes.

"I won't touch you again sexually until I can do so without making you feel bad about yourself."

"A hundred, huh?" she asked. Her smile didn't reach her eyes. They were resigned. Almost...dead. "You think you'll still be thinking about sex when you're a hundred?"

"If you're anywhere around—definitely."

Jamie didn't turn away, didn't even look away, but she felt strangely lost to Kyle anyway. The feeling was far worse than the sexual frustration he'd felt earlier. He could live without sex. He couldn't live without Jamie.

CHAPTER THIRTEEN

BRAD FAILED his midterm essay exam. Sitting at his desk at home, drinking coffee from a throwaway cup because he was gone so much he'd never gotten around to unpacking his real ones, Kyle read the paper a second time. Or tried to. Problem was, there were no sentences. Just thoughts. Jumbled ones, at that.

Though, in an odd kind of way, the jumbled thoughts did make sense. They were possibly even pertinent to the exam questions. Dropping the paper, and his glasses on top of them, Kyle rubbed the bridge of his nose. He really believed that Brad knew this stuff. That if the goal was an educated man who could convey intelligent opinions, Brad could at least make a valid comment or two if *Huckleberry Finn* were ever a topic of conversation.

Wasn't that the goal? Hadn't Brad then met that goal?

Picking up the exam again, Kyle shook his head. There was no way he could ethically give that paper anything more than the grade it had earned. An F. How could he hand this paper back to Brad, have the kid show it to someone, and ever be able to defend anything but an F? No matter what Kyle believed about Brad's goals, his capabilities, his improvement, the kid had still turned in failing work.

Red pen in hand, Kyle scored the paper accordingly. And then went to bed.

He tried to dream about happier things. Like Jamie. And Ashley. And all three of them living together as a real family. To take hope from the fact that she'd asked him to be her companion at a reception in Denver the next evening. She'd been attending a national accounting convention in the city every morning since they'd returned from the mountains three days before, and Saturday night was the culminating social event.

Kyle had decided that Jamie's desire to show him off to her professional peers was a good sign. Yeah. She was coming around. Hot for him. Fighting to keep her hands off his incredible bod. She'd be ready, any year now, to be his wife.

"YOU LOOK PRETTY, Mommy." Ashley perched on Jamie's bed.

Still wearing only her slip and panty hose, Jamie smiled at her daughter. "Thank you, honey." She held up two cocktail dresses, a light-gray one that looked good with her hair and matched her eyes, and a short black figure-hugging dress that she'd bought in an unusually vain moment—and never worn. "Which do you think?" she asked the four-year-old who'd already supervised her makeup application.

"The black one."

"This one?" Jamie held the black dress up to her body, studying herself in the mirror. "Why?"

"So you look more like a lady than a mommy."

"What?" Jamie dropped the dress.

"You're a pretty mommy, but Kayla and I watched on TV that daddies like ladies."

"Oh, Ash," Jamie said, sitting down to pull the little girl onto her lap. "Daddy likes me no matter what dress I wear."

"But he doesn't sleep here sometimes like Kayla's daddy does."

Looking into those earnest gray eyes, Jamie wanted to cry. "That's because your daddy and I aren't married, like Miss Karen and Kayla's daddy are."

Ashley nodded. "I know," she said importantly. "That's why you should be a lady. Daddies marry ladies."

"Would it upset you very much if your daddy and I just stayed good friends forever and didn't get married?"

With her little brow furrowed, Ashley thought that over for a couple of long minutes. "Would Daddy ever sleep here then?" she finally asked.

"No, but he'd be around all the time, just like now."

After more pondering, Ashley asked solemnly, "It takes a daddy to have a sister, doesn't it?"

"Yes." Jamie's heart sank.

"Then yes, it would upset me." The child nodded. "Very much."

KYLE HADN'T TAKEN his eyes off her all evening. Of course, she'd had to be staring at *him* to notice that. The man looked incredible in his black suit and white shirt. He'd even found a conservative tie. She'd never seen him dressed up.

She should probably plan not to see that sight again any time soon. Not if she hoped to maintain the promises she'd made to herself. And to her daughter the day she was born.

So what was the matter with her? Here she was, unable to keep her eyes off the man, pleased beyond compare that he was finding her irresistible, yet she was still determined to keep the relationship strictly platonic. Should she add "tease" to her list of sins? Or was he right? There *was* some nebulous force, stronger than either one of them, stronger than circumstances or justice, that just kept compelling them toward each other.

"You want to dance?" he asked, motioning to the tiny floor where a few couples were moving to the relaxed, low-key ballad the band had just begun.

Shaking her head, Jamie took another sip from the glass of wine he'd brought her. "I don't think we should."

"You have more business to do?"

He'd been great all evening, keeping her supplied with food and drink, making charming small talk when called upon and fading away when she couldn't avoid discussing business.

"No!" she told him now. "I don't want to discuss another ledger for the rest of the weekend."

"Then let's dance."

"No, Kyle."

"Why not? Other people do it."

"We aren't other people."

"I got it—you don't trust yourself not to jump my bones, right?"

Jamie laughed, glanced up at the handsome man at her side and sobered. "I don't want to be a tease."

"It's impossible to tease a man who already knows the score."

"This isn't fair to you, Kyle." She knew he wanted her. An expert on men's sexual needs, she could read all the signs.

"I'm a big boy," he told her with complete seriousness. "I can make my own choices."

Tempted, tired, vulnerable, Jamie could think of nothing but the need to feel his arms around her, to have his body there to lean against. "Okay," she said softly. "Let's dance."

Of course, the minutes she spent in his arms were pure torture. But never had torture felt so good. Jamie could happily have been convinced to stay that way forever.

They'd never danced together before, though she shouldn't have been surprised that they did so perfectly. Everything about her and Kyle fit perfectly— except the one thing that would never fit at all. The woman Jamie had been.

"Has Karen told her husband she's pregnant yet?" Kyle asked as they swayed to the music.

Jamie shook her head. Kyle wouldn't even have known about the pregnancy if Karen hadn't had a bout of morning sickness the week before, when the three adults had taken the girls out for pizza and skeeball.

"You think she'll tell him this weekend?"

"I hope so." Jamie was getting really worried about her friend.

Worrying seemed to be all she did anymore. About all of them. And now Ashley wanted a sister. She was going to want one even more when Kayla found out that Karen was having another baby. The thing was, Jamie would have given just about anything to grant the child her wish. But she just couldn't do it.

They were on their fifth song in a row when, suddenly, a male hand tugged at Jamie's shoulder.

"Little Jamie Archer! I don't believe it!" The man pulled her around. His voice was loud. And slurred from too much alcohol. But Jamie still recognized it.

She recognized the hand, too. It had touched her body enough times.

Panicked, she thought her knees were going to give out on her. "Do I know you?" she asked the man who had once been one of her most lucrative clients.

He'd always been sober back then.

He was also Tom Webber's accountant.

"Nelson Monroe," he told her. "Come on, baby, give an old man a thrill," he said, lurching sideways as he grabbed for her breast. "For old times' sake."

"You touch her, you die." Kyle put himself between the man and Jamie.

Crumbling inside, Jamie wished *she* were dead.

Nelson lurched again. "Oh, hey, man," he said easily, "I didn't know she was taken for the evening."

"She's taken, period." Kyle's voice left no room for misunderstanding.

Too stricken to do anything but stand there and wait for her life to come crashing down on her, Jamie watched the two men, horrified, transfixed, as if witnessing a fatal accident.

"No kidding," Nelson said, staring first at Jamie, then Kyle. "You managed to snag one, eh, little lady?" he muttered. "Good for you."

Kyle's face was red, his hands bunched into fists. "Where do you get off talking to her like that?" he demanded.

Jamie was afraid Kyle was going to hit the older man. "It's okay, Kyle." She couldn't bear another minute of this. She couldn't have Kyle risking arrest—not when he didn't have anything to defend. "Let's just go."

"It's not okay." He pushed her gently behind him. "You owe the lady an apology." Both feet planted firmly on the ground, he faced Nelson Monroe.

"Sure! Okay," Nelson said, holding both hands up in surrender as he took stock of Kyle's size through bloodshot eyes.

"Sorry, Jamie," he said, leaning far enough around Kyle to wink at her. He turned then and stumbled off.

Jamie had never hated herself more.

STILL NOT RECOVERED from Saturday night, Jamie reluctantly took Kayla and Ashley to school on Monday morning. The girls were going on an all-day field trip to the zoo, and all day seemed entirely too long for Jamie to be without them. She needed the comfort of innocent chatter, the security of Ashley's unconditional love.

She'd tried to be positive. Had taken time with her hair and makeup that morning, wearing her favorite pair of beige cords and a stylish black jersey that Karen said looked great on her—even put on the black boots that took ten times as long to lace up as the loafers she usually wore to drive Ashley to school. All in an effort to feel good about herself. It hadn't worked.

She desperately wanted to run away—so far away no one would ever find her again. Except that running would be wrong and she was determined to live her life right.

Besides, Ashley already loved her father so much. She loved her home, her school, her friends. To take her away would scar the little girl for life.

And Jamie wasn't going anywhere without Ashley.

Returning home for a morning of dodging thoughts, Jamie saw Karen waving frantically at her from her own front door.

After throwing the car into park Jamie hurried next door.

"I'm losing the baby!" Karen cried as soon as Jamie was within hearing. She was bunching the front of her denim jumper in her fists.

Oh, God. No. "Come on," Jamie forced herself to think, to stay calm. "Let's get you inside."

She led Karen to her living-room couch, where she helped her friend lie down. "Have you called your doctor?"

Karen nodded, close to tears. "She said to come in, but I didn't want to go alone, to drive myself."

"Are you spotting?"

"No. But I started having cramps right after you left with the girls. I just know I'm going to lose it."

"Have you called Dennis?"

Tears blurred Karen's eyes as she slowly shook her head. "I still haven't told him."

"Karen, my gosh, you're over four months pregnant! I'm surprised he hasn't guessed."

"I've only gained a couple of pounds so far. And...and he's hardly been home."

Looking at her friend's pinched face, Jamie considered calling Dennis herself. She would for sure if things got any worse.

"What did your doctor say, exactly?" Jamie wondered if maybe she should call an ambulance rather than risk driving Karen.

"She said that cramping is perfectly normal and there might not be anything to worry about, but she wants to see me just in case."

"Then let's go."

"I'm sorry I'm taking you away from your work, I know you're extra busy with April 15 right around the corner."

"Don't you dare apologize, Karen Smith," Jamie said firmly, helping her into a sweater. "You're my friend. You and the baby are far more important than any job.''

Karen started to cry then, slow silent tears that dripped down her face as she and Jamie stumbled together out to Jamie's car. Karen climbed awkwardly into the passenger side of the car, then leaned back with closed eyes as Jamie fastened the seat belt around her. ''This is exactly how it started the last time.''

''Shh.'' Jamie fumbled with the belt buckle, her fingers not quite steady. ''Don't even think about last time,'' she continued softly. ''Your doctor said cramping is normal. Let's go with that until we have a reason not to.''

Nodding, Karen lay back in her seat, eyes still closed, and rode the rest of the way without speaking. Hoping Karen had fallen asleep, Jamie drove as quickly as she could to the clinic, praying all the way that the baby's fragile life would be spared. Karen and her little family were Jamie's only personal experience of ''happy ever after.''

Two hours later, the two women were on their way home, exhausted but tentatively relieved. A thorough exam and an ultrasound had revealed that Karen's pregnancy was progressing in textbook fashion. Because Karen had asked, Jamie had accompanied her friend through both exams, cried with her when they'd seen the little body floating on the monitor during the ultrasound, then laughed and cried some more when they'd heard the little heart beating furious and strong.

''We've got a while before the girls are back. You

want to take a nap?'' Jamie asked as they walked
slowly up to Karen's front door.

"No." Karen shook her head. "I don't want to
be alone." She paused, turned apologetic eyes on
Jamie. "Unless you have to get back to work."

"Of course not!" Jamie chuckled. "Like I'd get
any work done now." She carried the manila envelope containing the film of Karen's ultrasound.
She'd made Karen promise to tell Dennis about the
baby the second he got home on Friday. Jamie had
already insisted she'd have Kayla at her house Friday night.

"You practiced your flute at all this week?" Jamie asked as she helped Karen out of the sweater
she'd put on to make the trip to the medical center.

"Nope."

"Me, neither. Think he'll fire us?"

"I don't think that's legal as long as we're paying."

"Good." Jamie left to get Karen something to
drink.

"You know…" Propped up with pillows on the
couch, Karen frowned, looking down into a cup of
warm milk a few minutes later. "I realized this
morning just how much this baby means to me."

Jamie stared at her friend. "You didn't already
know that?"

Karen shrugged, her eyes still downcast. "I knew
I loved the baby," she admitted slowly. "It was the
pregnancy I hated."

"Why?" Jamie sat on the end of the couch, pulling Karen's feet into her lap.

Glancing up, embarrassed, Karen said, "I'm afraid I'm going to lose Dennis." Tears flooded her eyes.

"What?" Jamie was shocked. "Why?" So there *was* trouble in paradise, dammit.

"Oh…" Karen took a deep breath that turned into a sob. "I just don't see how a fat housewife with baby talk for conversation can compete with the beautiful, professional women he sees at work every day."

"Do you really think Dennis is so shallow?" Jamie asked, rubbing her friend's feet. "He loves you."

"He's human," Karen said. She looked up at Jamie, tears streaming down her face. "You should hear him talk about Linda this and Christina that."

"He's probably just trying to share his day with you, Kar, keeping you involved in that part of his life."

"Or telling me what he really wants in a woman. He…he never even compliments me on my cooking anymore. But those women who—"

"Do you honestly think that if he wanted one of those women he'd be telling *you* about them?"

"I don't know." Karen shuddered. "But I'd promised myself that once Kayla started school in the fall I'd go to college, get a degree, be someone in my own right. Someone Dennis could respect and have an intelligent conversation with and—"

"You *are* someone," Jamie cried. "Don't you know your life is what gives me hope every single day? My gosh, Karen, you have everything I've ever wanted right here in this house. I *love* coming over here. You, your home and family give me hope that the world I want to believe in really does exist.''

Karen didn't look as if she believed her. ''Until this moment,'' Jamie continued, her voice almost angry, ''you've always been one of the most intelligent people I know. Education isn't intelligence.''

''That's easy for you to say. You've got it.''

''It's not easy to say,'' Jamie said. ''Life's full of tough choices, Karen, and it takes intelligence to make the right ones. You always do.''

''I wish I had half your confidence in me.''

Jamie resumed her massage of Karen's feet and calves. ''Has Dennis given you any indication that he isn't happy?'' she asked hesitantly. She didn't want to probe where she shouldn't, but neither could she leave her friend feeling as she did.

''No.''

''What about that weekend at the resort a month or two ago? Was it as great as you said it was?''

''Better.'' Karen blushed.

''I think you've just been letting your imagination run away with you,'' Jamie told her. ''Worrying over nothing.''

''I don't know.'' Karen sat up, wiped the remaining tears from her face. ''Can you honestly tell me you'd admire a woman who did nothing but change diapers, cook, clean house and watch *Sesame Street* as much as you'd admire that female lawyer on television or the doctor we saw today?''

''Yes.'' Jamie's answer was emphatic. ''Do you

know how much I'd give to be able to do what you're doing?''

Shaking her head, Karen grinned. ''I can't believe you're saying this!''

''It's true.''

Karen sobered. ''Do you have any idea how envious I am of you?'' she asked, looking straight into Jamie's eyes. ''You're so strong and confident. So perfect with Ashley. *And* you have a career. I'd have been a total loss at that convention you went to last week. But you go, wow everyone with your speech, take part in important conversations. And you look fantastic, to boot. I'll bet every man in the place wished he had a wife like you.''

Karen's words destroyed what little composure she had left. Trying to hang on, Jamie studied the threads in her friend's jumper, the pattern in the crocheted afghan covering Karen's legs. An afghan Karen had made herself.

She opened her mouth and before she'd even made the decision to allow it, words started tumbling out. ''You're wrong, Karen. So far wrong. You have no idea...''

Tears filled Jamie's eyes, but she refused to let them fall. Closing her eyes, she tightened her lips to stop their trembling. She could do this. Had to do this. She just couldn't run anymore.

''There is no decent man alive who'd ever want me for his wife.'' Her voice was devoid of emotion.

''You're nuts!'' Karen said, sliding her feet to the floor. ''You're every man's dream!''

Leaning her elbows on her knees, Jamie asked,

"You ever wonder why I never talk about my parents? About my life before I came here?"

"Sometimes," Karen said slowly.

"It's because I reinvented myself when I moved to Larkspur Grove. The person you know isn't the person I am at all."

"I don't believe that, Jamie." It was Karen's turn to sound stern. "I don't care who or what you think you were, I *know* who you are."

Swallowing, Jamie shook her head. She'd known this was going to be hard. She'd had no idea how hard. She could only hope there'd come a point soon when the hurt just couldn't hurt any worse.

"You don't know *me*, Karen. You know the person I invented."

"So you're telling me you aren't honest?" Karen snorted. "That you aren't loyal and caring? 'Cause let me tell you now—you're wrong!" Karen pushed the afghan off her lap. "This morning is only one of a million examples I could give to show the type of person you are."

Somehow she had to shut Karen up. Jamie just couldn't take any more of her praise, certain as she was, that once Karen heard the truth, she'd take it all back.

She opened her mouth one more time. "I was a prostitute."

Karen shut up.

CHAPTER FOURTEEN

A FULL MINUTE after Jamie's bald proclamation, Karen spoke.

"Excuse me?"

Head still bowed over her knees, Jamie said, "You heard right."

"But what—I don't believe you!"

Jamie turned her head just enough to meet Karen's shocked gaze. "Shall I tell you about some of my clients? What we did together? How much they paid to have sex with me?" With no idea what was driving her, Jamie was purposely crude. Almost as though she wanted Karen to hate her—in spite of the knowledge that the other woman would never hate her as much as she hated herself.

But as she dared to look into her friend's eyes, Jamie's wall of ice broke. Karen didn't seem disgusted or even angry at Jamie's deception, as Jamie had expected. Her eyes glowed with compassion. With love.

"Why?" Karen asked, her voice soft, without condemnation.

Jamie's tears fell slowly at first, one by one, sliding down her cheeks, until she was huddled over her knees, sobbing like she hadn't sobbed at any other

time in her life. She cried for all she wanted to be—
and wasn't. For things that could never be changed,
for innocence forever lost.

Karen's arms stole slowly around her, pulling Jamie back to rest her head against Karen's shoulder.

"It's okay, love. Go ahead. Cry it all out."

The anguish poured out of Jamie, completely out
of control. She tried to breathe and sobbed, instead.
There was too much hurt to store up any more. And
even with the tears, it didn't go away.

Karen's gentle fingers brushed the hair back from
her face, tending to her as though it were Kayla or
Ashley she cradled.

"I'm sorry," Jamie said when she could gulp in
enough air to get the words out.

"Who told me this morning that friends don't
have to apologize?"

It wasn't exactly what Jamie had said, and certainly not with such a connotation. She didn't know
what to do next, where to go. Who she was anymore.

"You never answered my question," Karen said
as Jamie's sobs finally quieted.

Sitting upright, Jamie looked at her, too drained
to do more than ask silently for clarification.

"Why?"

Jamie shrugged, trying to find the words to explain what she herself still didn't comprehend. Not
even sure how much she could bear to tell.

"My father ran out on my mom and me when I
was just a baby." She hadn't intended to go that far

back, but once started, the whole sordid tale tumbled out.

"The bastard!" Karen spat out when Jamie got to the night of her mother's funeral. "Oh, God," she said, her eyes filling with tears. "Tell me he didn't—"

Unable to speak for the fresh emotion clogging her throat, Jamie shook her head. She'd never imagined that telling someone about those years would result in anything but disgust. Karen's support was almost more than she could grasp.

She told Karen about running off that night, about the bit of money she'd had, taking a bus to Las Vegas, searching for a job, trying to get into school, find a place to live. And meeting Tom Webber.

"The bastard!" Karen cried again as soon as she mentioned Tom's name. "He put you to work! Just an innocent, frightened child! How could he?"

For the first time in what seemed like years, Jamie smiled. "No, he didn't."

"He didn't?"

"At least, not like you think."

She went on to explain her two-year relationship with her benefactor, the platonic first year, the support Tom had given her, the love.

"So what happened?" Karen's brow was furrowed as she gazed at Jamie.

"His wife found out about me. She showed up at my apartment."

"He was married?"

"Surprise, surprise."

"You didn't know."

Shaking her head, Jamie asked, "Can you believe I was so stupid? So naive? I actually thought he was going to marry me."

Karen reached for Jamie's hand and held it between her palms. "I'd have thought the same thing."

"No, you wouldn't." Jamie looked down at their clasped hands. "You'd have made the right choices everywhere I made the wrong ones."

"I haven't heard any wrong ones yet."

"The man was old enough to be my grandfather!"

"And he was the first person in your life who loved you!"

Jamie glanced back up at her friend. "My mother loved me."

Lips pursed, Karen said, "That's debatable."

"No, it isn't."

"Would you have stayed married to a man who was hurting Ashley?"

"No." No matter what. She'd give her life for her daughter. Jamie supposed that admission didn't reveal her own mother in a very good light.

"Sounds to me like she was too busy trying to cope with life herself to have anything left for you."

Okay. Maybe. Jamie didn't want to think about her mother anymore. Not today. She just didn't have the strength.

"You want a diet cola?" Karen asked, standing.

"Sure." Jamie followed her friend out to the kitchen, where she grabbed a couple of cans of cola from the refrigerator while Karen filled glasses with ice.

They sat at the kitchen table, a plate of cheese and crackers in front of them along with the sodas.

"So what happened after the jerk's wife came to your place?"

Jamie had known Karen wasn't going to let her stop where she'd left off. She wasn't even sure she'd wanted her to. The load was just too heavy to bear alone.

"Tom came by that night."

"The bastard!"

Again, she grinned at Karen's vehemence. Having such a loyal friend was more of a treasure than she'd ever realized.

"Not to sleep with me," Jamie assured her. "To break things off. If he didn't, his wife was going to divorce him."

"Which left you with an apartment you couldn't afford, and no ready way to pay your bills, buy groceries, cover tuition…"

Too ashamed to look at her friend, Jamie stared at the cracker between her fingers. "He offered me a solution."

"I knew it!" Karen cried. "He *was* a bastard."

"I guess." Jamie just didn't know anymore. "He said he had business acquaintances who'd be only too happy to pay for the same companionship I'd given Tom. Men who came to town infrequently…."

Reaching across to cover Jamie's free hand where

it lay on the table, Karen said, "Oh, hon, I'm so sorry."

Jamie shrugged. "It wasn't bad, Karen." She glanced up, meeting her friend's eyes as she finished her story. "By that point, it didn't seem like there was anything left to lose, and I have to admit they were all good to me."

"Thank God for that!"

"I don't think God looks out for whores, do you?"

"Absolutely. Besides, you weren't a whore, Jamie. You were a desperate young girl who made some desperate choices."

"I took their money."

"I take Dennis's money, too."

"That's different and you know it! You're married, the two of you—a team."

"Well, then, look at it this way. Students take handouts all the time to get through school. Sounds like these men could afford to help you out."

For a second there, Jamie almost saw herself through Karen's eyes. "I had my rules," she said. "Nothing kinky, no toys, and I never saw more than one man at a time."

"Basically, you dated Tom's friends while they were in town, and in turn they supported you."

"You make it sound a lot nicer than it was," Jamie said dryly. "In any case, I finished school—and got out."

Karen was frowning. "I thought you were still in your senior year when you got pregnant—" She broke off, her eyes wide. "Oh, no..."

Nodding, Jamie smiled sadly. "I was working the night she was conceived...."

"Oh, God."

She nodded, fresh tears brimming in her eyes, though she wouldn't let them fall. Not again.

"But Kyle—"

"Karen, the truth is, we met at a party of Tom Webber's and I *was* there to work. But what happened with Kyle was...different. We talked, we really connected and we...made love. It seemed so natural and wonderful—and it was the first time for me."

"Does he know?" Karen whispered. "I mean, does he know what you did for a living?"

"Not yet, but I'm going to tell him." Jamie watched the ramifications dawn in Karen's eyes. And saw the sadness—the worry—that followed.

KYLE STOPPED BY his favorite take-out place and bought them all teriyaki chicken and rice for dinner. Jamie had invited Karen and Kayla to join them; at Karen's suggestion they'd decided to meet at the Smith house. Karen was upstairs reading the girls a story when he arrived, laden with fragrant bags. He always looked great to Jamie, especially in his professor duds, but tonight he was like a lighthouse in a storm, calling out to her. His jeans fit his thighs as snugly as always; his jacket, a tweed, had patches on the elbows. And his hair was disheveled as though he'd been running his fingers through it all afternoon. But his eyes had warm lights in them when he smiled at her.

Jamie reached up and kissed him hello while he still had his hands full of bags. After tonight, she might never have another chance.

Gentleman that he was, he calmly kissed her back, as though her greeting had been a perfectly natural and everyday occurrence rather than the minor miracle it was. He then set the bags on the kitchen table and started divvying up dinner.

Although the girls were overtired, they were full of tales from their day at the zoo and kept the three adults entertained right up until dessert.

Which consisted of peanut butter, bread and jelly. Kyle had forgotten dessert, but he'd brought the sandwich makings in case either of the girls didn't like teriyaki chicken.

"This is lunch, not dessert, huh, Mommy?" Ashley said, turning up her nose at the offering.

"Usually it is, sweetie, but if Daddy says it's dessert, then tonight it's dessert."

"What's dessert about peanut-butter-and-jelly sandwiches, Daddy?"

"The jelly," Kyle said. "It's pure sugar."

"Then can I just have jelly and bread and no peanut butter?" Kayla asked, grabbing for a slice of bread from the bag Kyle had produced.

"Just jelly it is." Kyle rescued the bread from Kayla's tight little fingers and spread it liberally with jelly.

"Mommy? Can my daddy spend the night?"

Kyle dropped the slice of bread, jelly-side down, on the table.

Karen started to cough and buried her face in her napkin.

Jamie wanted to die.

"I don't think so, honey," she told her daughter. "Tonight's a school night and you know the rule about school nights."

"But daddies don't go to school."

"No, but little girls do."

"But Miss Jamie, if Ashley's daddy doesn't ever spend the night, then you can't be marrieds and live ever after."

"Yeah, and then I can't have my baby sister," Ashley whined.

"If Ashley gets a baby sister can I have dance, too?" Kayla turned to her mother with tears in her eyes. "I want dance like Ashley gets."

Karen stood. "I think it's time two little girls were in bed," she said, wiping the remains of Kayla's dinner off her face.

"But can I dance, Mommy, please?"

"We'll see."

Jamie reached for a cloth to wipe her own daughter's face.

"And my daddy can spend the night, too, huh, Mommy?" Ashley asked, avoiding her mother's cloth.

Abandoning the trash he'd been collecting from the table, Kyle scooped Ashley into his arms, dirty face and all. "Not tonight, sweets," he said easily. "Daddy does go to school, remember? I took you to my school, showed you my office and the classroom where I teach."

"Oh, yeah." Ashley was clearly disappointed. "But someday you will?" she persisted.

Kyle glanced at Jamie. "Someday, I will," he said.

Without conscious thought, Jamie sought Karen's gaze—and found what she hadn't even known she'd been seeking. Compassion. Commiseration. And courage. Tonight, as soon as Ashley was in bed, Jamie was going to tell Kyle the truth.

Beyond that, who knew?

"WHAT'S UP with you and Karen?" Kyle asked, Ashley on his hip, as they crossed the yard to Jamie's house.

"Nothing. Why?" She wasn't ready. Not yet.

She told herself she had until Ashley fell asleep— and hoped the child would take a long time to close her eyes that night. Surely once Ashley got home and into her bath she'd remember a lot more stories to tell them about her day at the zoo. Jamie hadn't heard any monkey stories yet, and Ashley loved monkeys.

"What's with the look she gave you right before we left?"

"Miss Karen had a bellyache today," Ashley reported, then promptly put her thumb in her mouth.

"I know, punkin, but she's all better now."

"She's made up her mind to tell Dennis when he gets home on Friday. I offered to keep Kayla." Conscious of Ashley's ears, Jamie worded the news carefully.

"We can take the girls to see the new Disney

film,'' Kyle suggested agreeably, automatically assuming that he'd be spending the evening with them.

After tonight, he probably wouldn't be.

AS MUCH AS he adored his daughter, Kyle was glad she went right down that night. Jamie had been nervous, cagey, all evening and he needed some time alone with her.

''We have to talk,'' she said, the minute they were alone.

Thinking positively, the memory of her kiss still tingling his lips, Kyle sprawled in the middle of her couch, inviting her to sit next to him.

She preferred to stand, with her back braced against the fireplace. If she'd had any idea how much she was turning him on in those tight cords, the sweater that outlined her breasts so clearly, he suspected she'd have climbed inside the fireplace, instead.

''Okay, so talk,'' he said.

She took a deep breath. ''I just want you to know that if, when I've said what I have to say, you never want anything to do with me again, I'll understand. And I'll always make Ashley available to you.''

Kyle sat forward. He didn't like the sound of this at all. Did she still not trust that he was in this for the long haul? Hadn't she figured out there was nothing she could do or say that was going to scare him off?

Meeting her gaze, reading the serious conviction in her eyes, he nodded.

''The night we met, at that party in Las Vegas, I

was working." She was like a robot, throwing out words that had no meaning to her.

Unfortunately, they had no meaning to him, either. "Okay."

"The man we met at the dinner Saturday night, Nelson Monroe—he was one of my clients."

Forearms braced on his knees, Kyle nodded. Was that it? She thought he'd disapprove of her clients? Of the fact that she did business at parties? Half the business transactions in the world took place at social gatherings. This was making no sense.

Jamie seemed at a loss for words suddenly, staring at him as though something was supposed to be clear to him now.

"Is he still your client?" he asked, more because he was baffled than because he cared if she did the man's taxes.

"No!"

"Okay."

"He wasn't the only one."

"Male clients, you mean?" He was really trying hard here.

Her lower lip started to tremble, but she continued to look him straight in the eye. "Yes."

"Okay." He hadn't figured all her clients were women. Neither could he figure out why they were having this conversation.

"I didn't do their taxes, Kyle."

That surprised him. "You baby-sat for them?" he asked.

"No." She wrapped her arms around herself as if warding off a chill.

"Did secretarial work?"

"No."

What in hell was going on here? "House-sat? Cleaned?" Was that it? She'd cleaned houses before she'd gotten her degree?

"No."

"Are you going to tell me where we're going with this, or you want me to keep guessing?" he asked. He'd do whatever he could to help her out, just as soon as he understood what they were talking about.

"You're so sweet, you know that?" She was smiling at him. But there was a sheen of tears in her eyes.

"And this is a bad thing?"

"No."

She shook her head, but the tears didn't fall. They just hung there, scaring him.

"It's a wonderful thing. It just makes this so much harder."

"Maybe if you'd tell me what 'this' is, it wouldn't be so hard."

Looking up at the ceiling, she laughed. Sort of. There was nothing light or humorous in the sound. "I'm trying to."

"All right," Kyle said, beginning again. "You were working the night we met—you have male clients—you don't do their taxes, clean their houses, type reports for them or baby-sit."

She shook her head.

"Monroe was one of your clients." Flashing back to the other night, Kyle listened again to Monroe's words, trying to find a clue there. And came up empty. The man had had nothing but sex on his mind.

"He wasn't as out of line as you thought," Jamie whispered. She'd opened her eyes very wide, as if she thought that could keep the tears from falling.

Kyle was finding it a little hard to breathe.

"Of course he was out of line, Jamie. It doesn't matter what you did for him, you deserve his respect."

"Even if what I did for him was exactly what he was asking for Saturday night?"

Mesmerized, Kyle watched two tears spill out and slide slowly down her cheeks.

The room was a little chilly. He wondered if Jamie was having troubles paying her heating bill. Maybe he should offer to light a fire.

He realized, suddenly, that she was waiting for an answer. "I don't believe you'd ever do what he was asking."

"I'm sorry." The whispered words were accompanied by more tears. "So sorry."

Kyle nodded. He believed she was. Maybe he should just head home. He'd left his thermostat up when he'd gone to work that morning. His house would be warm.

"Say something."

"What would you like me to say?" Seemed to him the conversation had gone on far too long already.

"I don't know, Kyle." She took a couple of faltering steps towards him. "Yell at me, tell me you hate me, but don't just sit there."

Standing, Kyle put the couch between them. "Okay, I'm not sitting."

She was so beautiful, standing there alone in the middle of the room, her eyes huge, pleading with him. If he wasn't so damn cold he'd pull her against him.

"What are you thinking?" she whispered.

"You expect me to believe you had sex with Nelson Monroe?" He didn't know where the words came from. They weren't the ones he wanted to say.

Hands still wrapped tightly around her middle, Jamie nodded. She must be cold, too, he thought.

"And there were others?"

Jamie nodded again.

"How many?"

He'd finally made her look away. The relief was almost overwhelming.

"I don't know, Kyle. What does it matter?" She was staring at the floor.

He didn't know what it mattered. "Ten, fifty, a hundred?"

"Closer to ten than a hundred."

His teeth clenched so tightly his jaw hurt.

Silence fell in the room. Kyle wondered how to leave.

"Somewhere between ten and fifty?" he asked when he thought neither of them was ever going to say another word.

"Somewhere."

"And they paid you."

"Yes."

"You took their money?"

"Yes, Kyle, I took their money. I was a prostitute, okay? What do you want, specific places, times, positions?" Tears were pouring down Jamie's face.

Kyle wondered where she kept the tissues. And whether or not she had a blanket or something for him to cover up with. Cold as he was, it might be a long night.

Then something she'd said earlier hit him squarely between the eyes. He felt his stomach cramp and almost threw up. "You were working that night we met."

Falling onto the couch, Jamie crumpled over her knees and nodded.

"That's why you thought my money was for the sex."

"Yes."

He wished she wouldn't cry so hard. It couldn't be good for her.

He wished he was alone. So he could cry, too.

"You were just waiting around for the next guy to offer and that was me?"

"No." She took a deep breath, as though she was trying to get a grip. "No."

He found that hard to believe. Having spent the first sixteen years of his life witnessing the business, he had a little experience with how these things worked.

"I connected with clients by referral only," she told him, surprising him. "And then only after meeting them myself. I was there that night to meet a friend of the party's host.''

''And did you?'' Like it mattered.

''How could I?'' she asked him. ''I was with you.''

Oh, yeah. That.

''Can I ask you something?'' He must not have sounded as calm as he felt, because she actually had compassion in her eyes as she turned and looked up at him. He would've thought they were full of love, except that now, of course, he knew they couldn't be.

''Yes,'' she said, ''anything.''

''Were you working when you spread your legs for me?''

He'd have given anything to take the words back, hadn't meant to be crude. Hadn't meant to hurt her. At least, he didn't think he had.

Only the back of the couch was between them, but he couldn't comfort her. Didn't know how.

''Would you believe me if I said no?''

Oddly enough, he would. Which didn't make any more sense than the rest of this horrendous conversation.

''*Were* you working?'' he asked again. More insistently.

She sat up straight, still turned to face him, meeting his gaze head-on. ''No, Kyle, I wasn't working. I never, ever, reciprocated when I worked.''

''What do you mean by that?''

''Others took pleasure, *I* never did.''

He needed it spelled out. "Surely a woman with that much experience knows how to enjoy sex."

"I knew how to make a man enjoy it. I knew how to pretend I was enjoying it." She shook her head. "But the first time I truly enjoyed sex, the only time I *ever* did, was that night with you."

This shouldn't mean so much. It shouldn't mean anything at all. "That wasn't the first time you…" He couldn't finish. Couldn't think about what they'd done that night. Not now. Not like this.

"It was my first climax, yes." She apparently wasn't as shy as he. But then, she wouldn't be. She'd had a bit more experience.

"After that you learned to enjoy it with others, right?" he asked, morbidly curious.

"No, Kyle." She looked him straight in the eye again, making him uncomfortable. "There's been no one else since then."

Ah. That hurt. Pain squeezed his insides until he thought he'd never breathe again. He loved her so damn much. And their night together had been so special to her there'd never been another.

Her *career* would have been so much easier to take if that night had meant nothing to her. Because then he could start convincing himself it meant nothing to him, either. How could it have mattered if he was the only one who'd felt the incredible bond between them?

Why couldn't those memories have been nothing more than the product of an overactive imagination? A particularly good fantasy?

"What are you thinking?" she asked softly.

Clutching the back of the couch, staring down at her, he told her the truth. "You don't want to know." His whole body ached with the effort it was costing him to stay calm. Unaffected.

"Yes, I do."

She was so cool. Even with cheeks still wet with tears, her composure was evident. He'd always liked that about her. Her self-control.

"I was wondering if Ashley's really mine."

But then, from the look on the other's face, she knew . . . she *recognized* the grief. The kind of grief she lived with every day. Nothing could ever replace what she'd lost. What she'd turned her back on. No matter how hard she tried. My children need their mother . . . Words that Jamie had spoken herself. Words that struck a chord that echoed through her life to eternity . . . and beyond.

CHAPTER FIFTEEN

SHE WAS RIGHT BACK where she'd started. Disgraced. As if the last five years had never been. From her stepfather to Tom to the wealthy, older men of her college years to the father of her child doubting his paternity. But this time, as she came face-to-face with the kind of woman she was, there wasn't any shock, outrage, confusion. There was something much worse. Resignation.

Oh, and the pain. It never stopped. Jamie knew that now. The kind of hurt she'd inflicted on herself was eternal.

"She's yours," she said. Not for her sake. What he thought of her didn't matter anymore. But Ashley needed her father. She deserved him. They deserved each other—this good decent man and the innocent child he'd created.

"How can you be sure?" Kyle asked, still standing behind the couch. "Obviously there were many others."

Breathing sporadically, she held back tears, promising herself that she wouldn't let them fall. She needed to be able to rely on herself for strength.

"I never had unprotected sex before that night."

But that wasn't why she knew. Biology wasn't even why she knew. She knew in her heart.

"Accidents happen." He turned around, moved away from her, ending up over by the fireplace. He took off his glasses, rubbed the bridge of his nose. "Do you know the names of all the men you were with in that last month? Would it even be possible to track them down, to narrow the child's parentage down to one man?"

She held up her head against the onslaught and faced the man she still loved. "Ashley needs you, Kyle. Please don't punish her for what I've done."

He blinked. "I'm not trying to punish her. I love her. Whether she's mine or not."

"Then don't punish yourself, either. Don't doubt what you know to be true."

Staring at her hard, he didn't move for several minutes. Solid and strong, he filled up her living room, her life, her heart.

Eventually, he reached the truth he'd had to reach. "She's mine," he admitted.

Jamie had known all along that he'd accept his fatherhood in every sense, biological as well as emotional. The special bond between them had brought them together in spite of what she'd been, and it still existed even now that he knew. It allowed him some kind of strange access to what she was really feeling; it denied the possibility of lying to each other. He could *feel* that the child she'd borne him belonged to him.

He just couldn't love *her* anymore. And she'd known that, too.

"I'd been under a lot of pressure for about six weeks before that party, studying for exams." She heard herself giving him the evidence she could have given him at the beginning. "I hadn't... worked...at all."

He was watching her.

"For more than a month."

"You'd had a period."

Jamie nodded.

"What about...afterwards?"

"I told you, I've never been with anyone since."

For the first time in more than an hour, his eyes softened. She caught a glimpse of the man he really was, the man she'd recognized as good, compassionate, a soul mate. "You meant that," he said, speaking almost to himself. "You've been celibate since that night...."

She'd had to be. After what she'd done with Kyle, what she'd allowed herself to experience, to feel, she *couldn't* sleep with anyone else. It would have destroyed her. She'd lost her indifference, her impartiality.

"When I worked, I went off to a little room inside me. A room I'd found when I was just a child." Why she was bothering with this, she didn't know, but she wanted him to understand how different their night together had been. Maybe it was for Ashley's sake. He needed to know that she was a special child, the consequence of an incredible night, a night out of time.

He was silent, so she figured he was waiting for more and eventually continued. "I'd occupy myself there for as long as it took.'' Jamie stopped, remembering, knowing she had to get through the next few minutes, just make it until Kyle left and then she could retreat to her invisible little room.

"Sometimes I'd make out lists of things I needed to do, make plans. I'd have conversations with a female friend, tell myself stories. I'd even sing songs that made me feel good.''

Kyle's jaw clenched, the muscles in his face working. The rest of him was frozen, motionless, as he watched her.

"Sounds crazy, huh?''

The strong emotions flaring in Kyle's gaze threatened Jamie's composure. She wanted so desperately to run to him, to bury herself in the safety of his embrace.

"It sounds like a way of coping,'' he said.

In his voice, she heard the warmth she'd come to associate with him during their many long phone conversations.

"I never experienced anything with the men I was with, have no memory of what a single one of them felt like.'' She hadn't even realized that until now. "I just remember places I've lain and the things I did in my room while I was lying there. I could even tell you who I was conversing with in my head or what song I was singing.''

"The mind's a pretty powerful thing.'' He was still her friend. Caring. "It takes care of itself.''

"I didn't go to my room the night Ashley was conceived,'' she whispered, losing her battle with the emotions thundering through her.

She could tell her confession moved him. Sitting beside her on the couch he took her hand, touching her for the first time since he'd learned her shameful secret. He didn't say anything for a long time. Just leaned back against the couch, staring down at their clasped hands.

"Why?" His question was tortured.

"Why didn't I go there? Or why didn't I tell you what I was?"

"Why any of it? Why you? Why me? Why was that night so different? Why, as much as I hate all this, do I still care so damn much?"

"Maybe you were drawn to me that night *because* of who I was." She'd been wondering that ever since he'd told her about his mother.

"I had no idea you were working."

"Maybe not consciously." She focused on their clasped hands. "But men have a way of knowing. Maybe you sensed it. Maybe, with all your doubts, your self-recriminations, you needed me."

"But why you? Why not any of a hundred girls I could have found—girls more obvious about what they were?"

Jamie had no answer. Except one. "Maybe because *I* needed *you.*"

For the first time, Jamie put into words something she'd always instinctively known. "You saved me that night, Kyle. You tapped into the good that was still left inside me. The integrity that desperately needed to break free, to live and breathe. That night with you gave me the strength to be the woman I'd always believed I was meant to be."

Kyle let go of her hand and raked his fingers through his hair. "So why'd you do it in the first place?"

She couldn't share that with him yet. Not while he was still so full of disgust. Not when his question came more from curiosity than concern. She needed him to accept her as she was. To care for her regardless. Or they could never have a future.

"I never sat down one day and made a conscious choice to become a highly paid escort, Kyle." She wanted to stand up. To get away from him. But she wasn't going to run anymore. "One thing just led to another, each little step leading me down that road. One little step at a time didn't seem so bad."

"Right, and next you're going to be telling me there was nothing bad about a woman who'd entertain two men at a time on her son's bed."

"No, Kyle, I can't tell you that. Because it isn't true." She tried to be strong. "The life of a kept woman—of any kind—can't be anything but bad."

"Well, this certainly explains your reaction the night I told you about her." His tone was cold again, distant. "You could relate."

"I'm not your mother, Kyle."

She didn't have to defend herself. Didn't need him sitting in judgment of her. She did that just fine all by herself. But neither could she leave him hurting this way, thinking he'd bedded a woman just like the mother who'd let him down so cruelly. So...

"I dated each of my clients—exclusively—until that particular liaison ended. If he was in town a week, it lasted a week. If he came back to Las Vegas later and I wasn't seeing anyone else, he'd have another week. If he lived in town, sometimes it lasted longer. I didn't pick up strangers. I never had one-night stands. I never once took a man to my home. I didn't allow kissing. And I never, ever, did anything you'd think of as…kinky.''

And then she remembered something. The champagne. The hot bubble bath. ''Until that night with you.''

LATER, LYING IN HIS BED, Kyle tried to sleep. He coaxed himself with the promise of eggs, fried potatoes and bacon for breakfast if he'd just drift off for a while. He got angry and demanded that he get his mind off it and go to sleep instantly. He lay quietly, eyes closed, trying not to move at all in the hope that he'd fall asleep in spite of himself. He counted old T-Birds.

Finally, he got up. Padding around the house in his underwear, he searched for something to do. He didn't feel like working or unpacking or reading. TV held no interest. It was too late to listen to music. Eventually, he ended up back in his bedroom, at the open window, leaning on the sill. As if the night held answers. The power to make his world right again.

At least the cool air brought relief to his heated skin. Earlier he'd been freezing. Now he was burning up.

He must be coming down with something.

Except that he never got sick. Didn't have the time for it. Or the patience, either. Besides, he didn't *want* to be sick. He couldn't see Ashley if he was sick, couldn't risk giving her a virus.

Not that he really had any worries on that score. He was perfectly healthy and he knew it.

Kyle stared up at the stars for a while, trying to remember a single constellation from his college astronomy class.

And remembered, instead, the shine of tears in Jamie's eyes earlier that night. No matter how disgusted he was by what she'd told him, what she was, he had to admire the way she'd come right out and confessed her terrible secret. She'd made no excuses for herself. Asked for no mercy.

That was his Jamie.

Thinking of her standing there at her fireplace, hands at her sides, bravery in every sinew of her body as she faced her one-man firing squad, Kyle felt his throat tighten up. The stars above him blurred and, blinking, he looked out into the darkness beyond the town.

The first tear was dripping off his chin before he finally acknowledged what was happening. And then he gave up, gave in and let them fall. The world was such a damn sad place to live.

He thought of Jamie's little room, felt honored that she'd shared it with him and sick to think of her hiding from her life in that make-believe place.

Kyle stood at the window until dawn was breaking, trying to make sense of it all. He couldn't turn his back on his daughter—or her mother. Neither could he tolerate the thought that Jamie had made a career out of bedding men. He'd grown up living with a woman who'd allowed strangers to touch her, to have sex with her for money. And he felt sick to his stomach just thinking about the fact that his own child had a mother who'd done the same.

But he couldn't stand the prospect of life without Jamie. He'd never felt as *good*, as valuable, as he did when he was with her.

He had no idea at all where that left him.

Finally, crawling into bed a couple of hours before he was due in class, Kyle drifted off with one last thought.

First thing in the morning he had to call his lawyer. He needed to find out how to get custodial rights. If anything ever happened to Jamie, he didn't want any doubts about who this child's father was.

ON THE FIRST DAY of April, Ashley rushed outside the minute she saw Daddy's car pull into the driveway. She'd been waiting for him ever since she got home from school.

"Daddy!" she yelled as loud as she could. "Daddy!"

As soon as he got out of his car, he caught her in a big hug, just like he was supposed to.

"What's up, squirt?" he asked her. "Is Kayla here yet?"

"Nope." Ashley was double happy. She had her plan for Daddy, *and* Kayla was going to the movies with her and spending the night.

Daddy rubbed his sharp face against her neck.

"Don't!" she squealed. "That tickles."

Daddy laughed, kept rubbing her neck with his cheek.

"I'll wet my pants!" she cried.

Daddy stopped really fast. He was always afraid Ashley was going to wet her pants, even though she didn't do that anymore.

"Guess what, Daddy?" she asked, exactly the way she'd practiced to herself as soon as she'd gotten her idea.

"What?" He was carrying her up the walk and she was going to have to talk really fast before Mommy could hear.

"Mommy's got a date with a other man," Ashley said, making herself sound as serious as if she was saying an answer to Miss Peters in school. Now Daddy would hurry up and marry Mommy, so some other man wouldn't take her far away and try to be Ashley's daddy, too.

Daddy stopped walking, which was good, but he was staring at Ashley like he might throw up, so she didn't feel happy anymore. "You're sure about that?" he asked in a very Daddy voice.

"April's fool!" she called. But the trick didn't seem good anymore.

HE WAS A FOOL all right. A damn fool. In that split second when he believed he'd lost Jamie, he'd felt as though he were dying. And his death would have been no one's fault but his own.

Hoisting Ashley a little higher in his arms, he forced himself to smile at her joke. It was difficult.

For an intelligent man, he was really pretty stupid.

He'd spent the last four days holding Jamie at arm's length when he should have been trying to hold her close, instead. How could he ever hope to salvage anything from this mess if he didn't try?

He still didn't have any answers—only an inkling that he shouldn't be searching for them alone. Unless that was how he wanted to end up. Alone.

"Daddy, I think Mommy's feeling sad. Could you help make her better?" Ashley pulled on his collar.

"What's wrong with her?" he asked quietly.

"Her smile isn't working so good."

Out of the mouths of babes... "And you think I can fix that?"

Ashley nodded. "Daddies can fix things. Kayla says so."

"Then I'll try my best. Okay?" he asked the child. His four-year-old was clearly smarter than her degree-totin' father.

"That's good, Daddy."

Chuckling, Kyle set Ashley on her feet inside the front door. He could smell dinner cooking—the savory aroma of wonderful things he couldn't identify. "Where *is* Mommy?" he asked his precocious daughter.

"Right here." Jamie came from the kitchen, wiping her hands on a dish towel, and Kyle's day suddenly seemed that much brighter.

EARLY SATURDAY MORNING, so early Ashley and Kayla were still in bed, Karen came knocking at Jamie's back door.

"I saw your kitchen light come on," she said as soon as Jamie had let her in.

"We're driving into Denver today. Kyle's going to be here soon." Jamie smiled as she noticed her friend's glowing eyes.

"What's so funny?" Karen asked, her brows drawn together. "You've seen me in my robe before."

"You look happy."

Karen's face broke into a wide smile, too, as she nodded.

"You told Dennis about the baby when he got home last night."

"Yep."

"And?"

The two women moved in unison to tend to the coffee Jamie had already started. Each with a steaming cup in hand, they stood leaning against opposite counters. Grinning like adolescents.

"Can you believe it?" Karen asked, taking a quick sip. "The idiot's been hoping for another baby for over a year. He just didn't want to pressure me."

"I can believe it."

The other woman looked down, blushing. "He says he loves my body like this."

"I knew he would." Jamie nodded, still grinning. All was well with her vicarious family again.

"And the only reason he quit praising my cooking and stuff around the house was that he thought his praise was upsetting me."

Jamie took a sip of coffee. "Was it?"

"Yeah." Karen nodded. "I thought he was humoring me."

"He loves you too much to do that."

"I know." To Jamie's amazement, and delight, Karen blushed again. Her friends must have had some night together.

"He made me feel a lot better about things," Karen confessed, taking another sip of coffee. "About myself. He thinks the crafts I do are great, said he couldn't learn to do them if he had years of lessons."

"I don't doubt it. After all, I saw him try to repair that lawn furniture last summer. You had to throw it out."

Karen laughed delightedly, then ran some potential baby names by Jamie, laughing again as she reported some of Dennis's more obscure suggestions.

"Cornelius?" Jamie repeated the last one. "Was he serious?"

"Yeah, and I can just imagine what the kid's nickname would be."

"Corny?" Jamie guessed, laughing. "Obviously, naming that baby is something we'll have to do when Dennis is out of town."

"Then it'll have to be quick," Karen set her nearly empty cup on the counter. "He's putting in for a job he's just been offered at the head office in Denver. Says he wants to be home for doctor visits and midnight feedings this time around."

"That's wonderful!" Jamie set her own cup down and gave Karen a big hug. And felt only a little jealous that life was working out so perfectly for her best friend.

WITH HIS RESOLUTION of the night before still in mind, Kyle collected Jamie and Ashley just after Kayla had left early Saturday morning. Jamie had suggested a family outing and in spite of the hour, she was all ready for their trip into Denver to attend the Family Fun Festival. She was wearing a lovely off-white pant suit, slacks with a long tunic jacket that belted at the waist. He felt a little underdressed in his black jeans and yellow oxford shirt.

Having had no idea what a Family Fun Festival entailed, Kyle was rather impressed with the more than three hundred booths set up, row upon row, in a large park somewhere in Denver. He'd never been to the area before, wasn't sure he'd be able to make it back there without Jamie's directions, but he liked what he saw.

"Let's go *there!*" Ashley cried, pointing at some colorful balloons before he'd even parked the T-Bird.

"We'll see it all, honey, as long as you can hold up," Jamie told the child.

Kyle finally found a place and parallel-parked in one try. He wondered if his ladies were impressed with his driving prowess.

"I wanna have my face painted!" Ashley announced.

Jamie turned around and grinned at her daughter. "How do you know they even have face-painting here?"

Ashley pointed out the rear of the car. "'Cause that little boy has *his* face painted."

Okay, so driving wasn't big with them. Never mind. "Can daddies have their faces painted, too?" he asked.

"Yeah!" Ashley hollered at the same time he heard Jamie say, "Not if they want to walk beside mommies."

As Ashley was about to dart off to six different booths at once, Jamie suggested they start at the beginning and try to work their way around the whole park. Kyle liked that idea best. With Ashley bouncing up and down at his feet, he paid the small fee for the three of them to enter the park, then followed his two festival experts inside.

"Look, Daddy," Ashley said, grabbing his hand. "There's a emergency man. Mommy told me about them. Wanna know what she said?"

"Sure."

She tugged on his hand in her hurry to share with him. "Their telephone number's 911 and you can call it if you're in trouble."

Intercepting a glance from Jamie, Kyle smiled at her.

It soon became apparent that not only did Ashley know about the fun to be had at the festival, she knew about all the hazards she was to watch out for, which games she was allowed to play, even which foods weren't so good for her. And she lectured Kyle on every one.

"You don't ever talk to strange people, Daddy,"

she said solemnly at one point. "'*Specially* if they got candy.''

Jamie was buying a handmade magnet at the time, and watching her, Kyle couldn't help remembering the night he'd talked to a stranger. A woman he'd never met but felt he'd always known. When he'd approached Jamie, it was the first and only time he'd approached a woman cold. And in spite of everything, he wasn't sorry he'd done that.

AFTER A FULL DAY of fun, one daisy face painting and more food than a four-year-old should've been able to consume, Ashley finally fell asleep in the back of the T-Bird. Jamie used the trip home to fill Kyle in on the latest with Karen and Dennis. She still got a happy little thrill whenever she thought about her friends.

Kyle carried Ashley into the house and straight into bed as soon as they got home.

"Shouldn't she have a bath or something?" he asked Jamie. "At least wash that stuff off her face?"

Shaking her head, Jamie led the way out of the little girl's room and into the kitchen. "I can wash her sheets in the morning a lot more easily than we'd get her into a bath tonight. She's exhausted and she'd only cry if we woke her."

She got out the makings for a pot of coffee. Got out a liquor bottle, too. She wasn't ready for him to leave. "Would you like an Irish coffee?"

"Sounds good." Kyle leaned against the counter. "I'd like to talk for a few minutes, if you're not too tired."

After a week of polite, meaningless conversations, the day's warmth had been a welcome change. But now she was afraid of what he might want to say.

"I'm fine." She tried to appear busy waiting for the coffee to drip. Anything to avoid looking at him. Though he'd been at the house every day that week, she'd missed him more than she'd ever thought possible. She'd come to depend on his friendship, his constant affection. She hated seeing the stranger's mask come over his face. Was too tired to pretend it didn't hurt.

She couldn't bear to have another session with him in her living room, so she took the coffee to the kitchen table and sat down. Kyle pulled out the seat she'd begun to think of as his.

"This past week's been hell," he said, placing his arms on the table on either side of his cup.

Jamie lifted her drink. "Can't argue with you there." She took a swig, needing the drugging bite of liquor, the surge of sweetness, and burned her lip.

Her hair a curtain around her face, she continued to hide from him.

"I've done a lot of thinking this week," he said.

"I suspect that's an understatement."

His only acknowledgment was a bowed head. "I can see where a desperate person might make some desperate choices."

She could tell what the admission cost him. And she heard the "but" in his voice. She wasn't strong enough for that. Not yet. Give her a year or two, a lifetime or two, to get over him first.

"I want to go back, Jamie, to be who we were before last week."

"And who were those people?"

Cradling his cup in his hands, he shook his head. "Friends, maybe?"

"Is it possible to go back?"

"Probably not."

"So what is it you *do* want—now, today—if we can't go back?"

He glanced up at her, his eyes looking straight into hers, connecting. Finally. "I want to bring what we had into the present, the future, to move forward together."

If he didn't get to the bad part soon, she was going to fall apart right here on her kitchen table. "I'm not against that."

"The only thing is—" He broke off, and his gaze broke away, too. He still hadn't taken a single sip of his coffee.

Jamie's was almost gone.

"Your past…"

She ran her finger around the rim of her cup.

"When I think of you taking off your clothes for those men," he blurted. "It bothers the hell out of me. I hate it."

Tears in her eyes, she looked at him. "Then that's just something else we have in common. I hate it, too."

"I can't promise it won't get the best of me someday."

Jamie nodded. "I understand."

"It's not fair to ask you to risk your heart on that."

"Life's not fair, Kyle."

Her cup was empty. She was tempted to reach for his.

"You're right," he said, "life's not fair. You know—" he slid his cup across to her, getting up to help himself to a shot of whiskey minus the coffee and cream "—I've been thinking about something you said last week." He came back to the table, sat down. "You were talking about your secret room."

She stared down, humiliated he knew about that. She'd been wishing all week that she'd kept that piece of information to herself. It made her sound so…weak. Weird.

"You said you'd been going there since you were a little girl."

So he'd caught that. Damn.

"Why, Jamie? What was happening in your life that you had to go there?"

She just couldn't tell him. Couldn't let him get that close. Not until he'd found a way to accept what she'd been, regardless of *why* she'd been that way.

"I just had a stepfather I didn't like."

His eyes were piercing as she tried to meet his gaze. "Why didn't you like him?"

She wasn't lying as she answered him. She gave him the truth the way everyone had seen it then. "Because I was jealous. Before he came along, it had just been my mother and me. I even slept in her bed with her. Once John was there, I had to sleep alone, had to share the rest of my mother's time."

"So you went to your 'room.'"

Jamie nodded. The rest just hung there, unsaid.

"Desperate people do desperate things," he said, almost to himself as he sipped at the small amount of amber liquid in his glass. "When did you start feeling desperate?"

She shrugged. "I couldn't name a particular time." She could name several of them.

"What made you desperate?"

Jamie wanted so badly to tell him the whole sordid story. But she couldn't give him that much of herself. She wasn't ready....

She had to be sure he was in for the long haul first.

"No one thing," she said, shrugging.

After finishing off the liquor, Kyle set the glass down hard. "I'm trying to understand here, Jamie. Because understanding brings forgiveness."

"Understanding doesn't change the facts," she told him, somehow finding the strength to look him in the eye. "And I don't need your forgiveness, Kyle. I need your acceptance."

For a long moment he stared across at her. And he nodded. "You're right. I'm sorry."

"It's okay."

"So we're friends—and heading beyond friendship?" He grinned at her.

Jamie nodded. And smiled. The first real smile she'd felt that week. She held no firm hope for the future, but she'd learned a long time ago to take life one small step at a time.

CHAPTER SIXTEEN

BRAD DIDN'T SHOW UP for tutoring the first Monday in April. His coach did.

"What's with you, Radcliff?" The coach stormed through the empty classroom, approaching Kyle's podium. "Your degree go to your head, make you think you're God?"

Glad he was standing—and with a podium between him and the irate gorilla—Kyle didn't bother to answer the question. "Where's Brad?" he asked, instead. "He missed his tutoring session."

"From what I heard, there's not much point in him being here. He's going to flunk anyway."

"That's possible." Kyle nodded. "Almost a certainty if he doesn't come to tutoring."

"You're something else, man, you know that?" Coach Lippert leaned over the podium, his big ugly nose in Kyle's face. "That kid's been trying. Really trying. He's missed conditioning sessions—sessions he needs if he intends to have a body that's still in decent shape ten years from now—to come to your damn *tutoring* sessions. And for what?"

The guy had some ugly teeth.

"I'll tell you for what," he continued without

giving Kyle time to reply even if he'd wanted to—
which he hadn't. "For a great big *nothing.*"

"We don't know that yet."

Lippert shoved the podium hard enough to move
it. "I saw his last exam, Radcliff. The kid doesn't
have a chance. Not unless you bend a little."

Kyle stood his ground. "What kind of message
are we sending Brad, and all the others like him, if
we tell them they aren't bound by the same rules as
everyone else, simply because they can play football?"

"Get off—"

"I'm not finished yet," Kyle interrupted. "The
world of professional sports is filled with young men
who think they're above and beyond the law. I read
the newspapers, Lippert. Athletes in jail for physical
abuse, for drug abuse, gambling, murder."

"Next you'll be telling me the prisons are full of
athletes!"

"No," Kyle said, supporting his elbows on the
podium. "That's just it. They aren't. Because these
athletes have managers, coaches and agents. They
have money for lawyers who buy them out of trouble time and time again. Is it any wonder the kids'
minds rot, that they don't think twice before breaking the law? We've basically taught them it's okay.
That their sins will disappear. They've never been
taught accountability."

Kyle shut up. He hadn't meant to lecture. Must've
been because he was standing behind the podium.
He also hadn't expected Coach Lippert to pay attention to anything he had to say, but the man was

staring at him, all signs of aggression gone from his body.

"You're right, of course," the big man finally said, though he didn't appear too happy. "But what kind of message are we sending Brad?" He frowned, apparently thinking out loud. "The kid's really tried, done everything that was asked of him and then some. He's done the absolute best he can do." Coach Lippert glanced up at Kyle. "Are we gonna tell a twenty-year-old kid that his best isn't good enough?"

"A college degree stands for something," Kyle said. "It tells any employer that the person holding the degree has mastered certain courses. Basic literature being one of them. If I pass Brad, I am in essence lying to anyone, at any point in his life, to whom his degree matters."

"The only employer that kid'll ever have isn't gonna care!" Coach Lippert came forward again, one hand on the edge of the podium. His arm bulged impressively from the strain. "Brad isn't ever gonna make it in the front door of any organization that'll give a damn about his degree. Not as a potential employee, anyway."

Kyle had to agree with the man there.

"Chances are, he's not even gonna *get* a degree. He's gonna be drafted before then. We just need to keep him in school long enough to get that offer."

Kyle listened. Really listened to what Coach Lippert was telling him.

"Yeah, I want to see my players make it big, but not at the risk of creating immoral human beings,"

Lippert said. Kyle had a feeling it wasn't very often the coach was this honest. He also had no doubt of the man's sincerity.

"Thing is, football is Brad's only chance," the coach continued, looking Kyle straight in the eye. "You've seen his work, Radcliff. You know as well as I do that the only kind of job he'd ever get out there would be menial labor, grunt work. And even that'd be fine, if it was all he was capable of doing. But it's not! The kid's got talent. More talent than I've seen in my twenty-five years as a coach."

Wishing he had some manual he could go to for the right answers, Kyle considered everything the coach had said. He weighed Lippert's unspoken request against his own standards. Growing up the way he had, the only thing that had seen him through was his principles. He always lived by the rules, always did what he thought was right, and because of it he'd been able to hold up his head.

But where were those rules written? How had they become a part of him? Who'd put them there? And how valid were they?

Did they leave room for compromise? For compassion? For occasionally making an exception?

"Brad *has* improved," he said slowly, as if hearing his own thoughts would help him put them in order.

"He's made every effort," Coach Lippert added, his elbow joining Kyle's on the podium.

"He's come to every class." Kyle took off his glasses, rubbed the bridge of his nose.

"Done all the homework and extra-credit assignments," Lippert said, scratching his chin.

"He participates in class."

"He's actually learned some things," the coach said, grinning at Kyle. "Do you know, he started rattling on about slavery in the South one day. We were talking about which NFL owners he most wanted to work for and he brought up the subject of racism."

Kyle stood up, glasses still in hand. "And that's the point, isn't it?" he asked. "That the kid learn something about life? That's what literature is all about, isn't it? Life?"

"You got me," the coach said. "I slept through my American lit class."

"And your coach got you a passing grade anyway, right?"

"Nope, I read the stuff and got Cs."

"I could give him an oral exam."

"That's his real problem you know—he can't write a coherent sentence to save his life."

"English 101 has to answer to that."

"He had it two years ago—"

Kyle raised the hand holding his glasses. "I don't want to know."

"That's probably best," the coach agreed, nodding.

"Have Brad come to my office an hour before the final. And tell him he'll still have to sit through the written exam—at least attempt it."

Technically, he supposed it wasn't fair to the other students, who could all stand a much better chance of acing the test if they could answer orally, too. But if there was one thing he'd learned in the past couple of months, it was that life *wasn't* always fair. Each life was lived on a case-by-case basis, and sometimes the old rules, the rules you'd established or learned or adopted, didn't work. Then you had to find new ones.

Coach Lippert smiled. A genuine, friendly smile. "He'll be there." He turned to leave. Made it all the way to the door. And then turned back. "Radcliff?"

Head bent over his calendar, Kyle glanced up.

"Thanks."

Nodding, he made the entry for Brad's oral exam. In both calendars. And made a note to tell Jamie, too. She still asked about Brad occasionally. She'd make sure Kyle remembered to attend the kid's final exam on time.

KAREN AND JAMIE had their last flute lesson the second week in April. They'd both decided to leave their flute-playing desires right where they belonged. In their adolescent pasts.

Kyle was happy either way. He kind of liked nagging Jamie to practice, mostly because there was so little she didn't do perfectly. But he was just as happy for her to have an extra free hour a week. He'd been keeping Ashley out of her way a lot during the past month or so as she got closer and closer to the tax deadline. But the fifteenth had just come and gone, and Jamie was smiling again.

In celebration of the last lesson, the end of tax

time and the fifth month of Karen's pregnancy, Kyle offered to look after both girls for the rest of the day so the two women could go out for a celebratory afternoon as soon as they'd blown their last note.

Which meant that Kyle got to take both girls to their dance lesson. Because Kayla had started lessons too late to learn the recital dance, Ashley had opted to skip the performance, as well, and would be finishing her classes next week. Having experimented with dance, they'd both be going on to tiny-tot tumbling in the fall.

"Daddy, I can't get my shoe on." Ashley hopped over to Kyle on one foot, her ballet shoe tangled around the ball of her foot. They were in a deserted waiting room in the studio, Kyle having taken the girls to class half an hour earlier than their scheduled time.

"Hold on, Ash." After setting Kayla down in a chair, one shoe on and one shoe off, he grabbed for Ashley. She had the shoe on backward, the elastic wrapped around her foot.

Just as he reached for her, she took one more hop. And slipped through his hands. Kyle's heart was in his throat as he watched her land on the side of her foot and topple to the floor.

"Daddy!" she cried, even before she fell in a heap.

Scrambling to get up, she stretched out her arms for Kyle, her eyes flooded with tears. Kyle scooped her up before her second wail.

"It's okay, honey," he assured her, feeling awful. "Let Daddy see."

"My foot hurts, Daddy," she cried, her eyes brimming over.

"Can I help?" Ashley's dance instructor hurried toward them, and she and Kyle examined Ashley's foot together. Her left ankle was already swelling.

"Swelling's good," the dance instructor said. "Means it's probably just a sprain. Let's get some ice on it."

"Mr. Kyle?" Kayla tugged at Kyle's shirtsleeve. "Is Ashley gonna die?" she asked, and burst into tears.

Squatting, Kyle grabbed Kayla onto his other hip. "Of course not, honey. She's going to be a hero!"

Both girls quieted at that, although Ashley still hiccuped with the occasional sob.

Fifteen minutes later, Kyle carried his daughter, who now had an ice pack taped to her ankle, to the front of the studio. He held Kayla's hand on his other side, both dance bags slung over his arm.

"I'll take her for an X ray just in case," he was telling their instructor as they reached the door.

"The swelling's gone down already," the woman said. "I'm sure she'll be just fine."

Kyle nodded, pushing open the door with his back. One of the two bags dangling from his arm caught on the handle.

"Let me get that!" The instructor freed him, then waved them off.

After that, he was on his own. And quite proud to be managing so well. As daddies went, he wasn't doing too badly. He'd handled his first crisis and there were no fatalities.

JAMIE PANICKED when she walked in the front door and saw two little crutches lying in the middle of the living-room floor.

"What happened?" She rushed in to find Kyle on the sofa, sound asleep, a little girl curled up under each arm, two little heads against his chest. And Ashley's ankle had tripled in size since Jamie had last seen it, due, she hoped, only to the elastic bandage wrapped around it. She no longer had to wonder who the crutches belonged to, only how serious the damage was.

Oddly enough, upsetting as it was to see her child hurt, Jamie was relatively calm as she stood there, smiling at the three sleeping faces. Kyle wouldn't be lying there so peacefully if Ashley's injury was serious.

And she hadn't had to handle the crisis on her own. She'd never shared the responsibility of caring for Ashley, the worry. Never imagined what a relief the sharing would be.

"Hi."

Kyle had opened his eyes and was watching her.

"Hi, yourself. Been busy?" she asked.

"We had a little accident at dance."

"I told you she wasn't a dancer," Jamie said, wishing she could get a look at the extent of the damage herself. "What'd she do—fall over when they were doing pliés?"

Shaking his head, Kyle sat up very slowly and laid the sleeping girls down on the couch, side by side. "Didn't even make it into the dance room," he told Jamie, a half grin on his face.

IT WASN'T UNTIL late in the evening that Jamie heard about the worst part of the afternoon.

"I take her to the emergency room and they won't let me sign for her treatment!" Kyle said, pacing between the counter and her kitchen table.

"That's ridiculous! What if she'd been bleeding to death?" Jamie stood with her back to the sink. They'd just finished the dishes, having left them earlier to give Ashley a bath and get the exhausted little girl to bed.

He shrugged. "I hope they'd have treated her and worried about legalities later. Thing is, I don't ever want to find out."

Picturing what could have been a horrific situation, Jamie didn't want to find out, either. Not the hard way.

She grabbed two glasses of iced tea, and motioned with her head toward the back door. "Let's take these outside."

Following her, Kyle pulled her little white parson's table between two lawn chairs. "We have to talk about this, Jamie," he said, sitting down only after she had. "She's not even on my insurance."

"She doesn't need to be. She's on mine."

"It's time I started providing for her."

"You've bought every single thing she's needed in the past three months, and paid for her dance lessons, too."

"And you've been providing a roof over her head, food for her to eat, clothes for her to wear and a million other things for the past four years."

Jamie enjoyed doing those things. "I had to have

food and a roof over my head, anyway. Besides, she's mine. I *should* provide for her.''

''Fine,'' he said, nodding, his hands linked across his belly. ''And so should I.''

''Fine. We split this fifty-fifty.''

''It's not that easy.''

''Sure it is. You get the school bill, I get household stuff and clothes, we buy birthday and Christmas presents together and we'll figure out the rest somehow.''

''I want to share more than her upkeep, Jamie.''

Kyle was looking at her intently. He meant business. And that scared her to death.

''Okay,'' she said slowly. ''Just what are we talking about?''

''I want custodial rights.''

His words took the breath from her lungs. Back in the beginning, when she'd first met Kyle again, she'd been terrified this might happen. That he might try to take Ashley away from her. But after getting to know him, after falling in love with him all over again, she'd never even considered such a thing.

What a fool she'd been.

''Hey.'' He leaned forward, rubbing the back of her hand where it lay listless in her lap. ''Don't look so hunted,'' he said. ''I'm not talking about taking *anything* away from you. I just want to share all the responsibility. To have all the rights of any other parent.''

Jamie tried to hear him, but the noise in her head was incredibly loud. She just sat there, frozen.

"I couldn't get my daughter medical treatment today, Jamie."

It was the pain in his eyes that got through to her. His request was reasonable. Honorable. Responsible.

She should've thought of it.

"Okay, we'll look into it," she said, convincing herself there was no threat in doing so. That, in fact, Ashley's well-being, possibly her health, depended on it. And if Kyle had legal responsibility for Ashley, wouldn't that protect Ashley's rights, as well?

They'd certainly never have to worry about paying for dance lessons again.

"What we need first is to name me as Ashley's father."

"That's done."

His head shot around as he stared at her. "It is?"

Jamie nodded. "Always has been."

"You named me as her father when she was born?"

Again Jamie nodded. It had been the right thing to do.

"I just assumed…" He looked shocked. "With you thinking I'd paid and left, like all the others…" He broke off again.

He grinned, so boyishly pleased Jamie smiled, too, glad now that she'd made the decision she had all those years ago. She'd anguished about it for months.

"Thank you." His voice was thick.

Eyes glistening with tears, Jamie nodded.

"Okay," Kyle finally said, "so what we need is joint custody."

Jamie started to relax—until Kyle proceeded to outline, in detail, all the steps necessary to obtain the type of custody in question. And that wasn't all. He knew the differences between the various types of child-custody agreements in the state of Colorado and what was necessary to obtain each of them.

Suddenly Jamie's blood ran cold. He'd sought legal custody advisement without telling her. Seeking the information, in itself, was understandable. But he had *extensive* information. And he'd never said a word.

Because he'd had something to hide?

She missed much of what he was saying after that, too overcome with horror to concentrate. Had he merely been biding his time, letting Ashley get to know him, to trust him, before he sued for custody? Like a fool, she'd given him every bit of ammunition he'd need to take the child away from her.

"Yes, I had sex for money, Kyle. I was working the night I met you…"

"That waiting period is…" He rambled on and Jamie had no idea what he was talking about.

"I have this little room…"

She wanted to curl up and die. Right there, underneath the lawn chair where the air was cool and fresh.

Had this whole "heading beyond friendship" thing simply been a clever ploy to get Ashley? Thinking back, Jamie realized she should have seen it all along. *"She's a two-bit whore…"* He'd hated his mother for what she was. How could he tolerate his daughter being raised by the same type of woman? Sure, his mother had been working when Kyle was growing up, and Jamie hadn't turned a trick since Ashley was conceived. But they'd both been women who sold their bodies—and for Kyle that was enough.

He had such strong, uncompromising morals *because* of the way he'd been forced to live growing up, and that was how he'd see things. He'd probably always intended to take Ashley away from her—at least, from the moment she'd been fool enough to confess her sins.

She had no idea how long he'd been silent when she noticed he was no longer speaking.

"You're very well versed," she said, trying to keep the tremors out of her voice. To think.

"This is important to me."

She was sure it was. "True or false, Kyle. Did you, in your research, find out how to go about taking Ashley away from me?"

She knew the answer before she even asked. He wouldn't have the information if he hadn't sought it.

His sudden silence was almost worse than an attempted denial.

"I knew it," she said, the bitterness rising up to choke her. It was never going to end. Hell was just the place she'd been born to live.

"Stop," Kyle said, reaching for her hand.

Jamie snatched it away from him and pulled both hands up to her breasts. "No, you stop, Kyle." She had to grit her teeth to force the words out. "Get out of my house now."

She might not be able to stop him in the long run, but for now, she could ban him from her life. From Ashley's.

"Jamie…"

"I said get out." She was going to be yelling in a minute.

He stood but didn't go anywhere. "You want me gone, fine, but listen to me first."

Only because she was so desperate to have him as far away from her as possible, she nodded her assent, allowing him two seconds to speak his piece and leave.

"I called my lawyer the morning after we talked—"

"About my past, you mean," she interrupted, bitterness controlling every nerve in her body.

"If I intended to take her away from you, honey, wouldn't I have done so then? Or tried to?"

"Don't call me 'honey.'"

"Jamie." He knelt in front of her. "I love you."

She didn't want to look at him but couldn't stop herself. She hadn't heard those words before. Except from Ashley.

"I will never deliberately do anything to hurt you."

She believed he meant that, but given her past, and his, she didn't figure the promise was worth much.

"You're a better mother than any I've ever seen or met or read about in my entire life."

She watched him carefully, sure he was humoring

her, making a joke. He'd never appeared more serious.

"Ashley needs you far more than she needs me," he continued, meeting her eyes.

He waited, as if expecting her to speak. She didn't have any words.

"I'm a scholar, Jamie, I thirst for knowledge of any kind. When I research something, I want to know every detail there is to know. Including the different procedures for custody."

She couldn't quite buy that. She knew he wouldn't lie to her, but it was just that—

"What if something happened to you, honey? I had to know what I'd be up against to make sure Ashley wasn't taken in as a ward of the state, that I'd know what papers to file, where to file them, and to be able to get it done before the state even figured out Ashley existed."

Jamie continued watching him carefully, but she started to breathe easier. The explanation sounded a little weak. And yet, with Kyle, it was a little plausible, too. Was she an idiot to believe him? Was she giving him the means and the opportunity to destroy her life while she waited at home, blissfully unaware?

She didn't think so. Kyle was a decent, honest man.

"Okay?" he asked, still kneeling in front of her.

She couldn't look into his brown eyes, soak up the compassion there, do anything but nod.

"She wouldn't have been a ward of the state anyway," she heard herself telling him. "Dennis and

Karen are her legal guardians if anything happens to me.''

Kyle nodded, as if he'd expected as much. ''I do love you, you know,'' he said, so serious.

''I love you, too,'' she whispered back. Because it was the truth. And she'd never said it out loud before. Except to Ashley.

Leaning slowly forward, giving her every chance to reject him, Kyle touched his lips to hers. Jamie didn't even try to escape. Didn't *want* to escape. His touch was comforting, not sexual—but only until Jamie leaned into him, deepening the contact, mating her mouth with his. It didn't seem to matter what went on between them, her explosive physical need for him didn't change. Except to grow stronger.

And yet, despite the insidious desire curling through her, Jamie's stomach was filled with other tensions. The knots got tighter and tighter.

CHAPTER SEVENTEEN

THE PRESIDENT OF THE United States was traveling through Denver in late April. He was making a public appearance out by the airport, and Miss Peters wanted to take Ashley's preschool class. Karen and Jamie offered to go along to chaperone, as did most of the other moms. Early that Tuesday morning, they boarded the bus that would take them to the airport, all chattering excitedly. It was hard to tell who was more excited about the outing, the children or their mothers.

It was a gorgeous spring day, and the children were in high spirits, all wearing red, white and blue in some form or other. Ashley and Jamie both had on blue denim overalls and white T-shirts. With their auburn hair, red wasn't a good color on either of them, but she'd bought them each a pair of red sneakers.

Karen and Kayla were in the matching red, white and blue striped jumpers Karen had made especially for the occasion.

"I figure if I make mine a tent, we can wear them for the Fourth of July, too," she'd laughed when she'd shown Jamie the material. Jamie had laughed, also. It just felt so good to see her friend happy again.

"So what's going on with you and Kyle?" Karen asked as the two women shared a seat in the back of the noisy bus.

Still getting used to having a friend she actually confided in, one who really knew her, Jamie shrugged. "He comes over for dinner almost every night."

"Just for a free meal?"

"Of course not. He always brings dinner or dessert or flowers or wine. Anyway, the man's loaded. He makes good money, doesn't spend much on himself, made smart investments. I'm his accountant—I should know how much money he has." Not that it made a difference to either of them. Money mattered only if you didn't have enough of it.

"You sure couldn't tell by his clothes."

Smiling, Jamie looked out at the huge trees zooming past the window. "That's just Kyle," she said. "He finds something that fits him, buys ten of them and figures he's done. Says it's much simpler that way."

"So, are you two—you know—happening?"

Karen's hands lay across the mound of her belly. Jamie envied her that.

Jamie shook her head. "I don't know what we are, Karen."

"You love him."

"Yeah."

"Does he know that?"

"Yeah."

"Well, he loves you, that's obvious."

"Yeah." Though Jamie felt a jolt of happiness at hearing her friend say so, she'd never get used to hearing those words.

"So?"

"So, he loves me, but there are parts of me he can't stand."

"Your past."

"Mmm-hmm." Jamie stared out the window again. She'd made her choices. She was accountable for them.

"He's a jerk if he can't see that you were just a desperate young girl making what seemed like your only choice."

"He's not a jerk." Jamie glanced back at her friend. "He just has a very strong sense of right and wrong. It's part of what I love about him."

If Karen had any more thoughts on the matter, she kept them to herself. Jamie didn't want to think about life at all. She just wanted to enjoy the day.

And she did. Until Nelson Monroe bumped into her right after an announcement that the President's plane had been delayed and he wouldn't have time for his address.

"Jamie! Hello. Twice in two months! I'm a lucky man," he said, giving her shoulder a squeeze.

Shoving Ashley back with Karen and Kayla, she tried to steer Nelson away from the other mothers and children. If she'd thought God would listen, she'd have prayed. Instead, she focused one-hundred percent on getting the man as far away from her daughter as she could.

"You're visiting in Denver?" she asked him, attempting to push through the crowd.

"No!" He grabbed her hand, pulled her to a stop—which wasn't hard, as the crowd wasn't moving an inch. "I thought you knew. I'm living here now."

"What about Tom?" The two men had worked closely together. "He's still in Vegas, isn't he?"

"Of course!" Nelson laughed. "You'll never get him out of that city. But he's semiretired now, and so am I."

The children were right behind them. Jamie could feel a little hand pushing against her leg. She could hear their chatter. But not Ashley's. She fervently hoped that Karen had managed to hold Ashley back in the crowd.

"Well, it was nice seeing you," she said with forced cheer. She had to get rid of the man.

And when that was done, when Ashley was safe from Nelson's dirty aura, then Jamie could fall apart. She might have climbed out of a hellish life into a good one, but there was just no way to obliterate history. It was alive. And dangerous.

"Wait!" Nelson's arm stole around her. "We had fun together once, didn't we?"

Trying to unclasp his hand from her hip, Jamie said, "I don't remember any fun." She couldn't pretend anymore. She had to get away.

"I've missed you, Jamie." He squeezed her hip. Not hard. But possessively.

Jamie almost threw up.

Pulling free from his hand, she cried, "Leave me

alone!'' She couldn't stand this. Couldn't stand what she'd been. Couldn't stand the fact that she was exposing her daughter to this scene.

"Hey!" One of the mothers came forward. "Leave her alone, you jerk," she said. Two other women moved up with her, circling Nelson.

Jamie would have cried at their support if she hadn't been so humiliated.

Nelson held up both hands in surrender, much the way he had that night with Kyle. "Hey, ladies, just saying hello to an old friend."

The first woman turned toward Jamie. "He's your friend?" she asked. She remained in her defensive stance while she waited for confirmation.

The women would walk away, leave her with Nelson if she admitted she knew him.

She wanted to deny his claim. And guessed, by the derisive look in his eyes, that he expected her to do so.

"Yes, I know him." The words were strong. Clear. She lived her life by the rules now. Honestly. She was buying back her self-respect, one instance at a time, and if it took until she was a million years old, she was going to keep trying.

"Oh, sorry," the mother said, embarrassed. "I can't believe I did this. I thought—"

"It's okay, ladies," Nelson interrupted, nodding at each of them. And then he looked at Jamie and she cringed, waiting for everything to blow up in her face.

"Nice seeing you again, Jamie," he said, and to her astonishment, he turned and left.

Jamie stood there a full minute, the crowd pushing around her, as she stared at the spot where Nelson had disappeared. She didn't know why, didn't know how, but she'd been spared.

BECAUSE MOTHER'S DAY was the biggest day of the year in the Archer household, Jamie and Ashley started making celebration plans by the end of April. They each came up with suggestions, which Jamie wrote down, and then when they had a whole list they'd put the day together.

Pen and paper in hand, Jamie called Ashley into the kitchen that Friday, just before dinner. They were waiting for Kyle, who was late. The table was set, casserole ready, salad tossed. Then they were all going to the drive-in to see a second-run showing of a favorite Disney film.

"Let's do our Mother's Day list," she said while Ashley was climbing into her booster seat. Mother's Day was not only a celebration of mother and child, but to Jamie, it was a symbol of who she herself had become. A celebration of everything that was good in her.

Ashley was watching her silently, eyes downcast.

"Don't you want to make a list?" Jamie asked, concerned.

"Uh-uh." Ashley shook her head.

Crushed, Jamie stared at her daughter. "Why not?"

"Mommy's Day is about God giving me to you, right?" the little girl asked, frowning.

"Yes." Jamie was scared to death of where this might be going, what Ashley might have heard.

"God gave me to Daddy, too, and it might hurt his feelings if we do our special day wifout him."

"You want to wait till he gets here to make the list?" Jamie asked, weak with relief.

The little girl nodded solemnly. And wait they did.

"I THINK we should all go to the zoo on Mother's Day," Kyle said after dinner when the list was once again on the kitchen table. "Ashley had such a good time there."

"Yeah!" Ashley cried. "We can see the mommy and baby and *daddy* monkeys!"

Jamie wrote down the zoo. "What else?" she asked.

"Your favorite, Mommy, Mr. Wallup's Ice Cream Shop!" Ashley's swinging feet were kicking her booster seat beneath the table.

Jamie added Mr. Wallup's to the growing list.

"I think we should have a picnic at the state park." Jamie threw out what she'd been thinking about. "We could have a cook-out with hamburgers or hot dogs and fly kites and take hikes if we want."

"Yeah!" Ashley cried. "A mommy, baby, *daddy* hike."

Kyle grinned at that last drawn-out *daddy*. If he'd had any doubts about where he placed in his daughter's affections, they'd surely been dispelled. Loving him as she did, Jamie felt almost as happy about that as he must have been feeling.

"Let's do that," he said, studying the other items on the list. "We could hike after the picnic and then go to Mr. Wallup's on the way home."

"Yeah!" Ashley cried, bouncing up and down in her seat. "It'll be the best mommy, baby and *daddy* day!"

Exchanging a warm, intimate glance with Kyle, Jamie couldn't have agreed more.

SHE TOLD HIM SO later that night, after Ashley was in bed and they sat together on the couch—another newly formed ritual.

"You sure you don't mind my coming along?" he asked as he looked down at her.

Snuggling into his side, Jamie shook her head. "I agree with Ashley. It wouldn't seem right without you this year."

"There *is* Father's Day in June." He gave her another chance to change her mind.

Jamie stared up at him. "We'll spend that together, too, won't we?" In spite of how well things were going, she couldn't ever seem to get rid of her doubts. Her insecurities.

"Of course we will."

Kyle bent, giving her a soft kiss to seal his promise. A kiss that, as on other nights, led to a heated exchange of the passion she couldn't allow free rein. And moments later, when Kyle's hands roamed to her breasts, when her own hands traveled the road to intimacy, Jamie froze. And Kyle dropped his hands.

Until there was commitment between them, they

could go no further than kisses. Jamie wasn't that kind of woman anymore.

Two mornings before Mother's Day, the second Friday in May, Jamie was in her home office, re-organizing now that tax time was over, when the phone rang.

Thinking the caller would be Kyle, on break between classes, she grabbed the receiver eagerly. "Hello?"

"Jamie?" The voice was male. It wasn't Kyle.

"Yes."

"Nelson Monroe here."

Oh God. Would the nightmare never end?

"How'd you get my number?" Not that it mattered. He had it.

"You're in the book, honey."

Of course she was. She just hadn't expected a john from her past to be looking for it.

"I'd really like to…see…you again, darlin'," Nelson said softly. "Your honesty the other day impressed me. A lot. You always were one hell of a woman—even if you were just a kid."

Tears burned her eyes. Her whole body trembling, Jamie said, "No, Nelson. I'm not that kid anymore."

"All the more reason for us to get to know each other again." He didn't seem to be grasping the point at all. "We'll have more in common now that you're a little older."

"We have nothing in common."

"We're both accountants."

"I get enough of accounting during the day."

"You've got a nice little setup there, haven't you, Jamie?" he asked, his charm slipping. "Does the man who came to your aid so heroically last month know what you really are?"

"He knows about my past," she was stung into telling him.

"Has he asked you to marry him yet?"

Her silence condemned her.

"Men like him don't marry women like you, darlin'," he drawled. "It's the way the world works."

Jamie couldn't say a word. She knew he was right.

"That's why there are men like me to make life easier for you," he said. "To keep you in the lifestyle you've grown accustomed to."

"I've been keeping myself for years, Nelson, and will do so until the day I die." Marriage, even if it had been offered, wouldn't have changed that.

"You're going to play hard to get, eh?" She could hear anger through the forced charm in his voice. "You were always an expensive filly, but I suppose, since you're somewhat more mature, I should up the ante a bit." He named a sum that would pay her mortgage for a year.

Something inside Jamie broke. Cracked in two.

She clutched the phone so tight it bruised the palm of her hand. "I'm an accountant, Nelson. Nothing more," she said coldly, and hung up on him.

When the phone rang again seconds later, she refused to pick it up. But she heard his message loud and clear as it blasted through her answering machine.

If she didn't come through for him, he was going to tell everyone in Larkspur Grove just what kind of woman she really was. He especially thought Dean Patterson would like to know he was recommending a *hooker* to all his acquaintances.

As Jamie sat there, the blood draining from her face, she could think of only one thing—what this would do to her daughter. The horror that Ashley's life would become.

And what about Kyle? Once her past was public knowledge, it wouldn't be long before people put two and two together and came up with five. They'd assume Kyle had been one of her clients.

Her mind in a fog, Jamie tried to think. To act, rather than react. But she couldn't move. Terror had robbed her of strength. She couldn't even raise a finger to erase the damning message.

She could refuse Nelson. Kyle would stand by her. And, of course, Ashley wouldn't know any better than to be on Jamie's side. But both of them would take unlimited abuse if they did. Kyle's position at the university could be threatened. Other kids would be mean to Ashley, their mothers not letting them play with her.

She could do as Nelson asked. He'd be discreet. He always had been. She had her invisible room to hide in, her way of coping. It would see her through.

Spurred on by nausea, Jamie found the strength to race for the bathroom. She barely made it in time. And being sick didn't bring any relief.

Because there *was* no relief. There was no way to fix this. No right answer. She'd already made her choices. There was no taking them back. No making them better. She couldn't rewrite history.

Finally accepting the truth, Jamie knew what she had to do. Ashley and Kyle stood to be hurt—unless she left town now. Alone. Then, when the truth about her came out, instead of the town's scorn they'd have everyone's sympathy. She had to leave them, taking her sins with her.

Ashley would miss her, of course. Head against the bathroom wall, she sat there and planned the end of any life that mattered to her. The little girl would be devastated for a time, but it was far more conscionable to allow that than to ruin the girl's entire life. Jamie could hardly remember being four herself—except the part where John came to live with them—and knew that Ashley's memories of Jamie would eventually fade. It probably wouldn't even take all that long with Kyle around. He'd love their little girl enough for both of them. Of that, she had no doubt.

And Kyle. While he'd be upset at first, he'd probably also be relieved. Maybe even surprise himself with the extent of his relief. She knew he loved her, but he couldn't let himself completely accept her. Doing that would mean he'd have to accept his mother, too. Which was something he'd never be able to do.

Jamie didn't blame him. His mother had done some disgusting, unforgivable things.

Surprisingly calm, numb, Jamie rose, found a duffel and started throwing things in. Her college diploma. She'd need it to work wherever she ended up. Some clothes. A picture of Ashley.

She couldn't decide which one to take. As she leafed through them, her pain broke through the ice surrounding her and the tears poured forth. Leaving Ashley was going to kill her.

Sobs racked her body as she carefully tucked away every single picture of Ashley she had. All the ones she had of Kyle, too. Their spring vacation at the resort, the first time he'd driven Ashley to school, the day he'd shown her his office and classrooms. Without looking at any more, Jamie added the rest of the pictures to her bag. Someday, when she'd found a way to live with herself, she'd look at them again. Maybe there'd come a time when she'd be able to see them without feeling as though she'd been ripped in two.

The camera she left for her daughter, setting it on Ashley's dresser, ready for the little girl to begin building new memories. Memories that wouldn't hurt her.

She couldn't look at the rest of the room. Knew she'd never find the strength to leave if she allowed herself to touch Ashley's things, to smell the fresh little-girl smells. Without a backward glance, she left the room for the last time.

Ashley was alone at school that day—Kayla being home sick with a sore throat—and due to be picked up from school in an hour. She had to be gone by then.

In the kitchen she saw the buns and chips on the

counter, purchased for the picnic they were to have had on Mother's Day. It was fitting, really, that she wouldn't be celebrating it with Ashley and Kyle. She'd made Mother's Day a symbol for something—someone—that didn't exist. She'd been trying to convince herself that being the best mother she could possibly be had wiped out the sins of her past. That simply by virtue of the fact that she was Ashley's mother, some of Ashley's goodness, her purity, became Jamie's own. But it didn't matter how much she tried or how much she pretended; the woman who'd sold her body to the highest bidder time and time again had been right there with them all along. That woman, the person she'd been, had dibs on Jamie's life.

But she didn't have to ruin Ashley's life. Or Kyle's. And she told him so, very briefly, in the note she left. She also told them both how very much she loved them.

The last thing Jamie did before she walked out of her house for good was pick up the phone to make three calls. One to Ashley's school to let them know her father would be collecting her. And no, she didn't need to speak to the child herself.

She'd never have lived through that conversation.

The second call was to Kyle, asking him to please pick up Ashley, since she had an important errand to do before their weekend together. He was as agreeable as she'd known he would be. She hung up without telling him goodbye. She couldn't do that, either.

The third call she'd planned to make was to

Karen. But in the end, she couldn't do it. As much as she needed her friend's loving reassurances, she couldn't risk the chance that Karen might talk her out of going. Because she knew that was what Karen would try to do. Knew, too, that Karen would probably succeed.

Then, slinging her purse over her shoulder and grabbing the bag, her vision blurred by the tears streaming down her face, she let herself out. Locked the door behind her. And didn't look back.

CHAPTER EIGHTEEN

KYLE WASN'T SURPRISED to find the house locked when he arrived home with Ashley shortly after noon on Friday. Jamie was gone—running her mysterious errand. Ashley couldn't wait to find out what her mother was up to, sure that she had a special treat for Mommy's Day. Kyle had to admit he was a bit curious himself.

Ashley ran off to her room as he opened the front door with the key Jamie had given him weeks before. Kyle wandered into the kitchen to get them both a cool drink and some cookies to last them until Jamie arrived home to have lunch with them.

Seeing the note on the counter, Kyle picked it up and was frowning over the first line when Ashley came darting into the kitchen carrying an expensive-looking camera.

"Mommy's camera's in my room!" The little girl was excited. "Can I take pictures?"

Kyle was getting a really sick feeling in his stomach. "Not now, sweetie," he said, reaching for the camera before the child dropped it.

"Maybe when Mommy's home?" his daughter asked, her little brow furrowed. Her long auburn hair, so like her mother's, was falling out of its ponytail.

"Maybe then," Kyle agreed. The note in his hand was burning his fingers.

"Okay." Ashley tore out of the room, apparently in search of more excitement than her father was capable of giving her at the moment.

With his back to the doorway, Kyle returned his attention to the note in his hand. He read it again, sure he'd missed something.

It said exactly the same thing the second time.

Kyle, I love you and Ashley too much to stay around any longer. Nelson Monroe is back. Wants me back.

Kyle glanced up from the paper, feeling dizzy and sick. Wasn't this exactly what he'd been afraid of? That his adult life would take on the same tones as his childhood if he lived with a woman like Jamie?

His gaze darting around her kitchen, settling nowhere, Kyle could feel Jamie there. In the cleanliness, the organization. In the wildflowers on the windowsill. The refrigerator covered with family goals, positive mottoes, reminders of promises and obligations. Ashley's drawings.

Suddenly filled with a burning rage, Kyle knew he was capable of hunting Nelson Monroe down and killing the man to keep him from bothering Jamie. Kyle didn't know why she'd made the choices she had before, but he was certain that desperation had driven her. She wasn't desperate anymore. She'd fought her way out of that life because she was a good person and she'd known the life she'd been living wasn't good.

And that was the difference between Jamie and the woman who'd borne him. His mother had never seen how wrong her life had become, how degrading, how damaging to her young son.

In order to protect their daughter from what Jamie had once been, she'd gone so far as to create an entirely new life for herself. In a new town, among strangers.

He could only imagine how horrifying it must have been to have had that safe harbor invaded by a man from her past.

Kyle needed to hit something. Hard.

Without even reading the rest of her note, Kyle could have told himself what it said. Because he knew Jamie. She hadn't gone to Monroe. But Monroe had driven her away.

He's threatening to tell Dean Patterson about me if I don't do what he wants, Kyle read. *Please take care of Ashley for me, Kyle. She'll need extra care for the next little while. Love her.*

Kyle had to look up from the note then, tears blurring his eyes, scrambling the words on the page. Blinking the tears away, he continued reading.

I love you so much, Kyle. And I love Ashley, with all my heart. But if it's easier for her not to know that, please don't tell her. Do whatever you must to make her happy....

The note was signed simply *J*.

He already had the phone in his hand by the time he got to that part. The note was wadded up in the pocket of his jeans when Karen answered.

"I need you and Dennis to keep Ashley for the night," he told her without preamble. He pushed the sleeves of his white oxford shirt up his arms. He was way too hot.

"Of course," she replied instantly. "What's wrong?"

"Jamie's gone."

"What? Where?"

"Some guy from her past's been bothering her. She decided we were better off without her."

"Oh, God." Karen started to cry. "She's the most honorable, decent woman I know. And she's paying for things she mostly didn't even do. It's just not right."

"I know." Kyle's jaw was clenched, his fingers damp with sweat as he removed his glasses and rubbed the bridge of his nose.

"Where is she?"

"I have no idea, but I'm going to find her."

"How long has she been gone?" Karen was still crying.

"Not long. She called me just over an hour ago."

"She probably had to stop for gas. She was low yesterday...."

Kyle's mind wandered for a second, reacting to something Karen had said a few minutes earlier.

"You said she's paying for things she mostly didn't do," he interrupted her. "You know details about her past."

"Some."

"I'm going after her, Karen, and when I find her, I'm asking her to marry me." He paused, but when she said nothing, he continued. "I'm not going to take no for an answer."

"Good for you," Karen sniffed. Crying again.

"It would help if I knew what I was up against."

Ten minutes later, Kyle wished he could take back the question. That he could roll back not just the last ten minutes but twenty years. He thought *he'd* had it rough. Freezing, he pulled down the sleeves of his shirt, buttoning them at the cuff.

He had to find her. To love her. To spend the rest of his life storing up so much happiness for her that somehow it would balance out the hurts.

When he thought of a grown man raising a fist to a child like Ashley he got physically sick. Somehow, someway, he was going to be worthy of the woman who'd mothered his child. Worthy enough to fill the next sixty years of her life with smiles.

KYLE HAD BEEN on the road about twenty minutes, heading toward a gas station on the edge of town, when he got the idea. He'd been hoping someone at the station might have seen Jamie, would at least be able to give him a direction to take on his trip out of town. But suddenly he felt sure he knew where she'd gone.

To the ski lodge where the three of them had spent spring break. She'd feel close to them there. He and Ashley were the most important part of her life, and he knew Jamie well enough to realize that the only way she'd survive this first night was to go somewhere she could feel their presence.

In spite of the speeding ticket he got on the way, Kyle made record time to the resort. And was rewarded when he stopped at a pay phone and asked to be connected to Ms. Archer's room. He hung up before Jamie could answer. He'd found out what he needed to know. She was there.

Now he just had to find out which room. Kyle started at the building farthest from the lobby and began knocking on doors. He was gambling that he'd locate her before someone reported him.

She was in the second building he tried, on the first floor, right by the pool. He recognized her voice as soon as she called, "Who is it?"

He also knew she'd been crying.

"Room service," he said, lowering his voice, afraid she might not come out if she knew he was standing there.

"I didn't order any."

And that was all the patience he had. "Jamie, it's Kyle. Please open the door."

The door flew open so fast Kyle almost fell through it. "Did something happen to Ashley?" she asked, fear making her eyes wild. She was wearing a pair of brown corduroy overalls cinched at the waist, with an off-white turtleneck underneath. And she was barefoot.

"She's fine," he said firmly, putting an arm around her to lead her back to the room. She was on the verge of collapse.

"You're sure?" Her gaze was still uncertain as she stared up at him.

"Positive."

Because he had no clue where to begin, Kyle pulled her into his arms and just held her. He'd stand there, holding her, for as long as she needed him.

When her legs gave out, he picked her up and carried her to the couch at one end of the minisuite.

Sitting with her, he stroked her back, her hair, occasionally laying gentle kisses along her brow.

What scared him most wasn't her silence but the fact that she wasn't crying. As if he was too late to save the tender person inside.

He knew his worries weren't unfounded when she started to touch him back. Not gently. But sexually. Like a woman who knew exactly how to get the response she was seeking. He cried out silently for the loving spirit that was Jamie, the spirit that had been so strong but maybe not strong enough.

Eventually her caresses moved upward, as did her lips, and she sought his mouth in a searing kiss that made Kyle's blood boil. His body sprang instantly, painfully, to life.

And he pushed her away.

"It's okay, Kyle," she said in a voice he didn't even recognize. "I'm not going to stop you this time."

He didn't know what to say, how to explain.

"My choices were made a long time ago," she told him matter-of-factly. "I'm not allowed to change them. So I might as well know the joy of having sex with the only man I've ever loved, don't you think?"

He might have thought so if there'd been any emotion in her voice at all.

"No…"

"Oh, I get it." She sat up, moving away from him. "You don't want to be dirtied." She didn't even sound as though the words hurt her. "I understand."

The thing that tore at him most was that she really believed she did.

"You're wrong, Jamie," he said, taking hold of her hand, caressing her fingers. "About so many things."

"I know, Kyle." She nodded. "I always have been. I think I was born that way, you know—with something wrong inside me." She could have been discussing the weather. She was completely and totally resigned. As though today's honorable act had drained all the life out of her, had sent the real Jamie, the true Jamie, far away.

Kyle hoped to God he wasn't too late to bring her back.

"Will you let me speak, please? Without putting words in my mouth?" He couldn't have any coherent thoughts, let alone express them, if she kept interrupting him. And he'd never needed coherent thoughts more than at this moment.

Obviously surprised at his frustrated tone, she nodded without another word.

"In the first place, the only thing I meant you were wrong about was how I feel about you—about making love with you. And mark my words—" he brought her hand up to his lips "—when we sleep together again, which we'll do very soon I hope, we won't be having sex. We'll be making love."

He thought he saw a spark of light in her eyes, but it was gone so fast he couldn't be sure.

"That's why I stopped you, honey. I couldn't let you compromise your principles. You aren't ready to make love yet. But when you are, we will."

She was staring at him, not even blinking. He

took that as a good sign. "I love you, Jamie. More than life itself. Without you, my life means nothing."

"I lost my virginity when I was nineteen, to a man old enough to be my grandfather," she said baldly, apparently expecting to shock him.

"After a full year of being friends with him first, and believing that he loved you and was going to marry you."

"How do you..." She was frowning at him.

"Karen." They both said it at the same time, though Jamie's rendition of her friend's name wasn't very complimentary.

"She told you everything." Her eyes were dead. He couldn't even determine if she was still looking at him or just through him.

"Enough," Kyle said, so filled with love for her he wished he could wrap her up in it. "The rest of the details are yours to give if and when you want to."

She pulled her hand away. "That's why you're here."

"I'm here to ask you to marry me." He had no idea if the time was right, knew only that he had to be honest. "That's why Karen gave me the information she did."

"You actually told her you were going to ask me to marry you?"

She didn't sound excited about that—didn't even sound as if she believed him.

"It's the truth." He took her hand again. "I was going to wait until Mother's Day, and since you left kind of suddenly and I didn't have any warning, the ring's at home in my silverware drawer.''

That seemed to get through to her. He was certain he saw a spark in her eyes.

''Your *silverware* drawer?''

''It's the only organized drawer in my house.''

She almost grinned, but sobered very quickly.

''I know how you feel about your mother, Kyle, and understand that in your heart you can't help resenting me for bringing you that kind of shame. Trust me, if I don't go, it'll only get worse.''

''I was wrong about my mother.'' He hadn't even admitted it to himself until that moment. ''I've been taking a good long look at things these past few months, at her life, her choices.''

Jamie was stiff beside him, barely breathing.

''I can't condone what she did or how she did it, but I can see that her intentions were good. She was providing a roof over my head, money for clothes, for food.''

''Which she could have done mopping floors.''

''That's true,'' he acknowledged. ''But there's something else I'd never considered before.''

Her raised brows questioned him.

''I'm grateful to her for having me when clearly she didn't have to. And—'' this next part was difficult, more difficult than he could ever have imagined ''—I'm grateful to her for loving me. That was one thing I never had to doubt.''

And that love had probably made him the man he was. It was the basis of his self-respect, his belief in himself—his mother's unconditional love.

It was a basis Jamie had never had.

"I only wish I could tell her so."

Jamie smiled at him, a warm compassionate smile, giving him hope. "I'm sure she knows," she said softly.

"Maybe."

They sat silently for a couple of minutes, her flight, Kyle's proposal, hanging between them. Jamie shifted, pulled her hand from his again, and when he glanced up at her, Kyle's dread returned. The moment of warmth was gone.

"There's no way you can expect fidelity from a woman like me," she blurted almost bitterly.

Kyle sighed. "I've been with you for more than four months, Jamie. I've felt the lust in your kisses, the heat in your hands as they move against my body. And despite that, I've yet to get inside your pants. So I hardly think fidelity is going to be a problem."

She frowned, crossing her arms over her breasts. "That's just because of who you are."

"No, honey, it's because of who *you* are." He was completely certain of that. "You may have been forced to compromise yourself when you were younger, but you're not forced to do anything anymore. Which leaves you free to be the woman you are inside. The woman you've been all along."

"How can you say that?" she whispered, and Kyle almost cried. She seemed to want so badly to believe him. But couldn't.

"Because I know you." Taking both her hands in his, he turned her to face him, gazing straight into her eyes with all the love inside him. "Your loyalty is something I've never questioned, Jamie. And I never will. Because loyalty is a part of the person you are, a part of the person you've always been. You were loyal to a mother I don't think deserved it, loyal to Tom Webber, who I *know* didn't deserve it. But most important you've been loyal to Ashley—and to us.''

''How have I been loyal to us?'' He could barely hear the words.

''Our night together was so different, so special to you, that you've been loyal to it ever since.

''The thing is, Jamie,'' he continued, never more serious in his life. ''You aren't sullied, as you seem to believe. You just had a series of unfortunate things happen to you, and you reacted to them in the only way you knew how.''

Tears started to slide slowly down her cheeks as she sat there, silently watching him. Her eyes begged him to be right.

''Considering the complete lack of guidance you had growing up, I think you're the most remarkable person I've ever met. I don't know how you didn't end up in the streets, on drugs, robbing, stealing, hurting the world as much as you've been hurt.''

''What good would it have done?''

''Bingo.'' Kyle did have to swallow back tears then.

''What?''

''That's you, Jamie—always looking for good. Don't you see, honey? An immoral person wouldn't have cared what good it would've done. People like that just automatically destroy. They don't even know good exists.''

The tears poured from her eyes then, soaking

Kyle's shirt as he pulled her against him. He held on tight, absorbing her anguish, thanking the heavens that she'd finally found a way home.

"Thank you," she whispered sometime later when she was spent.

"I didn't do anything." Gazing into her beautiful gray eyes, he knew that it was he who would be thanking her for the rest of his life. He'd been only half-alive before Jamie, too caught up in right and wrong to experience all the nuances of life.

"How can you say you've done nothing?" she asked. "You've just given me back the one thing I thought I'd lost forever."

He kissed the tip of her nose. "What's that?"

"My self-respect."

THEY TALKED FOR HOURS, long after it had fallen dark and the resort had settled down for the night. She told him about her past, things Karen had already told him and things she hadn't, but the telling was so much less painful with Kyle there, loving her more instead of less with every sordid detail.

"The greatest gift I ever had was Mother's Day," she said, snuggling into his side where they sat on the floor, leaning against the couch.

"What did you get?" He was nuzzling her temple.

"Mother's Day," she admitted. "That's it. The day."

"Why's that?"

She couldn't see his expression but was warmed by the genuine interest he showed in every single thing about her, every word she said.

"The first Mother's Day after I'd become a mother was the first time I ever felt good about myself. How could I not with Ashley staring up at me, adoring me, while I nursed her?"

"I wish I could have seen that."

His words stopped her for a moment. Stopped them both. And then she continued. "Besides, I'd done something good, turned my life around. Shown myself I could be a good person. Mother's Day is like my real birthday. The day symbolizing my rebirth. I was finally free from hell."

"No mother is more deserving of the celebration," he told her. "So it's a darn good thing we have one hell of a party planned, eh?" He poked her in the side.

Jamie squirmed, as he'd meant her to do, though she knew she couldn't go to that party. Whether Kyle loved her or not, some things hadn't changed.

They talked some about Ashley. About how excited she was to spend the night at Karen's. And about Karen. How distraught her friend had been. And how happy Karen and Dennis were these days.

And then they discussed the future.

"You know I can't marry you," she said, sometime after midnight. They were lying on the couch by then, her head on his chest, both still fully clothed. Their hands had been exploring intimate places on and off for the past hour.

"What are you talking about?" He sat up suddenly, setting her beside him.

"Have you forgotten Nelson Monroe?" she asked him. She certainly hadn't. "You could lose your job, Kyle!"

"They can't fire me for something they'll never be able to prove," he said. "You went out of business after that night with me. I wasn't one of your clients."

"But—"

"It doesn't matter anyway, Jamie," he said, silencing her with a gentle finger to her lips. "The town is going to take its cues from us. The way everyone else handles the situation depends largely on how we handle it ourselves."

She wanted to believe him. So badly.

"If you feel we should move, we'll move, but you have nothing to be ashamed of, honey."

"Right, Kyle. Tell that to Dean Patterson after Nelson gives him an earful."

"I don't think I'll have to, Jamie. You've already told the dean all he needs to know."

"I don't follow you."

"Ever hear the saying 'actions speak louder than words'?"

She nodded, frowning.

"You've been living in Larkspur Grove for more than four years. Living every day as the good, caring, committed, dependable person you are."

She almost grinned at his list of adjectives, except that she'd needed to hear them so badly she started to cry again, instead.

"All you have to do is stand proudly as that person and eventually even your most staunch critics will have to come around. Or show themselves for the unworthy people they are—and then who cares?"

"You really think so?" She could drown in the love in his eyes.

"I do." Leaning forward, he kissed her on the lips. Lingering there. "Everyone, including Dean Patterson, has a past littered with mistakes of one kind or another."

Once again, he was right.

"I'm not saying it's always going to be easy, but not many things worth having are."

"What about Ashley? How can we expose her to the truth? Kids can be really mean."

"She'll have us, honey." Kyle smiled at her. "And Karen and Dennis and Kayla. And maybe a little sister or brother?"

Gazing into his smiling eyes, Jamie felt the tiniest ray of happiness.

"Everyone has crosses to bear," Kyle told her. "Monroe may very well do as he threatened. Or he may not. Or we may run into someone else who knew you back then. And if we do, we'll deal with it. Together."

Kyle dropped a kiss tenderly on the top of her head, and Jamie finally understood. She had a family of her own now. A haven from the world. A fortress around her that couldn't be breached. Unconditional love. And as long as she and Kyle had each other, nothing else mattered.

"Love me, Kyle?" Jamie begged, kissing him hungrily. She'd waited more than five years. She couldn't wait any longer.

As the kiss ended, Kyle pulled back enough to meet her eyes. "Will you marry me, Jamie?"

She knew what he was doing. Making their coming together pure. With happy tears trailing down her cheeks, she said, "Yes, Kyle, I'll marry you."

"On Monday?"

"You have Brad's final on Monday."

"I do?" His face went blank.

"At one," she reminded him.

"And the class final directly after."

"Right."

"Four'll be safe then, don't you think?"

"For what?"

"To give us enough time to get to Vegas for a quickie wedding. Karen and the girls can come, too. And Dennis if he's in town."

Jamie laughed, hardly recognizing the happiness flowing through her. "Make it six and you've got a deal."

Kyle slipped off his glasses, dropped them on the floor and pulled Jamie against him. "That's one date I *know* I won't need a calendar to remember."

And he didn't.

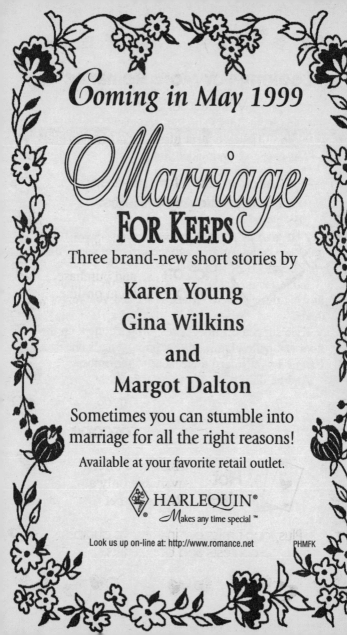

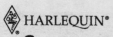

SUPERROMANCE

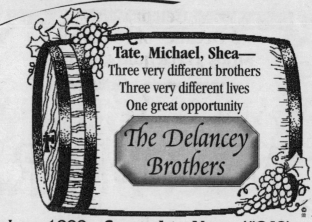

Tate, Michael, Shea—
Three very different brothers
Three very different lives
One great opportunity

The Delancey Brothers

June 1999—Second to None (#842)
by Muriel Jensen

What's a tough cop like Michael Delancey doing in a place like this? Mike was a hostage negotiator in Texas; now he's working at the Oregon winery he and his brothers have inherited.

Michael was ready for a change—but nothing could have prepared him for Veronica Callahan! Because Veronica and her day-care center represent the two things he swore he'd never have anything to do with again—women and children....

And watch for the third story in The Delancey Brothers series, Shea's story, *The Third Wise Man* in December 1999!

Available at your favorite retail outlet.

Makes any time special ™

#840 IF HE COULD SEE ME NOW • Rebecca Winters
By the Year 2000: Satisfaction!
Rachel Maynard was rejected by her best friend's handsome brother,
Nikos Athas, and now—years later—she's determined to win his love.
Except that when she meets his older brother, Stasio, she realizes she's not
in love with Nikos at all. Because *real* satisfaction can only come from
being loved by a man of strength, passion and honor—a man like Stasio.

#841 WINTER SOLDIER • Marisa Carroll
In Uniform
When Lieutenant Leah Gentry goes overseas as part of a team that
will provide medical care for those in need, she figures she'll spend
long days doing fulfilling work. What she *doesn't* expect is to fall for
Dr. Adam Sauder. *Or* to return home pregnant with his child.

#842 SECOND TO NONE • Muriel Jensen
The Delancey Brothers
What's a tough cop doing in a place like this? Mike Delancey was one of
the best hostage negotiators in Texas. But he left it all behind to work in the
winery he and his brothers inherited. He was ready for a change but nothing
could have prepared him for Veronica Callahan—a woman with a *very*
interesting past.

#843 TRIAL COURTSHIP • Laura Abbot
Life is a trial for nine-year-old Nick Porter. His grandparents make him
eat broccoli and nag him about his clothes. Aunt Andrea's a great guardian,
but she's always on him about school and manners and stuff. At least there's
Tony. For a grown-up, he's *way* cool. Nick's seen how Tony and Andrea
look at each other. Maybe if he's lucky, Tony and Andrea will get together
and Nick'll get what he *really* wants—a family!

#844 FAMILY PRACTICE • Bobby Hutchinson
Emergency
Dr. Michael Forsythe's marriage is in trouble. He and his wife, Polly, have
not been able to cope with a devastating loss or offer each other the comfort
and reassurance they both need. It takes another crisis—and the unsettling
presence of a four-year-old child—to rekindle the deep love they still share.

#845 ALL-AMERICAN BABY • Peg Sutherland
Hope Springs
To heiress Melina Somerset—pregnant and on the run—the town of
Hope Springs looks like an ideal place to start over. Unfortunately, her
safety depends on a man she met months ago when she was living under an
assumed name. But this Ash Thorndyke is nothing like the man she used to
know. She'd loved that man enough to carry his child. *This* one she's not
sure she can trust.